WEAKER THAN *Instinct*

BECCA SEYMOUR

RAINBOW TREE PUBLISHING

PRAISE FOR BECCA SEYMOUR

Becca Seymour is now on my list of writers to keep an eye on.

MYTHICAL BOOKS

Becca Seymour has put a unique spin on how shifters are turned that I haven't read before and I was 100% here for it.

LORE & LULLABIES

Emotional depth, fast-paced...a rollicking roller coaster of a read!

IND'TALE MAGAZINE

For Lana & Cat

WEAKER THAN INSTINCT

FANGS & FELONS
BOOK 2

BECCA SEYMOUR

RAINBOW TREE PUBLISHING

ALSO BY BECCA SEYMOUR

Zone Defense

No Take Backs | No More Secrets | No Wrong Moves

Fast Break

Rules, Schmules! | Facts, Smacts! | Regular Smegular

True-Blue

Let Me Show You | I've Got You | Becoming Us | Thinking It Over | Always For You | It's Not You | Our First & Last | Next For Us

Outback Boys

Stumble | Bounce | Wobble

Fangs & Felons

Thicker Than Water | Weaker Than Instinct

Stand-Alone Contemporary

Not Used To Cute | High Alert | Realigned | Amalgamated | Under the Blazing Stars

For information, contact the author: hello@beccaseymour.com

EDITING: HOT TREE EDITING

COVER DESIGNER: BOOKSMITH DESIGN

PUBLISHER: RAINBOW TREE PUBLISHING

E-BOOK ISBN: 978-1-922679-61-1

PAPERBACK ISBN: 978-1-922679-62-8

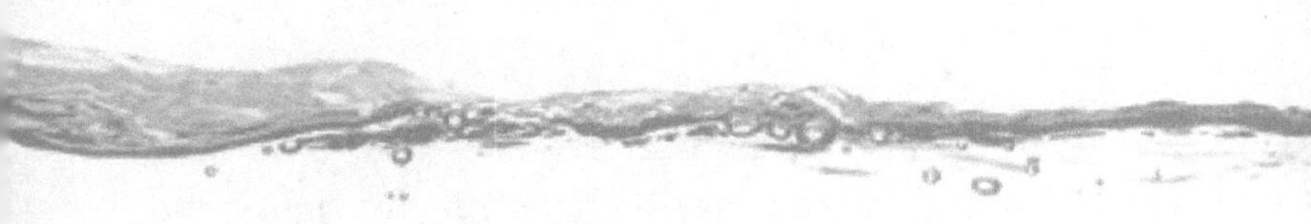

CHAPTER 1
MICHAELS

WEDGED TO THE GROUND, I TOOK STOCK OF MY limbs. Wriggling toes. Flexing fingers. Cracking neck as I turned it left, then right. Three good things going for me. Shoulders— there was no holding back the grunt of pain tearing out of me.

Red hot and intense, agony sliced through my stomach, my side. I screwed up my eyes, willing my breaths to even.

One breath. Two. All the way up to five before it was time to assess the situation.

I pried my eyes open and squinted through the smoke-filled air.

Debris surrounded me, disorientating and chaotic. Lucas was going to kick my arse. There were no ifs, buts, or maybes.

Obviously I'd heal. My shifter abilities came in super handy, but the blazing ache on my right-hand side couldn't be magicked or wished away.

Focussed on slow and steady exhales, I guided my hand to the area, already guessing what I'd find. A heavy sigh, followed by another throb of pain, trickled free when my palm connected with wet metal.

Blood. The sticky liquid coated the steel, the metallic scent thick and cloying.

Impaled was never a good look, let alone an ideal situation. But I wasn't dead, so there was that.

My comms sparked to life. "Michaels, this is Kent. Check in. Over."

Biting back my urge to grunt as I moved to touch the small device in my ear, I held my breath and finally pressed the button. "Michaels checking in. Over." With no quiver, no shake, my tone remained neutral, controlled.

The two-second beat before Kent's voice sounded in my ear was enough to warn me that she knew that shit had hit the fan. Her instincts were spookily accurate, even when a hundred kilometres away. "Status report. Over." There it was—her tight voice, her tone making it clear I should be more concerned about her kicking my arse rather than Mathew Lucas, the head of the ITU—the Infiltration Tactical Unit—I was a member of.

"I may need an assist. Over." I wasn't quite gung-ho enough to think I could pull the steel out of myself. Well, not without causing more injuries. The thought of taking longer to heal, which meant more time out of the field, was enough for me to admit I needed backup.

Kent didn't hold back her pissed-off snarl. "Two minutes. Over and out."

Yeah, Kent was definitely the vampire I should be more concerned about.

Waiting out the two minutes wasn't a hardship. The explosion had killed Muerso. The pool of blood decorated with ash and debris, as well as his prone form, was all the confirmation I needed. Plus the explosion was directly linked to the computer systems. I expected that would annoy Kent, our department whiz at all things cyber, but Muerso's death would put an end to his criminal dealings.

Three months of intel told me he hadn't been part of a wider ring. And with his servers destroyed, it was one more shady criminal enterprise dismantled. The metal piercing my side was totally worth it.

"You look like shit." Chris's grin was wide as he stepped carefully over the debris. His attention drifted to Muerso's motionless form before returning to me, his brow quirked high. "I take it you not waiting for your team was worth it?"

I studied him closely, assessing if he was as annoyed as Kent. With his grin still in place, his posture relaxed, he seemed okay, but as he crouched before me and prodded my wound, I reconsidered my evaluation.

There was no holding back my hiss at his touch. Narrowing my eyes, I stared hard, holding back my snarl.

"You're meant to wait for your partner." His dark eyes appeared black in the flickering lights and the smoke that had yet to settle.

I rolled my eyes, which did nothing to ease the guilt bubbling to life in my gut. "You were warned I was an arsehole in the first five minutes of joining the team," I grumbled.

"True, but you seem determined to push your reputation into uncharted waters. Putting yourself at risk like this is bullshit." The calm tone, the casual way he scanned me for further injuries, didn't gel with his words or the hardening glint in his gaze.

"Sorry. The wanker in me is strong."

Chris's lips twitched.

"While I'm digging the kebab look, you know, the whole wolf-on-a-skewer thing, you wanna help un-stab me?" I worked hard at controlling my expression, my voice. The injury in my side was a constant pulse of agony, and the sooner I was free, the sooner I could get pain meds and heal. While I was a legit arsehole lately, like right now for heading into the building without Chris, my partner of six months, I wasn't a masochist.

I wasn't that at all, and everyone in the team knew it, even Chris, the newest enforcer to join our unit.

At the sound of leather soles on rubble, he glanced behind him when a couple of medics entered, giving them a nod. "Looks like we can un-skewer you." With an effortless grace I was envious of right now, Chris stood and made room for Grace and Hansen.

The two medics made quick work of checking that pulling me from the steel was the best way to tackle my release, and within a few minutes, the three of them yanked me free. Chris took a little too much pleasure in my grunt and groan.

"Fuck." Lightheaded and shaky, I trembled, wavering on my feet. Hansen stopped me from face-planting by putting a strong arm around me. My head swam, a fresh wave of agony rolling through me and turning my stomach.

I swallowed hard. No way would I vomit. I'd never live it down. Chris would waste no time at all spreading that story about me in the unit. Would I deserve the shit talk? Absolutely. No chance would I make it easy for him, though.

"Let's get you a stretcher," Hansen said.

"Nuh-uh. I can walk."

The three of them rolled their eyes. Not that I gave two shits. The investigation was over. The crim was dead—honestly, the best place for the blood dealer. As far as I was concerned, this was a win.

Directing me forward, Chris tugged out his phone, beginning to record the mass of devastation I'd caused. "Kent is going to go for your jugular, man."

Not bothering to glance back as I unsteadily stepped over the rubble, trying not to stumble, I shrugged. "There might be something salvageable." There so wasn't anything left that could be rescued from the burst of flames and mini-explosions I'd detonated earlier.

Chris's snort called bullshit.

Ignoring him, I made it outside to the waiting ambulance. With blood trickling down my side and seeping into my tactical pants, I couldn't risk not getting patched up. I clambered into the open back, Grace following me inside.

"You need me to cut your shirt off?"

Wide-eyed, I stared at her in horror. "Fuck no."

Her lips thinned out as she waited for me to

unfasten my bulletproof vest and tug off my black SICB-issued T-shirt. These things were expensive as hell. The Supernatural Investigation & Crime Bureau budget was shit, and our unit's even worse, which meant if I wrecked the damn thing, I'd have to buy a new one.

Screw that. I'd wait till my yearly replacements.

By the time I eased the bloody shirt off, sweat trickled down my temples and my spine. A hot shower, a coffee, maybe some whiskey, probably a few stitches to help the wound along its way, and I'd be golden.

"Oh fucking hell." A gaping hole from the skewer had destroyed my shirt. I flicked my attention to Grace, who remained stoic as she stared at me, no doubt thinking I was a prize dickhead. "You could have told me it was wrecked." Petulance rumbled through my voice.

"Could I?" she deadpanned, swiping up some medical supplies so she could clean me up.

Keeping my mouth shut as she dabbed at my wound, I grimaced, knowing better than to complain. A wince and a hiss escaped as she cleansed the wound, and I glanced away quickly.

"You need an injection to numb the area?"

"I'm good," I said tightly, earning myself a grunted mumble about me being a pain in the arse. This wasn't

Grace's first rodeo of stitching me up, especially over the past year. If I were her, I'd be sick of me too.

A few stitches later and a bandage taped on, I was good to go.

"I'll be happy if I don't see you again." Grace shot me a pointed look, and Hansen snorted as he closed the rear doors of the ambulance.

"You won't miss me?" I tugged on a fresh tee that was shoved at me by Hansen. Unfortunately, not a new SICB one I could steal.

"Miss your surly arse? Hell no." She followed up with a smirk.

I waved her off, giving my thanks to both of them before seeking out Chris. Already in his car, he was tapping his fingers to whatever bad-taste beat was playing on the radio.

"You done?"

"Yeah."

He bobbed his head. "I've asked Tony to take your vehicle back to the main headquarters." Meaning, as opposed to our unit's covert location. "Thought it would give you a chance to heal before you head out later."

It would be easier if Chris was a dickhead. It would mean I could keep my distance and not like the man, but when he did stuff like this, it made it tricky.

"Thanks," I grumbled, settling down in the passenger seat. "You get my bag?"

He snorted. "You mean the one that's burned to a crisp?" The sound of the engine cut through his chuckle. "That'd be a no."

"Damn it. I liked that bag. It had my favourite Beretta in it." What a clusterfuck. I secured my seatbelt, readjusting the belt strap so it didn't press down on my injury. Not only would I be getting a bollocking from Lucas, but I'd destroyed my bag and one of my handguns.

But at least the bad guy was toast, and I could close my eyes for a few minutes while Chris drove us to the ITU headquarters.

Or maybe not.

Barely sitting up straight in the SUV, I grimaced as Chris took each turn fifteen kilometres faster than necessary. Despite his smile and ease with handling this situation, and the several others since he joined the ITU, the lion was pissed off.

I got it. Deserved it. Absolutely understood it.

Since Jenson's—my old partner's—death last year, I hadn't made life easy for myself or my team. I kept pushing the boundaries and had been reprimanded more than once for taking unnecessary risks. Add to that the number of times I'd gone lone wolf, and I was surprised I still had a job.

That I did such things, was so selfish at times, didn't sit easy. But I didn't know how to stop, how to process Jenson no longer being around. And no amount of talking about it, including the mandatary six sessions of therapy after the whole Lentwood shitshow, changed that one bit.

It didn't help that I'd refused to share a single thing the whole time. Well, nothing of value or truth.

"You doing okay there?"

I tilted my head to look at Chris and offered a chin lift. "Still alive."

He grunted in response.

"You got something to say?"

He sent a quick glance my way. "Not sure there's any point." His gaze returned to the road ahead.

The headlights caught on the late-night mist that had settled over Sydney. I always liked this time of night, especially on a weeknight. The busy city was virtually still with most residents tucked up for the night, ready for their early starts in the morning. So close to the headquarters, it was especially quiet.

While I registered Chris's words, I struggled to form a response that wouldn't simply piss him off even further. Landing on "Fair enough," I watched as the electronic gates whirled into action at the compound and thought about the report Lucas would demand I write.

We pulled into the underground parking, and Chris found a space and parked. I exited with a grunt, irritating my injury.

"Get to the infirmary. You're going to need all the strength you can get before Lucas sees you."

Not wanting to rile Chris up any more, I held back my refusal, since I'd already been patched up. Though some drugs that actually blurred the edges of my pain wouldn't go amiss. "He really that upset?"

His brows shot high. "I don't think upset quite covers it."

With a nod of thanks and a grimace, I waved off his help and headed to see the doc.

It didn't take too long to get the all clear—after having a couple of shards of metal pulled out of my back, which I hadn't noticed before—and make my way to the central workspace. This was really Kent's domain, and she was the first to spot me.

"You know what they call a dead shifter who goes in blind and plays with metal sticks?" Kent deadpanned, her unwavering attention on me.

Knowing not to bait the vampire, I simply looked at her.

"Whatever the fuck they want because the cockhead is dead." Her stare was hard, the only tell she gave that she wanted to lay me out.

I sighed, hating the guilt raising its ugly head.

When Jenson had been killed by our former division manager, it shook the whole team, devastated us all. Despite knowing how much it had impacted everyone, I found it easier to not focus on any of it. It hurt too fucking much otherwise. "I'm sorry I was a cockhead."

An unimpressed grunt filled the space as Kent narrowed her eyes at me. "Stop trying to get dead."

"That's not what—"

"Michaels, office, now." Lucas's usually quiet, steady voice was tense and filled with ice. My attention still on Kent, I widened my eyes.

The vamp simply smirked at me and flipped me off. "Enjoy getting your arse handed to you."

Locking my jaw, I shot her a stink eye, which only had her chuckling as I made my way to Lucas's open door. The man was at his desk, his focus on me as I loosened my limbs, trying not to appear affected.

"Close the door and sit."

After doing so, I sat as still as possible, working hard not to twitch under his intense stare. While Lucas was so unlike Thatch, the old head of the ITU, they had one thing in common. Both of them knew how to make you squirm with their annoying-as-hell silent glare. For years under Thatch's leadership, I'd battled to wait him out. Not once had I won, and Lucas had the same frustrating determination that Thatch did.

Too sore to last the distance, I relented in twenty seconds. "So, that went well. Case solved, mission over." Inside, I grimaced, knowing I was playing with fire.

Lucas remained stoically silent, and another twenty seconds passed.

"Perhaps I should have waited for Chris."

A quirked brow from Lucas was at least a reaction.

"I should have waited for my new partner and not put myself or the case in jeopardy," I admitted.

"I've got something new for you," Lucas said, surprising me. "Tomorrow morning you're to head to the academy." I groaned and was sure there was a damn twinkle in Lucas's eyes at my reaction. "Plan for four weeks, and I'll let Thatch brief you."

"Seriously?"

"Seriously." Lucas grinned. That reaction right there told me so much. "The doc said by the morning, your wound should be closed, and by tomorrow evening, just some minor bruising should be the worst of it." He scanned his computer, no doubt reading the doc's report. Talk about efficient. "Doc says, nothing strenuous for forty-eight hours, so I'll let Thatch know to give you a hall pass."

"Is this an investigation or—"

"Kent has your academy pass and has sorted your paperwork. On paper, you're there for a month-long sabbatical as part of the academy's teaching and training program."

"No." I gasped, legit struggling for breath at the horror of it all. "Me with recruits? Have you lost your mind?"

"We need someone from the team in there, and Thatch is going to be assisting you however you need it. Active agents from different divisions do four-week stints all the time, usually for official reasons, to share skill sets, assist with training, and give recruits an insight into the different fields available. You can offer all of those things while on the job. You're to use your official ID." As opposed to my unofficial role in the SICB ITU, which was a hush-hush, need-to-know unit.

Narrowing my eyes at the man, despite knowing it would have no impact, I tried to keep my petulance at bay, asking, "Is there really an investigation, or are you punishing me for being a dick?"

Lucas quirked his brow. "You think I'd fabricate something like this to punish you?"

I thought about that a moment and figured Lucas wouldn't be the one to do that. But I knew someone who would.

"Maybe not you, but I'm sure as shit Callen would." My former colleague, who was also Lucas's best mate and the man Thatch bumped uglies with— admittedly it was more than that with the whole domestic-nuclear-family thing they had going on, but still, this had Callen Blackheath written all over it.

"Are you suggesting the SICB division leader would fabricate an investigation while punishing you with green recruits, just so you'd pull your head out your backside?"

"Abso-fucking-lutely he would. He's your BFF or whatever. You know he'd totally do this."

His lips twitched and amusement shone in his eyes. "Well, you perhaps have a point there. We all know exactly the sort of things Callen's capable of when he's worried about someone he cares for." All of Lucas's humour slipped away, and once more I felt a punch of guilt in my gut. "But no, this isn't such an occasion. Kent will send you an encrypted file, and Thatch will be briefing you at 0800 tomorrow. Your only orders for today are to file your report, get home, pack, and rest. Got it?"

Nodding, I stood, the fight bleeding out of me. Once I was at the door, Lucas's voice stopped me.

"Listen, Vaughn, you know the whole team has your back, and I'm at the top of that list. This assignment is going to take some unravelling." I glanced over at him, and a small smile lifted his lips. "Perhaps use the time while you're there to get back to the root of it all. Maybe inspire a recruit or something along the way while you're at it."

It didn't matter that I understood what he was saying or that his heart was in the right place. My reasons for being in the task force had changed. They had the moment one of our own had put a gun to Jenson's head and pulled the trigger.

To protect and serve was like a distant memory. Instead, seek and destroy all the fucked-up criminals in our world had become my new mantra.

Being locked in the training academy for a month was not part of that mission.

That meant whatever it was that I was sent in to investigate needed to take a lot less time than the prescribed month. No way could I handle longer than seventy-two hours in the place.

· · ·

I GATHERED MY THINGS AND JUMPED IN MY SUV, relieved there was enough time to grab a coffee before starting the hour-long journey to the academy. The traffic was shit, a given when trying to navigate through the roads of Sydney, but with spring only just started, at least I didn't have to put the air-con on full blast. It all but destroyed my senses—the blast of cool air tended to mess up my ability to scent clearly, as well as screwing with my hearing when in such close confinement of my car.

Once I had my caffeine fix in hand, I gulped the black coffee, wincing at its heat. Last night, after I'd picked up food from a local restaurant, a place that was known for its generous portion sizes to accommodate its nonhuman clientele, I got to my place, inhaled my food, then was out for the count.

It meant I hadn't looked through the file Kent had sent me, too tired to get a heads-up, which I would have preferred. There was no doubt Thatch would talk me through the investigation when we met. As my old unit leader, I trusted him implicitly. It helped that Thatch never cut corners.

When I pulled up to the security gates of SICB Academy, I tugged my ID from under my shirt, holding the lanyard so the tiger on duty could scan me in. I nodded my thanks when he gave me the all clear and followed his directions to the C-block car park.

Thatch stood sentinel before an empty parking space, and since he was smiling, I figured I wasn't in the doghouse too badly. He met me at the door with a hug when I stepped out, something he'd never have done pre-Callen. Me either, for that matter.

"Good to see you, Michaels." He patted my back and released me, and as frustrated as I was about this assignment, seeing the man who'd been my mentor was no hardship.

"I'm still standing." I tugged my bag from the back seat of my SUV, noticing immediately that Thatch had taken in its size, his lips twitching.

Instead of challenging me about my lack of packing, he indicated for us to start moving. "Just about standing after yesterday, I heard."

"You in the loop for all classified shit these days?"

"And don't you forget it." He smirked, and I rolled my eyes, barely holding on to my grin. Sure, I liked to wind the man up, but I had no concerns about the fact that he was in the loop of all things SICB related. If anything, that he had Callen's ear was reassuring. "It's been a while since I've seen you. You've ducked out of the last couple of get-togethers," he said, nodding at a group of recruits kitted out in black fatigues and jogging in formation past us.

"Blame Lucas for putting me on assignments that keep draining me," I jested, knowing full well he wouldn't buy my bullshit.

"Well, it's a good job I've got you for a month, then. It'll give us time to catch up while we're figuring things out."

Refusing to bury myself under the added guilt of distancing myself from those I cared about, I instead focussed on his last words. "So there really is a genuine reason for me being here?" Yesterday when I'd challenged Lucas, it hadn't been in jest. Callen really was the sort of guy who would totally set me up to try to get me to see sense.

"In my office." Thatch swiped his card through a security door, then reached a second door, this one with a print scanner.

I frowned. "This level of security normal for campus?" The green light beeped, and as I stepped inside the office, I caught the sign on the door. *Chief Instructor* was spelled out in gilded letters. That was new, or at least I thought it was. It was something I would have heard about, right?

The door closed with a soft hush, and a moment later, my ears popped. I grimaced at the sensation, knowing immediately that Thatch had activated a sound blocker. The plot was seriously thickening, and for the first time since hearing the news about this assignment, my interest was piqued.

Thatch tugged the visitor's chair to his side of the desk and turned on his computer, going through a series of safety checks. I sat at his side. Thatch was not a man to be rushed, and I could be patient when I needed to be.

"Jack Chambers, the academy's chief instructor, disappeared approximately forty-two hours ago." My brows shot high as he opened an email containing a folder with numerous files. "We started a covert internal investigation rather than a red alert after I received this email on our encrypted server."

He toggled open a document and eased back in his chair so I had more room to read.

"Kent traced the particulars of this email. It was sent one minute after an email from Chambers's account to the board and headquarters indicating an emergency and he would be leaving town."

So basically he'd broken every protocol going. Not only had he sent an email rather than going through HR to request time off, but emergency leave required verbal and visual confirmation from HQ.

As if already knowing where my mind had gone,

Thatch continued, saying, "Chambers was a stickler for protocol. Him doing this goes against everything I know about the man."

I nodded in understanding. "So a red warning flag and not something he'd even do in an emergency?"

Thatch shook his head.

"What's in the folders?"

Thatch clicked on one. "This is the only one we can open. The rest have some serious security encryption. Kent's been at it, but she's struggling."

My brows shot high at that. "What about Lucas?" Before Lucas joined our unit to take over Thatch's role, he spent his time buried neck deep in coding and tech. Between him and Kent, there shouldn't be an issue.

A grim expression appeared. "They've been working on this since the moment I received it, and nothing yet."

"Shit."

"It's going to take time. There seems to be some sort of activation key that they're struggling to get around."

I glanced around the tidy office. Activation codes tended to never be written down, for all the obvious reasons. "But why send them if you'd need the code to open them?"

"Now that's the question we're trying to get our

heads around. Either he has faith in the ITU, knowing that with time they'll crack it, or—"

"Or it's somewhere we can find it."

"Exactly. I'm going to focus on that while you keep your ear to the ground. Focus on the staff, the recruits. Everyone."

I bobbed my head, understanding a little better why he called me in. Pulling someone in with fresh eyes was a no-brainer. But reading people, cutting through the bullshit, discovering their secrets was a skill set I was particularly proud of. "Got it." I indicated the file he opened. "And what's the one file you can open?"

He double-clicked on the one document, using a password.

"My tax file number." He rolled his eyes, and I snorted, wondering how many attempts it had taken him to work that out.

The page opened, and I froze.

HUGHES. GALLAGHER. SMITH.
SHADOWFALL.

"Shadowfall? The clandestine op?" Goose bumps startled to life on my arms. "As in, Captain Hornell?" A quick glance Thatch's way was enough to have my gut twisting. "They were shut down four years ago."

"I looked into the general SICB database for those other names, which was a nightmare."

"The Smiths?"

"You know it. I switched my focus to the academy's enrolment. Martin Hughes, Kate Gallagher, Paul Smith. All quit the academy in the past three months."

I scooted my chair so I could see Thatch better. Since he'd been turned into a wolf shifter last year, he had even better control of his tone, his expressions. But sometimes his tells gave me a clue as to what he was thinking.

"Three dropouts. What's so special about them? When I was training, at the beginning of my two-year course, there were ninety-eight recruits. Only thirty-three made it."

Thatch's startling green eyes shone with intensity, a vivid contrast to his dark skin. "All three dropped off the face of the earth within sixteen days of leaving."

I frowned, waiting for him to continue, certain there was more he'd put together. He didn't disappoint.

"You know the SICB keeps a close eye on dropouts for the first two weeks. After that, they do spot checks."

I bobbed my head, knowing that SICB checked to ensure the health and well-being of recruits who didn't make the cut. Or at least that was the party line. The reality was, they were also ensuring the former recruits were on the straight and narrow, as it were. Not selling bureau secrets—not that recruits were exposed to many, but the bureau was a secretive bunch for a reason.

"All three were excelling in hand-to-hand combat. Top ten of their class, in fact. The same for tactics and weapons."

"So what's the bottom line here?"

"Preliminary digging shows families are not concerned that their child—and in one case, husband— are not around, but they all have one additional thing in common."

I quirked my brow at him and held back my smirk. Thatch had always been a straight shooter, but the way he was unravelling the information was on the cusp of telling a tale, complete with dramatic pauses. Callen was rubbing off on him, and I was half tempted to let him know as much, but I wasn't sure I was that brave.

"All three next of kin have a connection to AXF."

"The medical research lab?"

"One and the same. They're the second largest in Australia and conduct ground-breaking trials and a whole shitload of medical projects. Several government approved."

My mind ticked overtime, wondering if Thatch's deductions were leading him in the same direction as my own. The missing chief of staff and former recruits, the links to AXF as well as the academy.... I frowned. "What aren't you telling me?"

A barely there smirk was directed my way as Thatch leaned forward and pressed a small button underneath his desk. Once again, my ears popped as the soundproofing deactivated.

A second button unlocked the door.

Immediately, my gaze was drawn to the opening door and the dark-haired panther who entered. Like most panthers in human form, his skin was golden brown, indicative of their species' heritage. Lithe and with eyes that struggled to blend in with the human world, the young panther was mesmerising.

Securing the door behind him, he didn't take his gaze off me. It was only after the pop of the sound-proofing being engaged that he finally flicked his focus to Thatch. He stood at attention before the desk, his gaze ahead.

"At ease, recruit," Thatch ordered. "Take a seat."

Curiosity fluttered to life inside me, not only at the reason for Thatch bringing him in, but at the young man himself.

I expected I had at least eight years on him. Likely more. It was the confidence he exuded, though, that sparked my interest.

Sure, SICB recruits could be cocky bastards, but there was something more about this one, different somehow. Yeah, he was good-looking, ridiculously so, something I could usually see past within an instant, especially of late. But with his golden eyes sparking with intelligence and pouty lips that I struggled to glance away from, I was ensnared.

Thatch clearing his throat jerked my attention away. His brow was quirked high, amusement seeming to battle with concern in his stare. I clenched my jaw and gave him a firm nod, returning my attention to the recruit, who now sat before the desk, interest clear in his eyes as they roamed over me.

"Jett Shaw, meet Agent Michaels. Shaw here is going to be supporting you while you're on campus."

Snapping my eyes in Thatch's direction, I frowned. Any amused expression he may have had earlier was gone. This was full-on "I will kick your arse if you question me" mode.

"Shaw's already in the loop, and yes, there's a reason why you're on campus, as this will be the focal point of our investigation. Shaw here is the top of the class for—" Thatch tilted his head, gaze on Shaw. "—well, everything."

That got my interest as I refocussed on Shaw. While I wouldn't exactly describe it as challenge evident in the young panther's eyes, there was certainly a boldness there I kinda liked.

"He'll be graduating in two months and is already in talks with Lucas."

"No shit?" My eyes widened. Lucas was interested in this kid joining our unit? Not that I needed to look at Shaw with renewed interest, since he already had my attention, but if Thatch had recommended him to Lucas, our team, which I had no issues declaring was fucking awesome, then he must be good.

"Yes shit," Shaw responded, a smirk on the cusp of being cocky forming.

It took effort to hold back my grin, but I did, not wanting to make Shaw think we'd become best buddies or some shit. I'd had one of those.

Never again.

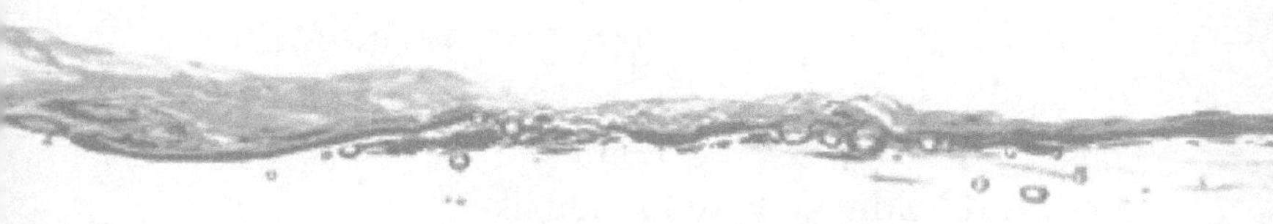

CHAPTER 2
SHAW

For two hours I'd kept my cool. Only one of those had been spent swallowing down my excitement.

Vaughn Michaels was here, his face at times inches from my own as we looked over paperwork. It took the interim chief giving me a hard stare when I may have gushed over recalling one of Michaels's ops we'd studied—even though when we had, the whole class were not made aware of the agent's actual name, let alone the unit he was from—to get me to finally pull my head in.

But holy shit, it was hard.

This was *the* Vaughn Michaels, one of SICB's ITU specialists, whom less than a handful of trainees and staff combined on campus knew about. It was Agent Thatcher who'd brought me into the fold just four months ago, seeing something in me that hinted at a future I had only dreamt about achieving.

Before learning that the covert ITU truly existed, I'd heard enough rumours of small division pockets that, while they weren't quite off the books, they flew under the radar. When I was a kid, my mum whispered about such units, always with awe in her voice. It was then I'd known, if such a unit really existed, I wanted in.

And it was happening.

Not only that, but I'd be working covertly with Michaels over the next month, the badass who Agent Thatcher—or Thatch, which he'd given me permission to call him behind closed doors—had told me stories about. The boon—because I refused to look at it any other way—Michaels was freakin' delicious.

Ignoring the whole dark intensity of his eyes was all but impossible. Teamed with his built frame, one packed with hard muscle and defined ridges, there was an undeniable presence about the wolf.

After two hours, I was finally able to control my boner—a total win. But a nervous excitement sang in my veins. As soon as I stepped out of this office, I'd be officially on a covert op. Admittedly, I'd still be doing exactly what I did every day in training—attending lessons, studying my arse off, and pushing myself through the paces to make sure I stayed on top. The difference was, I'd be keeping my eyes and ears open, as well as laying down the groundwork for news about a distressing "situation" back at home.

"What time will they be arriving?" I glanced at Michaels, already trusting he was in charge and wouldn't let anything happen to my folks.

"Your parents are en route to the safe house and are due to arrive at 1300."

I bobbed my head, reassured they'd be safe soon and that Kent, the computer-whiz agent in the ITU, had already set the trail.

"You're due in the mess hall at noon," Thatch said, eyeing the clock on the wall. We had half an hour to make sure we were ready.

I straightened in my seat, alert and needing both men to know I could do this. "My dad's been struck down by the D34R virus. He's in Cardstone Hospital, in secure isolation. My mum is with him. The cost of treatment is going to be crazy. Selling the house and our limited assets is the only solution. I need to keep kicking arse and being on top, while bitching about the government and the health system, the unfairness and expense of it all. I also start asking around for any side gigs going on. Subtle-like." My gaze flicked to

Michaels, whose butt was perched on the desk, his focus unwavering.

"The mission is baiting. Based on the intel we've pieced together, someone, likely within the academy, is pulling high-attaining recruits to join a black-ops, probably privately funded, military group led by Hornell. I need to get myself an invite."

The room felt warm after I'd gone over the basics of my task. The whole thing was surreal. The thought of a privately funded organisation seducing, forcing, possibly paying—we weren't sure which, though the medical research company was a main player somehow—trainee operatives to join them boggled my mind. I still didn't know much about the Shadowfall—my barely there clearance was a hundred million levels too low for that.

I'd known Hughes and Smith vaguely, both a year behind me. But I'd shared a lot of training time with Kate Gallagher. In a couple of fields, she was close to my standing, heightening my competitive streak just enough to make those training specialisms more fun.

When she'd left four weeks ago, shock had rippled through the academy, especially for me. In eight more weeks, she'd be graduating and would likely have had her pick of fields to join.

Yesterday, when Thatch had approached me with

information about possible reasons why she'd left, and with the information about her now being MIA, it had been enough to make me want to step up. But throw in the news about Chief Chambers being missing too, and that my dad used to work for AFX, and any semblance of doubt I may have had fizzled out immediately.

"I'll be taking on *limited*"—Michaels eyed Thatch—"classes, covertly checking out staff, and I'll be running two one-on-one sessions to make sure we"—he directed this at me—"get opportunities to meet regularly. It'll also explain why you're kissing my arse and trying to spend time with me." He actually grinned, the expression sweeping away some of his intensity and brightening his gaze.

Swallowing my tongue was a real possibility at the visual of kissing his arse. How was I meant to answer that without going tongue-tied, falling on my knees before him, or turning into a red, needy mess?

Calling on my almost two years of training, I evened my breathing. Getting kicked off this mission and losing a place with the task force was not an option. Once in control, I rolled my eyes, as was expected.

"I'll help corroborate your story about your parents and your situation, since I've stepped up into the COS position while Chief Chambers has been pulled out for a family emergency." It was the story that Thatch had circulated.

"We need Thatch far away from this, with this meeting being the only time we're all together until this is over. You have problems, you come to me. You have doubts, I'm your point of contact. You have—"

"Okay, Michaels, I think Shaw gets it."

I slid my gaze to a relaxed-looking Thatch. I wondered if anything got him worked up. Since he'd joined the academy early last year, he'd been so cool and calm. He'd already had one hell of a reputation, and since discovering where he really used to work, the unit he led, I finally understood why.

Michaels didn't take his focus away from me, all humour gone. "We need results. You need to push without making anyone suspicious. If Hornell is involved and Shadowfall has new life, this shit is real and likely dangerous. Got me?"

Aiming for a stoic expression, I nodded sharply, alert, and aimed my stare straight at the wolf before me. There were a lot of pieces in play. That much was obvious with only a fraction of information.

It was up to me to help get answers and work out what had happened to the chief and the former recruits.

Lunch started as normal. I sat with Henderson and Rickman, which was the norm, deliberately keeping tight-lipped and tight-jawed. After trying to engage with me a few times, they gave up, Henderson with a look of concern, Rickman shrugging it off completely, as was her way.

I had to play this right. While I had moments when I could be over-animated and talk shit like the next person, everyone knew I planned to be a lifer. The academy had always been my dream, both parents having careers in the SICB—even though Dad didn't stick it out and went into private medical research. Rather than my parents' experiences putting me off, I'd loved the stories they could share and leapt all over any training or wisdom they gave me.

They'd always indulged me and supported my choices. I could only imagine what they were thinking with the new turn of events and them being ushered into protective custody.

I was grateful that with Mum being a former field agent—before she settled into a desk job—and Dad spending years in often top-secret medical research, they'd handle the unit's urgency and plan. Fingers crossed they didn't freak out too much about my involvement in the investigation.

Being so close to graduation was a possible hindrance to this mission, since I might not be seen as perfect bait with so little time left. And me being a lifer could prevent someone from taking the bait. That I was top of the class also posed a problem. But Thatch thought I could do this. Given that I was so focussed and committed, I had every intention of making this work, regardless of the consequences.

I tugged out my phone and kept it low under the table, checking for messages I knew weren't there.

The conversation cut off immediately. "Shaw," Henderson rushed to say, his voice quiet, but in a room filled with supes, it wouldn't take much for someone to listen in.

Flipping my gaze in his direction, I dipped my brows low, aiming for a winning combo of panic and pissed off.

His eyes were wide, and he stared hard at the phone he spotted in my hands, giving me a pointed look.

I tensed my jaw and bobbed my head, slipping the phone in my pocket. All communal areas were deemed restricted, and as such, communication devices were not allowed. The only exceptions were the two-ways staff carried with them. Me pulling out my phone was the trigger I needed.

"What were you thinking?" Henderson mumbled.

My jaw clenched, and I gave a sharp shake of my head.

Rickman shifted in her seat. "Bullshit. What's going on?"

They'd known I'd disappeared for a couple of hours earlier. I expected most of my cohort did too. "I was called to take an emergency call with my mum." With a purse of my lips, I counted to five, allowing the quiet to fill the space before continuing. "Dad's been admitted to Cardstone." I swallowed hard and once again clamped my jaw tight. I had to play this right, figure out how I'd behave and react if the news were real.

"Shit, what's wrong?" Henderson asked, concern in his voice.

"Not sure yet, but clearly something serious if he's been transferred to Cardstone." Placing my hands on the table, I picked up my fork, playing with my uneaten pasta. That in itself was a huge tell right there to anyone who knew me.

I never fidgeted or twitched. I certainly didn't get agitated or play with my damn food. Since an early age, in my almost obsessive need to prepare for the academy, I'd trained myself to not do any of that—give no signs, provide no opportunities for anyone to read.

"I'm sure you'll hear something soon, and when you do, whatever it is, he'll be okay." Henderson offered me an awkward smile. I appreciated the effort. Henderson was a good guy, friendly, with his whole cute nerd thing he had going on. Nerd thing meaning he got revved up by gadgets a lot more than I did.

"Thanks, mate. I'm sure you're right. It'll be good to know something for sure. I'll be able to get my head around everything then."

Rickman picked up her plate and stood. "Best distraction is to get our butts into gear." She offered me a chin lift. "Heard a rumour that the new instructor's here. Let's hope he's not a prick like the last agent they sent on his month-long."

Henderson and I stood too, following Rickman's lead.

She wasn't wrong about some of the month-longs we'd encountered over the two-year training course. Some clearly didn't want to be here and were probably being punished or something by their superiors, while others were so enthusiastic, their hyped-up energy was overkill and edged towards exhausting.

Fighting hard, I held back my grin as I dumped my plate and headed to the gym. While I knew exactly why Michaels was here, I wondered how he'd play it. I already knew he'd be using one of his position aliases, but the man was impossible to read—not a surprise from his time in the field, especially in his unit.

Perhaps it wasn't the right time, but I wanted to impress the shit out of him. Yes, we had a mission, but the hot wolf could end up being my colleague, all going well. That, and I liked his attention on me. Just the two hours we'd spent together let me know that keeping my lusty and so-not-the-right-time thoughts to myself would be a challenge.

A collection of recruits already stood in formation as we stepped into the gym.

There were only twenty-four of us left in our year, most having dropped out after the first month of training almost two years ago. The reduced number made Kate Gallagher's leaving more noticeable.

Gossip had been rife at the time of her leaving, and knowing what I did now, I admitted I was pissed off at myself for not reading more into her departure.

Resolve slammed into me as I stood side by side with Henderson and Rickman. All thoughts of flirting with the man who entered the room with Trainer Rogers flittered out of mind. How could I be the best agent if I didn't see something was amiss? The thought sat heavily on my chest. I had to make this right.

I had to do better. Be better.

"Recruits." Rogers stopped in front of us. "Agent Michaels from the Global Response Shifter Force will be joining us for four weeks."

I snapped my attention to Michaels, who stood stoically at Rogers's side.

"He has over ten years of field experience and will be running a handful of sessions a week with junior and senior recruits but is also offering specialist intensive training to two individuals. One from this senior class, one from the junior recruits." Rogers faced Michaels, giving him the floor.

"Thank you, Trainer Rogers."

The deep gravel of his voice snaked up my spine, and I barely held back the shudder at how the sound caressed my skin. I bit the inside of my cheek, pissed as hell at my reaction and my inability to control myself.

"Recruits, if you look around, you'll see part one of a series of tests, if you will. After this, we'll step outside to the rifle training grounds, then to the hub, and finally, we'll reconvene here for sparring. Trainer Rogers has already provided me with a detailed rundown of each of you, and he'll join me in the selection process. Yes, I'll be looking out for the winner, but also the exceptional, watching for your tells, observing how you approach each task."

When I'd entered the gym, I'd noted a series of stations dotted around. Some with puzzles, some with physicality-based tasks. I swallowed hard, knowing I had to take the lead and outperform everyone. But jumping through so many hoops seemed a little overkill. Hell, talk about the man pushing me to see what I was really made of.

If he'd asked, I could have easily given him a rundown of all my amazing qualities and skills. But no, rather than one simple arm wrestling match or something, he'd organised all this.

"Trainers Duncan and Leopold will also be joining us to observe and help with the assessment process." Rogers eyeballed us, his silent order to not screw this up and embarrass him easy to read. "Listen up for your name and head to your assigned area. The buzzer will sound. Each task will have six minutes on the clock."

At my side, Marge Trenton shuffled, earning Rogers's gaze, which snapped in her direction.

"There will be no questions, no clarification. You read the situation and act on the buzzer. Understood, recruits?" Rogers's tone allowed no room for comment.

"Yes, Trainer Rogers," we chorused.

"When you think you have finished the set task, stand at ease."

We spoke in unison. "Yes, Trainer Rogers."

A thrum of energy picked up around the room. Desperate to glance around and try to get another look at the different stations, I exhaled instead. No chance would I risk doing that and receive the wrath of Rogers. A hard-arse at the best of times, he was ten times worse when showing us off with a visiting trainer.

Keeping my gaze straight ahead, I listened intently to Leopold, who entered the room and listed off our names and station numbers. As the last name was read off, I prepared myself. Alertness buzzed along my skin, ready to move to station four along with Smythe.

"Thirty seconds to find your station, and then the first buzz will start. Go."

Turning on my heel, I scanned the area. None of the stations were numbered, but they were laid out in a large circle at the northwest of the large gym. Locating the wall clock, I refocussed on the stations, aware most recruits had charged ahead, searching for some sort of label or sign.

In the centre of the circle, a mark on the floor caught my attention. Barely a speck, it was blue and misshaped, and absolutely had been positioned there. I took five steps in its direction, still on the outskirts, zeroing in on the shape until I finally registered what it was.

An arrow so tiny, it couldn't have been bigger than a couple of centimetres in length.

Pointed at one of the stations, it was a clear signal.

A clock. The arrow signifying a clock arm.

Acting fast, I took controlled steps to station four, figuring the arrow was pointed at twelve. Two other recruits were already there. As soon as they saw me, their eyes widened, and I arched my brow in challenge. The flare in their gazes told me enough.

They knew they'd screwed up.

They spun around, checking on their location, then raced off to station seven, which was their correct assignment.

"Time," Rogers called just as Smythe skated to a halt beside me. Red-faced and looking panicked, he blew out a loud breath, his limbs vibrating.

Jesus. I held back my head shake and instead offered him a tight smile and the barest of nods. Smythe could be painfully shy. While we spent a lot of time together in group and whole-class training, he wasn't someone I chose to hang out with in my downtime.

He was a whizz at tech, especially secret coding. These sorts of exercises should be right up his street. One thing I'd learned about the guy, though, was that he got distracted easily when there was so much noise and movement.

I expected being human and not having supernatural senses didn't help either. It was probably why he missed the arrow. Too small for his human vision.

He was potentially off his game in this sort of setting.

Not that he didn't do well overall in training, though. I wasn't questioning him being here, or his ability to be a good agent. In two months' time, as long as he was behind a desk with tech at his fingertips and in a controlled environment, he'd excel. Of that I was sure.

Though why he chose SICB rather than sticking with the human division had always baffled me. Not that there weren't plenty of human agents who worked in the SICB, but some appeared better suited to it than others.

Standing at ease, I raked my gaze over the double station, my lips twitching once. LEGO, of all things, were in a bucket. Next to it was a LEGO structure of a gun. The buzzer sounded, and I got to work.

A kick-arse LEGO gun, a straw structure, a crossword puzzle, a game of Connect Four, of all things—which I totally won... twenty-five times—achy arms from six minutes of push-ups, and a whole host of random tasks, including putting together four different guns from a mixed-up pile of parts, and we were on our last task.

We'd been at this for over an hour, but rather than feeling tired, exhilaration sparked beneath my skin, eager to get this next successful task under me. I had no idea how anyone else had done, beyond Smythe who stuck doggedly to my side and watched me with an intensity that should have bothered me. But I was convinced I'd nailed this session—and the tasks—so far.

The end buzzer sounded, and I darted for the final station, almost stumbling when I saw Michaels sitting cuffed to a chair, another trainer with his back to him in the same position.

Over the last hour, I'd been viscerally aware of the wolf, so I knew he hadn't been the person chained to the chair, wrists cuffed on his lap, chain dropping down to his cuffed feet, before.

With his gaze locked on mine, I stared back, barely daring to breathe. And then the buzzer went off, and it was time to react and get him the hell out of the cuffs. No way would I let Smythe work with him.

Making my intentions clear, I blocked off Smythe from reaching Michaels. He darted to the other trainer with a sigh, giving me the chance to focus on the man before me. Pausing a metre away, I examined his body, his position, the slack of the chains, the tightness of the cuffs.

He wore glasses, which he hadn't worn earlier and something a shifter would never need. I angled around and looked at the other trainer. In the same position, also wearing thin-rimmed glasses, the trainer remained still, his focus on Smythe, who was on his knees, yanking on the cuffs and chains.

A minute must have passed, but I still hadn't moved closer. Something about this one seemed off.

Returning to Michaels, I crouched low, far enough away not to be in kicking distance. A bulge on his right ankle had me pausing, wishing I had X-ray vision to see beyond the fabric of his agency-issued pants.

And not at all for nefarious reasons of looking to see any other bulges he may have been sporting.

Studying every part of him that I could see, I knew I could swipe his glasses and use them as a pick. I could have the things open in under thirty seconds.

"How you doing?" I hadn't heard a single other recruit speak in the past hour, but it looked like I was all in at changing that.

"I've been in better situations," Michaels answered.

I bobbed my head. "Any idea what those cuffs are made of?" Human-issued handcuffs wouldn't keep a supe contained. Our agents carried specialist tungsten handcuffs containing added drendoine, a metal that neither shifters nor vamps had any way of breaking.

Michaels shrugged. "No idea."

I stood up slowly, gaze unwavering. "You want to lift your hands up so I can see your reach?" What I wanted to do was see if he was packing something.

"They're pretty restrictive. Maybe you could help me."

"Or," I said with a smile, "you could try for me, just so I know what I'm dealing with." There couldn't be anything more than two minutes left on the clock. This was a risky call I was making, but given the slackness, the bulge at the ankle, and that I was sure he was concealing something in the waist of his pants, I trusted my gut.

Picking cuffs was too easy. Sure, so were some of the other tasks, but the fact that Michaels was before me and not another trainer had me on high alert.

The sound of metal hitting the ground caught my attention, and while I was aware of Smythe standing there, grinning, and that he was, I was sure, wondering what I was playing at, my gaze didn't waver.

I didn't have a weapon—no recruit did unless on a field or weapons training exercise. That meant I couldn't keep him in his chair with a gun pointed at him, so it couldn't have been a part of the exercise.

Sixty seconds.

I released a slow exhale and took a step away from Michaels. Decision made, I stood at ease and waited in silence, staring at the man cuffed to the chair before me.

The final buzzer sounded, and a collective sigh rippled through the group. From everyone except me.

With a barely there tug, Michaels snapped the cuffs, yanked the chain, and dropped them to the ground. He stood and took a step in my direction. "Recruit Shaw, care to tell the rest of the class why you were the only person who didn't unlock the cuffs and free the person you were assigned to?"

I fought the urge to swallow. "After assessing the situation, it became clear from the lack of glaze in the metal that the cuffs were human issued. Plus there was the fact that you're packing a weapon, a blade against your right ankle and possibly a Glock, maybe a Berretta, in the waist of your pants. I didn't expect you would need rescuing when armed."

The shuffling of feet echoed around me.

"Oh, and the glasses. Remove the plastic end from an arm, and they make a formidable weapon, often dipped in poison." Something we'd had a fun session on when looking at old cases.

For five long seconds, Michaels's gaze didn't stray.

I'd been under the microscope so many times since being at the academy, a given considering the nature of the training and what the agency was training us for. But in those five seconds, it felt like layers were being peeled back and Michaels was seeing into my damn soul or something.

"Impressive, Shaw. Each of the other recruits would have been dead."

In response to Michaels's words, Trainer Duncan, who Smythe had set free, pulled out his own gun from his waist and a blade from a strap at his ankle.

"Fifteen minutes." Rogers cut off the collective groan of my fellow recruits. "Meet us at the rifle training grounds. Collect your training weapons en route. Dismissed."

As one, everyone's feet moved around me. Staying stock-still, I stared at Michaels, who continued to assess me. I should have moved and beat the crowd to pick up my weapon, but with Michaels's intense brown gaze on me, pulling away proved impossible.

And then he nodded, a barely there bob of his head, but fuck if his approval wasn't everything. It was what I needed to spin on my heel, grin stretched wide, and race after the other recruits.

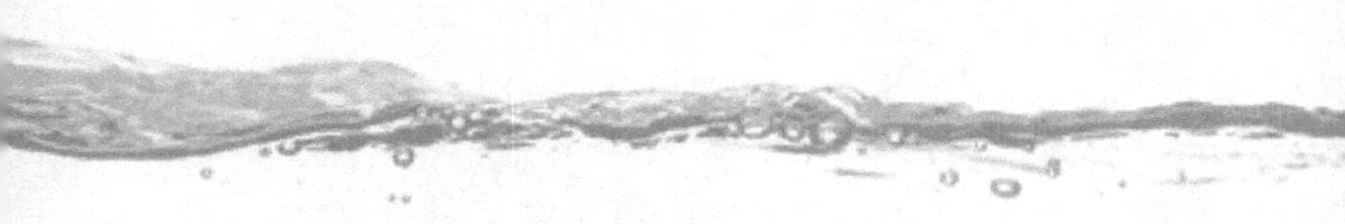

CHAPTER 3
MICHAELS

Test after test, Shaw aced every single thing I threw at him. Thatch had been right. Not that I'd doubted him as such, but still, I'd held back my judgement until I'd put the panther through his paces.

But the whole challenge wasn't just a ruse to get alone time with Shaw. Observing the reactions of the recruits offered some enlightenment. There were those who were impressed, envious, while some didn't give two fucks about Shaw's successes.

And there were the three members of staff.

Rogers growled regularly like the bear he was, frustrated at those recruits not bringing their A-game. The two other trainers quietly observed while providing interesting on-point feedback.

None of the trainees concerned me.

There were currently twenty-four recruits in their final weeks. Fifty-two still in the rookie year. With twenty staff consisting of trainers and admin, there was plenty of ground to cover, but Thatch's plan to focus on Shaw's story seemed like the best option.

We had to play it carefully, though. That he'd earn one-to-one training time with me would be great so we could meet daily and give him the hall pass he needed, but with this plan, we ran the risk of whoever had infiltrated the academy having even more reason to stay away from him. I knew my getting close to Shaw was a risk, but it was one we had to take.

"Koen."

"Agent Michaels."

I stifled my smile as I reached out and shook his hand. There was no reason any recruit here should technically know me. "Congratulations." While a glance around us didn't reveal anyone in hearing distance, there was no telling how many eyes and ears were focussed on us. With this in mind, I stayed true to the narrative and acted like Koen was a stranger.

"You did well with the exercise," I continued, telling the truth. While I didn't organise the same number of exercises with the rookies, time spent at the assault course and the shooting range provided one very clear winner.

This kid had come a long way since relocating last year to move into Thatch and Callen's guest house. He'd protected Callen's niece, Lucinda, with his life, a debt the division leader and my old boss happily repaid however they could.

But it was his determination, his strength of character that enabled the shifter to secure a spot in the academy. And from what I'd witnessed a short while ago, the past ten months at the academy suited him. Hell, his display on the course and with the rifle was impressive.

Of course it meant he knew who I really was, but since Thatch hadn't mentioned Koen during our meeting, I had to assume he didn't know the real reason I was here.

"Thanks." A happy smile lifted his lips, revealing bright white teeth and making him seem younger than his twenty-two years. That didn't mean I didn't see him as a kid, though. My old arse thought anyone under twenty-five was a juvenile these days.

"I'll reach out to you about the extra sessions once I can align our schedules." Honestly, I was relieved as hell Koen had aced the challenges. Giving my time to him wouldn't be a hardship.

"Great. I look forward to it." He bobbed his head, his gaze landing on the wall clock. "I actually have to get going. If not, I'll be late for the session with Zenmire."

"Sure thing. I'll see you tomorrow." I watched him leave as I considered my next move.

With no official plans until tomorrow, I supposed I should work out a time to meet Shaw and Koen. I also had a close-combat-skills demonstration tomorrow. Not that I needed to prepare for it as such. I could do that shit with my eyes closed.

Deciding I should check out my quarters in more detail than the "head around the door and dumping my bag on the bed" perusal I gave it this morning, I made my way to the staff residence.

On the way I passed by a lecture room. The door was open, blinds up. I peered inside, my attention immediately landing on Shaw. Our gazes connected for a beat before I forced myself to look ahead. The panther reeked of danger—of distraction—and try as I might to ignore the reason why, it was no good.

Jenson. The similarities were eery, and it had nothing to do with their looks. Heck, Jenson had been human. But in just the few short hours I'd spent with Shaw, I recognised he had the same spark of determination, a thread of pushy personality—one determined to make everyone who met him like him—that Jenson had.

Unnerved, I ploughed on to my room, needing to get as far away from Shaw and the memories of my best friend as possible.

After I'd shoved my unpacked bag in the small wardrobe and had sought a coffee from the staff kitchen, I tugged out my phone and called Callen, my previous colleague who'd since become the big boss—something that still boggled all our minds.

Not that he wasn't kick-arse in the role. My surprise had everything to do with him not having been known to follow the rules when he was a field agent. But since closing a huge investigation, he'd earned his stripes and the new appointment into leadership.

"How are you settling in?"

I snorted down the line at his greeting. "And hello to you too."

"Shit, is this finally a social call, and you've pulled your head out of your arse and are inviting yourself around for dinner? I'll stop the fucking press."

With a heavy breath, I tilted my head back and looked up at the ceiling. My friends, my colleagues, had given me a free pass since Jenson's death, but their patience was wearing thin. Yesterday's behaviour and my now-healed wound were a stark reminder of why they were pissy. "I suppose I deserved that."

"Considering how many times you've not been

written up, you could say you deserve a hell of a lot more."

Tightness ached in my chest. Letting go, moving on, whatever I was expected to do, plagued me, threatening to take my legs from under me when I thought too hard about it. "I'm sorry."

Silence greeted my words, the shallow breaths through the line the only reason I knew Callen remained on the call.

"I'll do better." I wanted to. Hell, maybe Lucas was right to send me here. While there was a real investigation at the academy, perhaps being around trainees would help. No idea how exactly, but how I'd been tackling life wasn't the answer.

"I know." Understanding coloured those two words. Callen knew loss, and he'd found a way through to the other side. "So what can I do for you, other than let you know I expect your arse at ours on Saturday afternoon for a barbeque?"

With no room for negotiation in his tone, I smiled, the sensation surprisingly easy. Callen was a tenacious bastard. I liked it. "I'll be there." After that I had nothing to say. Talking about the case wasn't the reason for the call. The possibility of someone overhearing my side of the conversation was too high for that.

When Callen said, "Good, I'll let Thatch give you

the details," gratitude that he didn't push for an answer calmed my tense shoulders.

"Sounds good. I'll see you at the weekend."

"You will."

When the call cut off, I slipped my phone in my pocket and pulled out the swivel chair at the small desk in my en suite room. Reaching out to Callen had been unplanned. I expected seeing Thatch had stirred the need to make amends somehow. At least I was trying. It should keep everyone in my unit off my back.

Not that they could be on my back for the next four weeks.

I smiled and eased back in the seat, linking my fingers around the back of my head. At some point in the past eight hours, my reluctant few days on campus had morphed into my acceptance of being here for the whole month.

Being in the infiltration unit had its bonuses, this being one of them.

A knock on the door had me angling around and calling, "Yeah? Door's unlocked."

The door opened, and I blinked in surprise. "Prescott?" I jumped out of the office chair and took a step forward, extending my hand to shake John Prescott's. "Shit, man, what the hell are you doing here?"

Prescott pumped my hand, an easy smile on his face. "I swear I didn't believe it could be the Vaughn Michaels I knew, but here you are." He chuckled, a sound I hadn't heard for maybe twelve years.

I shook my head in wonder. This was the last place I expected to see Prescott. We'd been at the academy together. "Seriously, man, what are you doing here? Are you working here?" The question reminded me I'd been slack and had yet to read through the document Kent sent me yesterday.

"Let's head to the cafeteria, and I can catch you up."

Grabbing my keys, I followed him out, walking at his side as he led me to the cafeteria. The hall was quiet, but it wouldn't be for much longer, with most sessions finishing in the next fifteen minutes.

"Getting a jump on the cadets, huh?" I chuckled, eyeing the large tiger shifter at my side.

"You know it. Today's curry day. Those greedy arseholes tend to wipe out the naan, leaving the chapatis."

Grabbing a tray, I peered around the room, taking stock of my surroundings. Only two tables were currently occupied. One with two young shifters who looked barely old enough to be here. Another had a vampire wearing a bright pink tee and an odd hair-wrap thing on her head. Her nose was buried in a book.

The cafeteria accommodated the whole recruit and staff population easily, which I imagined never reached capacity. Easy was not a term associated with the academy. The two-year training provided by the SICB very quickly differentiated between those cut out to be agents or other SICB employees and those who were not suited to the commitment and skills needed.

After the first year, the cohort split into the first stage of specialisms.

"Let's go grab a table." Prescott pulled me away from glancing around the open space filled with large tables.

I bobbed my head, letting him know I'd follow after serving myself some food. The curry smelled delicious, so I took a healthy couple of scoops along with rice and naan.

Once I sat opposite Prescott, I accepted the water he poured me with thanks. "So, spill," I started, saluting him with my glass of water. "You're a trainer here?"

"Third year," he said before taking a mouthful of curry.

"What's your specialism?"

"Tactics."

Considering the last I'd heard about Prescott was him joining the counterterrorism division, I was surprised by his answer. "What happened to counterterrorism?"

Two lines appeared between his brows. "A prosthetic leg and a steel plate in my sternum."

"The fuck?"

A humourless snort escaped him. "Pretty close to my reaction too."

With horror battling it out with my shock, I shook my head. "Shit, man." What else could I possibly say? Supes healed at an accelerated rate, some species faster than others. For a shifter to need such medical intervention was almost unheard of.

Not that we could grow a whole limb back or anything. That sure as hell would be helpful, but there was a limit to how much healing a body could do.

Prescott shrugged and met my gaze. A smile pulled at his lips. While it didn't touch his eyes, there was acceptance there. "It is what it is. We took down Levy Canceca, so it was worth it."

"Fuck. That was you?" Canceca had been behind a series of attacks on and off Australian soil. The list of deaths his group had been responsible for was too long to memorise.

"Me and my team, yeah. Lost two good men."

"Fuck." Placing my hand on his forearm, I squeezed. Sometimes there were no words to express the sorrow or anger at the injustices in the world, let alone what we experienced trying to keep our communities and country safe.

At the sound of voices edging closer, I pulled away.

"It's all good, though. Working here has its moments." He scooped up a spoonful of curry, the tightness around his eyes easing. "Not cooking for myself being one of them." He bounced his brows and got to chewing, the tension fizzling away.

Focussing on relaxing my shoulders and brushing away the effects of Prescott's story, I glanced at the incoming bodies. The recruits were noisy fuckers. Some laughing, joking around, some in quiet conversations, while a few solo cadets entered.

A punch of heat rushed into me when my gaze caught Shaw's. While his weren't the only golden eyes in the incoming group, they may as well have been a beacon.

A signal to get my attention and keep it.

At his side were a female wolf shifter and a vampire, the latter probably just forty or so, young for his species to be at the academy. Vampires were known to join a little later in their immortal lives, usually needing a break from monotony, and often after having lived at least one human life cycle.

The shifter was speaking animatedly at Shaw's side. The words were undecipherable within the volume and number of conversations. Her worry was clear, though. Good. It meant Shaw had begun to lay the groundwork for his story.

With most of my attention on Shaw and his complete attention on me, the stumble came out of nowhere. Amusement slammed into me at the look of horror morphing Shaw's features as he displayed no grace whatsoever while he stopped just short of falling backwards, having run into a large bear shifter who'd stopped in the queue.

Heat flooded his cheeks, his gaze dashing away from me as he mumbled an apology and spoke in hushed voices to his two friends.

Meanwhile, I swallowed down my laughter, entertained he hadn't been paying attention.

"Who's got your attention?"

Prescott's voice snapped my focus back to him, but not quickly enough, as he was already staring at a red-faced Shaw.

"I heard Shaw had won some sort of challenge with you. That right?" He turned his gaze back to me, interest in his tone and in the depth of his oak-brown eyes.

"Yeah." I chuckled, loosening the muscles in my shoulders. "Set up a bunch of tasks." We were still alone, a good distance from the cohort and the slowly filling tables. Not that my volume was foolproof. It wouldn't take much for someone to overhear.

Which meant every word I said while on campus had to be deliberate. Concise. Have meaning.

"That kid won. Seemed decent enough, if not a bit of a try hard. Seems a bit distracted, though." I shrugged, making sure I didn't look in Shaw's direction. "Not going to hold my breath that he'll do something of worth." I held back my wince, knowing I sounded like an arsehole.

The importance of remaining low-key and staying under the radar was essential. It meant that while I'd be meeting up with Shaw regularly, to anyone paying close attention, it had to appear like I had a complete lack of interest in the man.

"Honestly, I'm already looking for ways to get the hell out of here."

Prescott arched an eyebrow at me. "You piss someone off?"

"Ha. Just a couple of times." I shrugged it off. For years, I'd been known for nothing beyond being smooth and laid-back. My new partner, Chris, wouldn't have recognised that version of me. I needed to figure out how to play this with Prescott.

Sure, years had passed, and people changed, obviously, but my official role and background in the bureau said nothing about the death of my human partner. Just like it didn't mention the covert ops I'd run point on over the years. Hell, our unit's very existence remained on a need-to-know basis.

The version I presented of myself now would be it. The character I played. The Vaughn Michaels who worked in the Global Response Shifter Force. And since I'd already played the pissed-off arsehole card, it made sense for me to stick with that.

Considering my attitude over the past year, it wouldn't be too much of a challenge. Or any at all depending on who you asked from my unit.

"Just see the next month as a mini-break. Little paperwork. No report writing. It's cruisy."

With a quirk of my brow, I grinned. "Sounds like a plan."

"And I wouldn't worry too much about Shaw."

"No?" I asked casually.

"Nah. He might be top of his classes, but he keeps his head down most of the time. Doesn't usually demand attention or even have a big ego."

"Top of his classes yet doesn't parade like a peacock?" Real surprise lifted my question. It wasn't uncommon for brilliance and arrogance to go hand in hand.

"Not that I've seen. Keeps to himself. Is dedicated. Give him some crazy challenging tasks, and he'll be out of your hair while figuring them out."

"So he's determined and is going places?" I asked innocently, more than aware of Callen and Thatch's plans for him.

Prescott shrugged and placed his utensils down on his empty plate. The tables were filling up around us, and while I couldn't see Shaw from where I sat, I was acutely aware of his position. "Time will tell." He bounced his brows. "Let's grab a dessert and take it back to the staff quarters. The volume of these guys inhaling food gets old fast." He stood with a smirk, and I followed suit.

As soon as I turned, my gaze once again connected with Shaw's. This time he immediately looked away. I barely held back my eyeroll. The kid needed to stop seeking me out.

Talk about potentially blowing our cover.

Not that I was any better, and damn if that didn't piss me the hell off.

I didn't sleep for shit.

It took two strong coffees to get me to function. This morning, I was due to observe special-ops training. It would give me time to get a read on Cramer, one of the technicians here, and observe some of the cadets.

While I was itching to meet with Shaw to check on his progress, which had been planned for later this afternoon, it didn't mean I was looking forward to it. That totally wasn't the reason. Because, Jesus, I didn't even know the kid—though that wasn't strictly true.

Last night I'd stayed up late finally studying the files Kent sent over.

Not only did it contain the details of the case—the missing trainees and the chief instructor—but it also had overviews of the assessors, trainers, and other academy staff as well as everything the SICB knew about Shaw.

Unsurprisingly, the information was detailed and concise. What did take me by surprise, though, was Shaw had studied at university for three years, receiving an honours degree in supe and human relations, alongside a minor in law. After that, he'd spent two years working for Legal Support Services, acting as a court liaison.

It meant he wasn't exactly a kid or as green as I'd thought.

Not that you had to be young in the academy. Hell, one of the cadets was a seventy-two-year-old vampire.

I shovelled down my breakfast, half listening to a conversation between Prescott and one of the human instructors. At forty-eight, Sandra had spent ten years out in the field before she'd joined the academy. The files stated she was dedicated and passionate. What they didn't have a record of was how she was in a romantic relationship with Prescott.

It took just ten minutes for me to figure out they were at least sleeping with each other. Beyond that, I didn't know if they were serious or just screwing around.

"It's time to get our arses into gear. You know where you're going?" Prescott stood as he spoke, attention on me.

Swallowing my last swig of coffee, I bobbed my head. "Yeah. Got the lay of the land yesterday."

"In that case, I'll see you later. Try not to scare any of the recruits off. There's not many left." He rolled his eyes good-naturedly.

"That right?" I asked, leaving from the same exit as Prescott after Sandra left in a different direction.

Keeping my tone mildly amused, I asked, "Even fewer making the cut than in our day?"

"Nah, not really. Just a few dropped off later than normal. Par for the course, though, right?"

"Not in the final year, from memory." Lifting my shoulders in a careless shrug, I focussed on the group a few steps ahead of me, spotting Shaw immediately. Thankfully, there'd been no eye contact or acknowledgment so far this morning. "Anyhow, catch you later." Walking away, I offered an up-nod, deliberately not waiting for a response.

Instead, I kept my eyes on the small group ahead, following them, since they were scheduled for ops training.

I held back my twitching lips when I tuned in to their conversation.

"—stripping. You'd make a killing." The shifter Rickman nudged Shaw's side, amusement in the action and her tone.

A humourless snort spilled out of Shaw. "I don't think that's going to cut it, but thanks for the seal of approval." With his face angled towards Rickman, I could see his side profile. A soft smile played on his lips, but everything else about him reeked of despondency.

Impressive.

"He's right." Henderson, an interesting character, based on his profile notes, bobbed his head. "I've heard that meds for the D34R virus are crazy expensive. Crippling almost." A tight, sad smile sat on his mouth. "I'm sure you'll get it figured out. Your mum's still working for the bureau, right? Won't your family get assistance or something?"

Shaw started shaking his head halfway through Henderson speaking. "You know the system doesn't work like that. Nonhumans have a limited budget assigned per year for medical support. No way will whatever healthcare my dad needs cover that."

It was true. My mood soured at the reality of Shaw's words.

Financial support for medical care was virtually non-existent for the supernatural community. Since supernaturals had the ability to heal at an accelerated rate, the government, in its wisdom, had prioritised human healthcare. While I understood the fundamentals of that, shifters and vamps still got sick and injured.

A bone of contention amongst the political parties, especially with virus warfare becoming more prominent over the past thirty years.

"Just..." A defeated sigh preceded Shaw's next words. "...if you hear of any jobs or anything, let me know, yeah? If I can't get anything on the side, I'll have to...." He trailed off, shook his head, and released a heavy breath.

"You'll what?" Concern filled Henderson's words.

"Nothing." Shaw looked away. "It'll be fine, I'm sure."

Having reached the large building used for field operation scenarios, the group stopped talking and filed in. While I followed, my brain ticked over the possibilities of what was going on and what the missing recruits were involved in.

At present, the biggest concern was that the instigators wouldn't take the bait. While Shaw had a reason to need money, we weren't even certain that was the draw factor. Plus there was the fact that his father hadn't worked for AXF for five years, and since they were the links—the research company and the academy—would it be enough?

But with no other students having AFX connections, a fact confirmed by Kent's diligent report, we just had to hope this fishing trip would be fruitful.

Fuck knew what we'd do if not.

The morning proved interesting. Not exactly related to the case at all, but watching the recruits in action kept me entertained.

Fumes circulated through the building. The scent

of lead, heavy in the air, unavoidable with so many rounds of ammunition being fired.

I loved it. The smell reassuring, familiar.

With the recruits so close to passing and joining the SICB in their official capacity, the unit layout wasn't simple and static. Where would the challenge be in that?

Like a well-oiled machine, the area was rigged with moving targets, sensory deprivation blocks, and after discussing the setup with the technician, more than five thousand possible patterns. That, and walls could actually be moved.

It was an impressive structure.

The team I observed, which included Shaw, his two friends, another vampire, and two humans, worked almost seamlessly as a unit. In action, amongst the flashing lights, the smoke screens, and the random targets, there were only two mishits.

Mildly impressed, I called out, "Who took that killing shot on target seven?" While there were cameras dotted throughout, my eyes couldn't be everywhere.

"Shaw." Rickman smacked her group leader on the back as they removed their headgear and clicked on their safeties. Because of course it was Shaw. That he'd stepped into the role of group leader for the task, each member happily accepting his authority, wasn't even a surprise.

For the first time today, Shaw peered my way. Bright-eyed, he grinned. Jesus. That stare, his hunger, his joy, the exhilaration flooding his features threatened to catch my breath.

It looked good on him: success of the win, the thrill of the mission.

It had been so long since I'd experienced those emotions, let alone saw them expressed by anyone in my team. What I wouldn't give to feel that way again, and with a partner who read me like the pages of their favourite novel.

Aware of my silent stare, I bobbed my head. "Good shot," I offered. "What happened with target five?" Since Shaw was the team leader, I directed the question to him.

The smile on his face slipped, and my gut tightened. This, my reaction, me pushing, not being too impressed was a necessary evil. The reminder had me throwing up my shutters.

"The team split to cover the two areas."

"Why?" Voice devoid of emotion, I stared him down.

"There were four possible entry points and five obstacles obscuring the view. It was the only way to ensure full visibility and to provide clear shots."

"Clear shots? Really?" I quirked my brow and held back my smirk at the slight tick in his jaw. That there he needed to control. "If the shots were clear, why the two mishits? If the targets had guns, Bennett and Rickman would be dead."

The click of his swallow hit my ears. "There were eleven targets, all were taken down. The smoke made the visibility of number five tricky, but the team got the job done."

The group around him stood straighter. They had his back, trusted him. It was a good sign.

"The targets also weren't firing at you. If they had been, you'd be the one reaching out to the next of kin, letting them know your call had got them killed."

"Respectfully, Agent Michaels, Shaw took the only option possible. There was no—"

"Bullshit." My word was clipped and shut Henderson up. Returning my gaze to Shaw, I sized him up, wondering if he had what it took to follow my lead, read me despite us not having worked together before.

Units should be able to work by osmosis, anticipating their leader's and their teammates' moves. Curious to see how Shaw would handle himself under real pressure, I stared at him hard.

He didn't move under my scrutiny. No more clenching of his jaw. No fidgeting. It didn't mean he wasn't pissed off, though.

"You. Reload your ammo." Not waiting for a response from Shaw, I turned to the rest of the group, saying, "The rest of you, go to the observation room." Not checking to make sure they carried out my orders, I walked over to the technician. "Can you run the same programme to have the same issues and obstacles, but repositioned so we don't know what's coming?"

"Yeah, of course."

"Do you have the capacity to arm your targets?"

Wide-eyed, the technician nodded. "With live ammo or paintballs?"

"Live ammo."

The guy shifted a little uncomfortably. "I'll need the approval of the chief."

"That's Agent Thatcher, right? Acting as interim chief?"

"Yes, sir, it is."

"He's already given me carte blanche while I'm here."

"I'll need—"

"Check your email."

While Thatch had provided instructions for instructors and trainers to allow me to take over and run things how I wanted, I didn't expect he'd be happy about live ammo. But still, these wannabe agents had to learn.

There was no room for excuses out in the field.

A mistake could cost someone their life.

Something I knew all too well.

And if Shaw was as good as Thatch thought he was, as the assessors here believed, plus if he did join our unit soon, hell yes, I was going to push him. See what he was really made of.

I turned my back on the tech when his brows shot up while reading the email and went to suit up.

Shaw waited for me in silence, his gaze steady and unwavering.

"We're doing the exact same scenario."

"I heard."

My lips almost twitched at his practically monotone response. "You okay with going in with live ammo? Can I trust you to have my back, follow my lead?" Searching his gaze as I spoke, I saw the shift in him. It was slight, but enough for me to be sure he was in this.

"Yes." Resolute and firm, his voice held conviction. The spark I'd squashed in him earlier roared back to life—obvious in the uptick of his breathing, the way the hairs on his arms lifted. "I will not let you down."

The way he stared at me, the sincerity in his very being, was like a punch in the gut. Rather than pain slamming through me, awareness and excitement awakened.

Like a soothing balm, his eagerness, his determination, coated me. Energy thrummed through my limbs as a smile split my face. I couldn't hold it back, couldn't bury the elation down. And hell if it didn't feel like I was coming alive, waking up after a dark, miserable sleep.

Surprise morphed his features before they settled into happy expectancy. With his smile so big, so real, Shaw locked and loaded. Once he was done, he bobbed his head. "You lead and I'll follow."

Fuck me dead.

Those words called forth a brand-new need in me. But for now, I wanted to see what Shaw's capabilities really were. I just hoped I wouldn't be pulling bullets out of my chest for the rest of the day.

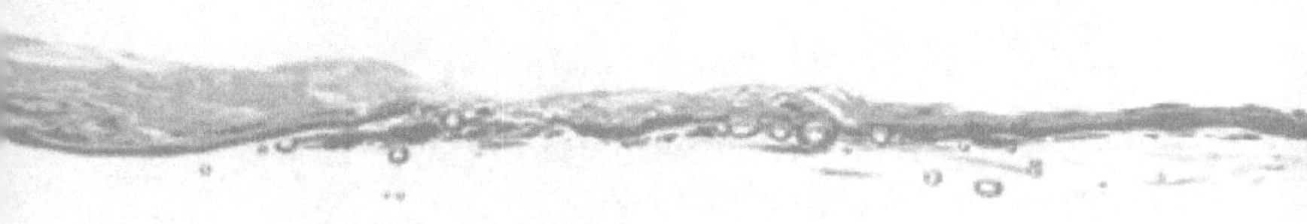

CHAPTER 4
SHAW

Two against eleven. We totally had this.

Anticipation battled with nervous excitement in my veins. Working with live ammo was one heck of an adrenaline rush. But what got me buzzing even more was doing this with Michaels.

"Comms open," he instructed, peering back at me at the entrance of the course.

The area was set up to replicate a multi-room building. Grinding, shuffling, groaning cogs drifted out of the training space. Blinker, the tech, was working his magic and mixing things up while we waited to get started.

Walls would be shifted by the press of a button, targets hidden away in discreet storage in the walls, while new targets would be repositioned, this time armed with weapons containing live ammo activated by a high-tech computer program.

"You keep your eyes and ears open. If either senses are compromised, use your nose."

I nodded my understanding.

"Follow my lead, read my body."

I locked down the roaming thoughts that surfaced at his words, remaining focussed, intently listening to his instructions.

"Trust your gut."

Startled at the intensity of his words, my brows shot high before furrowing in question.

"Everything at the academy is all about following the rules, staying on the mission. It's not real life. Shit goes wrong all the time. If something feels off, even if it doesn't make a lick of sense, react and follow through. But never compromise your unit. You got me?"

I gave a short, sharp nod, my pulse picking up speed. "Yes, sir."

"And that right there." He pointed a finger at my chest. "Keep your heart pumping. It'll help you stay alert. You guys having breakfast, then strolling on down here for this training, is something you should never do out in the field. That sort of relaxed state can be detrimental to your focus and ability on mission. A high-pumping heart will boost your mental awareness. You need to activate your brain and not rely on your strength or your reflexes."

He waited until I nodded before he cracked his neck side to side, checked his weapon, patted his spare guns and ammo, then he smiled so big and wide that it was like seeing a different man. "Sounds like we're ready."

The thundering of my heart pulsed in my ears, but I couldn't hold back my smirk. We hadn't even started, and I knew this was going to change everything. Blow my mind wide open and make it clear that joining the ITU, working alongside Michaels for real, had to happen.

A quick triple-check of my weapons, and I turned off my Glock's safety and stood in position. With my eyes on Michaels, I scanned my surroundings with my other senses, waiting for his instruction.

His two-finger go signal had us moving.

With Michaels taking point, we edged through the entrance.

In position, I scanned the small room, relying on my shifter vision to cut through the shadows rippling with heat and smoke.

Michaels was five steps ahead. "Clear," he whispered. With just one door out, no windows and no places to hide, he continued forward, close to the wall at a steady pace.

A sound a few metres ahead in the other room had me pausing and tapping on my comms twice. Immediately, Michaels paused. His nod was miniscule, but enough to let me know he'd heard and was on it.

With my Glock in position, I stepped closer before shifting over to the opposite side of the doorway, zeroing in on the section of the room I could see. Pausing, I scented the air. Chemicals, oil, plus the distinct aroma of chemically enhanced shifter scent—a special blend created by the tech team to allow trainees to use all senses.

A quick glance at Michaels and I nodded, signalling to him.

As soon as Michaels indicated he was in position, I prepared myself, ready to follow his lead. One hand movement and we stepped into the room, Michaels dropping low.

I was at his heels, focussed on the right, taking out one threat a half a second before Michaels neutralised another. Heat beat down at us, the aim to disorientate and slow our reactions.

But not on my watch.

Another sound and two possible exits. Targeting the threat, I moved, dropping low and firing two rounds as the third target moved into view. Once the hits made their mark, the rigged device pulled the target out of the way, clearing our path.

Sweat trickled down my spine, the heat stifling as we pushed ahead.

In the third room, the smoke obscured my vision. I held back, stepping to Michaels's side before edging away. Tingles shot up my spine, fast and impossible to ignore. I turned, pressing my sweat-soaked back to Michaels as we both opened fire, taking down two more targets in quick succession.

The red light spotlighted direct hits.

Another room, another three marks. This time a shot hurled in our direction while we took out two and ducked for cover. Hidden from the next room and opposite me, Michaels focussed on me. Even in the darkness, his exhilaration was obvious.

He loved this shit.

Bouncing his brows once, I knew he was about to take action. My lips twitched as I looked at Michaels, my heart stuttering when he threw me a wink before we moved in synch, the next target taking two hits, mine right in the heart, Michaels's in the centre of his forehead.

We couldn't be sure there were eleven hostiles like

last time, but the mission would remain the same. Take down the enemy and secure the two hostages.

We edged to the next door and faced each other. Trying to get a read on Michaels, I stared hard. But there was no time to communicate, no time for a breath.

Multiple shots fired in another room. We ducked. Raced towards the sound. Michaels two steps ahead, me on his six. A target appeared to my right. I took it down, still charging, not willing to let Michaels go in alone. A loud shot rang when he incapacitated another target.

I scanned and ran, keeping so close that if he stopped, I'd likely slam into him if I didn't keep my bearings. A moment later, we were in the room. I shifted, taking out two more assailants, rolling to my left as a bullet whizzed past me, splintering the doorframe.

"Fuck." With my heart in my throat, I zeroed in on the two hostages, aware of Michaels creeping ahead on my left, easing towards another door and a stack of boxes. Neither of us knowing if there were any more hostiles, every step was cautious.

Not only did I have to activate the rescue signal attached to the hostages, but the rooms needed to be cleared. All hostiles taken down.

Slowing down my breathing, I took careful steps towards the hostages, trusting Michaels to have my back. The corner was clear, enabling me to head towards the hostages. A sweep over them, checking for weapons and positioning, and I was sure the dummies were in fact the prisoners—the memory of yesterday's test with Michaels at the forefront of my mind.

Standing in front of the captives, my back to them, I aimed at the open doorway to the uncleared room. Thick smoke rolled out of the room, picking up intensity. Anticipating final players to take down, the hairs on my arms stood on end.

I couldn't leave Michaels to clear the space, my gut screaming at me to be at his side. Positive nothing would be coming up behind us, certain we'd swept our route carefully, I left the hostages. Sure, in a real situation, I would have perhaps stowed them away in the corner of the room, but that wasn't possible in this scenario.

Once at Michaels's side, he offered me an up-nod and signalled for me to go right.

With my finger on the trigger, I took point, going low, sweeping right, and unable to see a thing. Not only was it dark, despite the beam of light filtering in from one window, but the chemically enhanced smoke was too thick to cut through.

With no idea if there were additional doors in the room, I kept close to the wall, Michaels behind me.

A shadow.

Movement.

Yanking Michaels down, I fired just as a bullet lodged into the wall where his head would have been. A thud followed by a red light gave me some direction.

With my heart threatening to explode from my chest, I locked my jaw and reined in my reaction, stopping my body from shaking at the close call of seeing Michaels with a bullet in his skull. It would be highly unlikely anyone could come back from that.

We darted fast and low, taking out one more hostile before we returned to the hostages. As soon as I was before them, I hit the release button. A green light flared to life as the lights turned on, heating cut out, and ventilation kicked in, clearing the room of smoke.

"Holy fucking shit." I snagged Michaels without thought beyond my relief, tugging him towards me and wrapping my arms around him. "Jesus. That was fucking intense."

His low chuckle at my ear left me grinning. "Good save there, Shaw." He hugged me back with two hard slaps.

Still smiling, I eased away. Laughter stirred in my chest, exhilaration buzzing in my veins. "That was insane. Amazing, but shit." I shook my hands out. With so much energy pumping through me, I needed to do... something.

The smile directed my way caught my breath, and fuck if I could pull my gaze away. My mouth went dry. I darted out my tongue, swiping it across my bottom lip, still focussed on Michaels's mouth.

When his smile slipped, my throat clicked as I swallowed hard. It didn't stop me from taking a step forward.

His lips parted, chest moving with his heavy breaths.

"Mission successfully completed."

I jumped, the sound over the speaker system scaring me half to death. "Fuck." I pressed my hand against my chest, my heart hammering so hard, I could feel the vibrations in my fingers.

Michaels snorted. "Good job there weren't any surprise announcements during the scenario."

I rolled my eyes, flipping him off. Was he my superior? Sure. But fuck if I could hold back any of my inappropriate reactions around the man.

"Come on. Let's get out of here." He cast a glance at one of the three cameras I'd spotted.

"They all turn off as soon as the green light signals, ending the scenario." And it was a good job, too, considering how I'd eye fucked him and got all up in his space with that hug. I cleared my throat, checked that I'd remembered to put my safety back on, and slotted the Glock back into the holder at my waist.

Side by side, we walked out, my pulse calming as we got closer to the exit. Tension remained thick between us. I was so aware of every breath, every movement, every blink.

Keeping my stare ahead, I thought about the mission, thought about what I needed to share with him at our meeting later.

My parents are in protective custody because I agreed to take on this mission.

The thought hit me where it needed to. Straightening my shoulders, I took one last calming breath before we stepped out of the simulation.

What we were doing wasn't a game.

It wasn't a test.

A real, dangerous situation lay before me. Keeping my head in the mission was my focus. Whatever pull towards Michaels I felt was inconsequential.

For now.

Nerves, oh how I hated them.

It didn't matter that they held hands with my excitement.

It was my first official meeting with Michaels. The whole way to the private conference room, I worked at talking myself down. What that meant was getting my heart rate to behave and my libido to toe the line. The reason for the latter?

This morning we were tasked with swimming pool time, to keep pushing our speed and practice holding our breath. While it sounded a little kindergarten-esque, apparently both were skills we were expected to excel at in the SICB.

As a panther, swimming wasn't my favourite, but that didn't mean I was bad at it.

But hell if Michaels joining us, complete in board shorts, revealing his ripped abs and toned muscles and all that expanse of skin, didn't nearly have me drowning.

All that session achieved was working me up for this meeting, making my "whatever pull towards Michaels I felt was inconsequential" thoughts a mockery.

He was already waiting for me by the time I arrived.

I took a second to fully compose myself before stepping inside, closing the door behind me. The *pop* followed.

"Hey."

Shit, was that too lame? Too informal? Should I be greeting him as "Agent Michaels?"

"Take a seat."

Relieved he directed me to sit, I went gladly, preferring the safety of a table separating us rather than standing and not knowing what to do with my hands.

"What do you have so far?"

Shoulders relaxing, I smiled. *This* I could do. Discuss the mission and get to the point. "The rumour's out there. I've made it clear I'm looking for a quick way to earn cash. Said loud and clear about my dad's specialism in medical research."

He bobbed his head. "If you get a bite, it's going to take some time." His tone indicated a begrudging acceptance.

"Yeah. The last thing I'm expecting is someone to corner me and simply offer me a side gig. I'll step it up. Add in more details, more phone calls."

"I'll make sure you receive a couple of emails from your mum. Perhaps get the first bill for medical care."

"That makes sense." It was a good idea. Medical costs could be astronomical for nonhumans, especially since the government provided barely any funding.

"I've been looking through the files on staff and recruits. There's a couple of potential amber flags, but honestly, nothing to really go on. If there was anything blatant, I'd be more concerned about the academy's interview process and background checks."

I listened intently, agreeing completely. "I plan to spend less time holed up in my room for studying or the gym for practice. Make sure I'm around other students more," I offered. It was my norm to put focus on study and training. While I had a couple of close friends, I wasn't exactly a socialite. Sure, I could shoot the shit, but I didn't make a habit of lazing about or hanging out for the sake of it.

I supposed it could get lonely at times, but I figured there'd be plenty of opportunities for that once I'd been sworn in and was with my new team.

"Stealth eavesdropping, huh?" Michaels quirked his brow, intensely studying me.

"It's fun." I grinned.

He snorted. "Until you get caught."

I rolled my eyes. "That's where the stealth comes in."

Two lines appeared between his brows as though he was deep in thought.

"What are you thinking?"

Surprise flooded his features, understandable since I was outright asking, but a wallflower I was not.

"Just coming up with a plan to check how good your stealth skills really are."

A flutter of anticipation found life in my chest. Learning from Michaels, being challenged by him, sounded like my idea of a good time.

"And that there"—he pointed at me—"needs to stop."

I clenched my back teeth, knowing exactly what he was talking about. "I'm not usually this bad," I admitted, fighting hard at keeping my tells to myself. I seriously wasn't. It was all his damn fault. Michaels and his sexy abs. Michaels looking like a dripping lollipop I wanted to lick clean when he'd stepped out of the swimming pool.

"You're not, huh?"

I counted to three, controlling my pulse, containing those traitorous fluttering wings going wild and trying to take flight.

"Nope."

His lips twitched. "Better. That was fast control."

Swallowing back my inner peacock at his praise, I nodded. "So, stealth. What have you got for me?"

His smile turned positively wicked, and I was

certain by the time I locked myself away in my room after this, I'd melt or explode. Maybe both.

With his roguish grin in place, he stood. "Follow me."

It didn't take long before I realised where he was leading me. I freaking loved the holo room. The training space offered physical props to help with the programmed simulations. But I also knew there were cyber specialists working on replicating matter, which would offer solid projections.

The tech was out of this world.

We weren't quite there yet, but I expected—hoped—it wouldn't be long.

We stepped inside the large warehouse-style space, sealing the door behind us.

"You spent much time in here?" Michaels asked.

"As much as I can get away with."

He chuckled. "It's fucking awesome. This tech was only in the early stages of development when I was training."

"Jesus, how old are you?" I sassed.

He flipped me off, and I couldn't do anything about my heart flip. That he was being so casual with me was a hell of a thing. "We'll run a stealth programme."

"*We* as in you're joining in?"

Something close to excitement filled his eyes. It

suited him. "Fuck yes. I love this tech. I've only been able to have a play a couple of times since being an agent."

Getting any sort of emotion from Michaels would be an extra mission of mine, I decided. It looked good on him.

"Being out in the real world doesn't offer much opportunity for playtime, huh?" I teased.

"Well, I don't know about that." His voice dropped low, the gruffness making my breath catch. He looked away quickly, focussing on the wall pad while I stopped myself from swallowing loudly, refusing to give away just how much the sound of his rough voice affected me.

"I'll grab the devices." It was the safer option rather than standing here staring at the man.

I returned a moment later and handed him the small unit. We fit the tech over our eyes, like eyeglasses. After attaching the tiny neuron reader to my temple, I slotted in the earplugs, which doubled up as comms and simulation instructions.

"You ready?" Michaels made eye contact with me. The excitement wasn't completely lost, not now he was kitted out and ready to start the simulation. While his smile was so minuscule it would be invisible to most, I latched on to the gesture, grinning wide, keen to get started.

"Hell yes, I'm ready."

His lips twitched as he passed me the laser gun that could be programmed for different types of weaponry.

"Stealth mission, here we come."

The countdown began at the click of a button. With it came the computer's mission instructions.

"Your mission is to tag five key targets with a tracking device while remaining undetected. You have fifteen minutes to complete the task."

Just like the outside training space, there were a multitude of variations to the programme, so this mission would be different to others I'd practiced. And doing it with a partner wasn't something I did in my free time.

We'd have to pay attention to the patrols' behaviour patterns and stay under the radar. There'd also be security systems I expected, like cameras, volume alerts, possibly tripwires in place.

I flicked the switch on my gun to the correct mode, one that would fire out tiny cyber tracking devices.

A buzzer sounded in our headsets, and the scene before us changed.

The sun set behind a rugged terrain. Bushes dotted the area outside a building. Without speaking, Michaels and I made our way through the darkness towards our target—what looked to be a high-security facility.

Moving quietly through the shadows, we navigated the perimeter. I spotted a sensor ahead and indicated to Michaels. He nodded and we continued, avoiding motion sensors and security cameras with slow moves and precision.

As we approached the first target, a high-ranking enemy official from the looks of it, the sound of footsteps approached. Quickly, we took cover behind a nearby bush, silently watching as two of the holographic enemy soldiers passed by, oblivious to our presence.

Once the coast was clear, we emerged from our hiding spot and approached the official. Aiming at the target, Michaels fired his laser gun. The device hit its mark.

We retreated into the shadows, heading towards our next target located in the heavily guarded building. A quick scan showed a possible path ahead. I directed Michaels with a series of gestures. Rather than studying my suggestion, he indicated for me to take point.

It was a hell of a thing, his trust.

We worked together to slip past the guards, quietly making our way to the next target's location.

As we approached the target, once again the sound of footsteps approached. Spotting a desk, we took cover, holding our breaths as three enemy soldiers entered the room. Determination thrummed through my veins, adrenaline vibrating and threatening to make my pulse race. We waited until the soldiers had passed before tagging the target and making our escape.

With three more targets to tag and time ticking down, we had to be quick. We moved swiftly through the facility, avoiding detection and tagging our targets with ease. Just as we were about to mark the fifth and final target, two enemy soldiers entered the lab.

With the mission to remain undetected, we had a decision to make. And it all came down to our interpretation of the mission wording.

Did it mean no alarms and we could take down the bad guys in silence? Or was it complete incognito—that no one would ever know we were here?

Making eye contact with Michaels, who pressed against my side, I silently questioned him. The tilt of his head let me know it was my call.

I pressed a button on my glasses. We had two minutes to complete the mission and get out of enemy territory.

Time was not on our side.

I indicated for Michaels to go right and circle one of the armed guards, letting him know I'd head in the other direction. We needed to incapacitate them without alerting the fifth target.

By the time the attack was discovered, there'd be no focus on checking for tracking devices, effectively securing the tracking device without giving the target the heads-up.

With my focus on the guard, I moved stealthily around the shelves and stack of boxes, keeping my senses alert for any signs of danger. Once in position, I waited, eyes penetrating the darkness, seeking Michaels out. Already in position, his gaze was on me.

The only way to do this was a combined attack.

He signalled three and gave an up-nod.

Three seconds it was.

On three, I darted forward, grabbing the unsuspecting guard from behind, wrapping my strong arms around his neck in a chokehold. The man struggled against my vice-like grip, but it was no use. No way was I letting go.

I tightened my hold, cutting off the guard's oxygen supply, rendering him unconscious. Silently, I lowered the man to the floor—having learned the correct pressure to use with holograms to make it work—seeking out Michaels, who was still crouched at his guard's side.

With a quirk of his lips and a nod, he gave me the go-ahead.

I grinned, chest feeling full, and aimed at the target a few metres away. Her back was turned to us as she stood at a desk. A pull of the trigger and the tracker found its mark.

A second later, the lights flickered on, the hologram faded away, and the computer system announced our victory.

I pulled off my headset, not giving a shit that Michaels would be able to hear my racing heart. "Fuck, I love this programme."

Following suit, he tugged off his glasses, a grin appearing and nearly knocking me on my arse with how perfect it was. "It's impressive."

"Right. Just imagine what it's going to be like when they fully develop the system to include solid projections." There was a little substance already with the guards we had to wrestle, but not quite enough to make it feel real.

Was I standing there with a dopey grin on my face, revelling in the high of the session? Damn straight. And with the way Michaels looked at me, his eyes wide and bright, I kinda figured he loved it too.

"So, was I stealth as fuck?" I bounced my brows for good measure.

"The stealthiest." The hint of teasing in his voice caught me by surprise. I latched on to it.

"And we make a pretty good team, right?"

His smile slipped a fraction, some sort of emotion bleeding into the depths of his eyes. My stomach bottomed out, wishing I could take my words back, hating that the sparkle in his gaze had dimmed.

"Yeah." He tilted his head, studying me. "We made a pretty great team."

And while I missed the joy from a few moments ago, I still smiled, high on the thrill of spending time with Michaels and kicking holographic arse.

"So, another round?"

At his words, I laughed, agreeing immediately. I didn't doubt meeting with Michaels was going to quickly become the highlight of my day.

IT TOOK FIVE LONG, FRUSTRATING DAYS TO GET A lead. At least I hoped that was what I was about to discover. While it didn't sound like a long wait in the grand scheme of things, with the chief still missing and

Michaels's cover having a finite time, it felt closer to a month.

Not that the five days had been a total bust.

I'd spent alone time with Michaels every day. Technically that time was meant to be spent engaging in one-on-one training, which it was. The fact had surprised me.

With little to go on, so little conversation of sharing intel to be had, Michaels had used our time to give me genuine instruction. He'd shared what missions he could with me, gave me pointers about my training sessions he'd witnessed, and we'd grappled. A lot.

And hell if that wasn't fast becoming my favourite way to spend time with him.

Up close and personal, bodies close and sweaty. Heavy breaths in my ear. Needless to say, each hand-to-hand combat session I walked away from resulted in a cold shower and me taking myself in hand with Michaels's name on my lips.

It was dangerous and wrong, but so damn hot, I wasn't willing to stop.

But finally, a lead.

I headed off campus and made my way towards the large public gardens about three kilometres away. Cars passed me by, their engines humming with the buzz of electricity. The spring sun dipped low, close to touching the taller buildings lining the CBD in the horizon.

Unable to speak to Michaels in person given the short notice of this off-site meeting, I'd asked Henderson to get word to him that I would be late for our six o'clock session, using the excuse that I had to take an urgent call with my parents.

While Henderson had looked uncomfortable about passing the note to Michaels, courtesy of Michaels not being especially warm and fuzzy around campus, he'd promised to pass it on. The message should alert Michaels to some sort of development. While it was a risk to leave site with no backup, this off-the-books job had potential.

I'd found the note in my laptop bag. From there, I'd been led on a wild-goose chase, to the library, to the gym, until finally I found a third envelope with coordinates and a time.

And with the instruction to come alone.

Ominous for sure, which made me think this could actually lead to something.

It had left me just twenty minutes to get off campus and to the east side of the gardens.

Spotting the entrance to the public gardens, I picked up the pace. The colour and scent of flowers filled my senses as soon as I stepped inside the confines of the ten-acre space.

A wall of frangipanis lined my way as I followed the concrete path before splitting off towards the east. It led me to a small pond where a couple of swans drifted gracefully as though travelling along a steady current rather than working their feet in the still water.

Checking the time, I slowed my pace. I had four minutes, plenty of time. The unhurried steps gave me the space to think and prepare myself for any upcoming conversation.

My parents remained in protective custody. The story of my dad's illness and my mum with him in quarantine was holding strong. Two email exchanges between my mum and me, discussing the illness and the first bill that had come through, along with the financial forecast, had been fabricated, unencrypted, and easy to find and read should anyone need to.

Reaching the area, I glanced around. No one was in sight. Beyond flowers, shrubs, and trees, there was nothing but a single bench and a trash can. The whole thing felt cloak-and-dagger, and while I'd never admit it to anyone, a thrill of excitement pulsed in my veins.

Figuring it was best to sit, I did so, facing the way I came, which gave me the view of three pathways. The entire area remained quiet. With dusk closing in, most people were already home, no doubt preparing their evening meals, kids hooked to their devices, maybe doing their homework rather than kicking around a ball.

On the way, I'd passed by just seven people on the gardens' grounds. Five supes and two humans. None had spared me a second glance. None had trailed after me. Other than the birds fluttering by and the insects buzzing around, the only sound was the trickle of water from a small water feature and the breeze rustling the leaves.

A check of the time told me whoever I was meeting was three minutes late.

Unless no one was meeting me.

Placing my hand under the bench seat, I trailed my fingers along the edge. My heart stuttered when I made contact with paper. Tugging it clear, I held a white envelope.

Scent-free and flat, it didn't scream dangerous, but not wanting to open it while out in the open, I tucked it away in my back pocket, stood, and headed towards the south exit, which wasn't the closest way out, but it was different to the way I'd entered.

Was I being overly cautious? It was likely. But with such little information at hand, it paid to be overzealous.

Back on the street, I closed in on a row of shops, ducking into a side alleyway. With my back to the wall, I took a surreptitious glance around, then opened the letter.

```
$12590
33.8793° S, 151.2155 E
RETRIEVAL: GUNNEBO
BROWN FILE
DROP OFF: 33.7793° S, 151.2159 E
DEADLINE: 0400
```

My pulse thrummed loudly in my ears. The exact value of the first invoice for my dad's care.

This was happening. And clear as hell, a test.

The brand name Gunnebo clued me in to what I'd be expected to do. Safecracking was part of our training, though I didn't imagine the SICB ever intended for our skills to be used for nefarious reasons.

I wanted to talk this out with Michaels, the desire to seek him out pushing at me. Without a doubt, he'd want me to follow through, but with the time sensitivity, I couldn't hover, couldn't second-guess or hesitate.

I definitely couldn't find a secure location to make a call. Shit, why the hell hadn't I been issued with an untraceable, unbuggable mobile or something?

First things first.

The beginning numbers of the coordinates told me I needed to head into the city.

Train it was.

It took over an hour to get into Sydney and find a back-alley internet café. As expected, it was rough as hell. But the place was discreet, without cameras, and boasted an impressive VPN.

After I searched the coordinates, the location before me in black and white, surprise slammed into me. The museum. The hell?

Looked like I was taking a trip to look at dinosaur fossils.

Four hours later, after completing a job that was ridiculously easy—the museum really needed to up their security—I shoved the brown envelope I'd stolen from the safe into the honesty box of a home-grown produce stand, the only structure I'd spotted for three kilometres within range of the coordinates in the white envelope. After that, I jumped back into the rideshare car and directed them to the train station.

The whole journey in the car, then later on the train, I focussed on playing a game that required minimal effort on my phone. It was enough of a distraction to stop my heart bouncing out of my chest.

Nervous energy spiralled through me at the rate of this high-speed train.

Fuck knew what I'd stolen from the museum.

What I'd delivered. I didn't check, take a peek. Today had been about establishing trust. That much I knew.

With how easy the break-in and safecracking was, I didn't expect my skills at breaking and entering were the point of the exercise.

The buzz of an incoming text had me freezing. I glanced around the empty carriage before opening it. A deposit receipt direct to my bank account. Details I'd never provided.

Fuck, this was intense.

Even more so, I had no clue what the hell was going on.

I had to trust that I was smart enough to get through this. Trust that Michaels had my back, even though he wasn't here.

The announcement for my stop filled the carriage. Relieved, I pocketed my phone and waited by the doors, desperate to get out and head to bed. It was past midnight, and I had a five-thirty start. Sleep beckoned, but fuck if it didn't feel like I'd been zapped by a live wire.

With a yawn, I stepped onto the empty platform and trudged to the exit. It was a five-kilometre walk back, which I could do without, but with no other options and wanting to remain under the radar, I placed one foot in front of the other and left the station.

I considered shifting, knowing it would save me so much energy and time. But that would mean stripping down in the middle of the street and abandoning my clothes.

About half a kilometre down the road, I froze. A car was up ahead. Nothing should have been strange about that, but the outline of someone in the driver's seat was visible, making my senses go on high alert. There were no houses around. No shops. No reason for anyone to be pulled over at all, let alone sitting in their car at this time of night.

I relaxed my shoulders, prepared to turn and sprint, when the door opened. No light appeared inside, but after a deep inhale, I relaxed, a rush of air escaping.

Michaels.

Taking long strides, I was at the car in no time. With an arched brow, he indicated the passenger door. Silently, I climbed in, tugging the door closed, and a few seconds later, Michaels started the engine and pulled away.

"Are you okay?"

It took me a second to register that his first question was for my safety rather than the intel. "Yeah," I all but croaked, not having used my voice since I left the campus early yesterday evening. "Tired, but wired."

He nodded. "Yeah. That's normal. Did you come in contact with anyone?"

"No one. Picked up an envelope, jumped through a few hoops to get the job done, and now my bank account is twelve K healthier. Exact same amount as in the hospital invoice."

"No shit?" He shot a look my way, his brows lifted in surprise. "Okay, talk me through it."

So I did. I explained everything from the wild-goose chase, the final note, how I infiltrated the museum and broke into the safe. I went on to describe the drop-off, the location, right to the point of me jumping on the quiet train and returning in an empty carriage.

"You did good."

Heat flushed my skin at his praise. "Thanks. Wish we knew what the contents of the envelope were, though."

"It doesn't matter."

"It doesn't?"

Michaels shook his head, indicating right and pulling into a quiet service road a few blocks from campus. The headlights cut through the pitch-black, revealing a dead end.

He pulled up, cut the engine, and we were shrouded in darkness. Only the three-quarter moon in the cloudless sky provided enough light for me to see his face.

"No, it doesn't. The contents were probably insignificant and likely already destroyed."

While I'd previously expected it to be a test of my will, my skill, and just what I was willing to do, that the whole thing was bullshit shouldn't have been a surprise. It did make me feel better, though, to believe what I'd stolen wasn't a threat to anyone.

"I also got more intel through from Kent this afternoon, which the unit believes is linked to Shadowfall." Something shifted in Michaels's gaze as he turned in his seat to face me. "The director has cleared you for the history of Shadowfall."

My heart galloped, which of course he'd be able to hear. Thankfully he didn't call me out on it. "Okay. It'll help to know what I'm potentially walking into." I wasn't even being sarcastic. The reality of working for the SICB meant I'd come across a lot of blacked-out documents and never know half of the shit the bureau was involved in.

"The whispers about Shadowfall had been circulating for two years before the SICB finally had enough intel to shut it down and take out the key players. No one was sure exactly what it entailed, but the rumours were disturbing. The project was run by a shadow government agency, which Captain Hornell was revealed to be heading. It involved dangerous medical experiments conducted on unwilling subjects."

Michaels's jaw tightened as he took a deep breath, and I thought back to a project taken down just a year or so back, which Thatch had disclosed the UTI had led and were responsible for shutting down. He'd also told me they'd had a loss, and I wondered who it had been and how close Michaels was to the person killed in action.

"Captain Hornell had always been a brilliant and respected officer, or so I've heard, but somewhere along the way, he'd apparently grown 'disillusioned,'" he said, rolling his eyes, having used air quotes. "I just call bullshit, as that's a sorry excuse."

My lips twitched at his side jab.

"Anyway, it led to him becoming a ruthless bastard and a greedy fucker. He organised a team of medical scientists and soldiers. The results...." He shook his head, his wolf rising to the surface with anger in his gaze. "Shit, they were horrifying. Some said groundbreaking, but fuck that."

"Jesus," I said, unable to keep quiet. For Michaels to be visibly shaken by the project, the case must have been bad. "What were the experiments and their purpose?"

"It seemed to start off with an almost worthy mission. It pains me to admit it, but it's true. Cell regeneration at a level far beyond supes' natural abilities. It was clear that's where it started. Research had even been approved by the medical research board about eight years back, but it was when the cells started mutating that the project was officially shut down by the board. Not long after, Hornell took it up as a clandestine project. Most of those involved thought it was government approved, just supersecret. Thought they were doing good to continue the research.

"It would have been incredible," he continued. "Saved the lives of so many humans and supes, but after the mutation, Hornell's focus shifted."

I hung on to every word, goose bumps lifting the hairs at the back of my neck. Hell, just the word "mutation" had my gut twisting.

"The experiments were designed to create a new breed of soldier capable of surviving even the harshest environments and equipped with abilities far beyond those of a normal supe. But the cost of these enhancements was the loss of their humanity."

"Holy shit." At warp speed, my brain attempted to process the information.

"The project was finally deactivated four years ago. That means there's been four years' worth of continued technological and medical development happening in the world. The possibility of Shadowfall now being successful...." He shook his head. "Hell, they may not have even been shut down completely like we assumed."

"So," I finally said, having gathered my thoughts, "based on the encrypted message received by Thatch—the names included, the missing dropouts, the findings from interviews with the family—what else is there?"

"Meaning what?" Curiosity lit his words.

"As in, are there any increased thefts linked to medical stuff or technology? And are there more missing trainees from other locations in Australia, or even active agents who have disappeared? Hell, any cadavers gone missing?"

His brows shot up at that. "You think bodies are being stolen for research?"

I couldn't hold back the twitch of my lips at the horror on his face.

Over the past five days, I'd received nothing but scowls or complete disinterest from him publicly around campus. Not that I'd admit it aloud, but each cold shoulder and hard look stung. It was only in our training sessions that he lost the steel in his eyes. So anytime he let down his guard and didn't keep me at a distance, I liked it a lot.

"Not really. Just thinking outside the box a little. Trying to consider areas that could raise warning bells."

A slow nod followed as he pulled out his phone. Getting through the variety of security measures he appeared to have in place, he started reading, his eyes flickering over the text as he scrolled.

"How about this? Milton Technologies reported a break-in ten days ago. Nothing was reported as stolen, and they couldn't find a system breach. Want to hazard a guess what the company specialises in?"

I stayed quiet, mesmerised by the uptick of his lips forming a self-satisfied smile. Everything about Michaels did it for me.

The way we'd worked as a team a few days back had added fire to the flames that licked my skin whenever I saw him. I was close to the point of not caring if he burned me so intensely that I'd not bother struggling to escape from the kindling he kept throwing my way. Intentional or not.

Was I clinging to every second we spent together? That'd be a hard yes.

When I didn't answer, amusement flashed in his gaze. "Gene editing."

"Just what every Frankenstein wants, right?"

Michaels's chuckle swept over me, pressing against my skin and forcing me to fight for even, steady breaths. Jesus, it was rich, dark, and delicious, a sound I could get addicted to hearing.

From the little I knew about the man, he rarely let down his guard, nor did he laugh often. A tragedy, considering how it changed his features, lighting an emotion from within and brightening his gaze.

A slow smile formed on my lips as I watched him come to life, luxuriating in the gift of his genuine amusement. My gaze roamed his expression, drinking in every crease, every movement, until his shutters came back up.

It happened so fast—his smile dropping, laughter cutting off, shoulders tensing—that I lost my breath, unsure what had happened.

"I'll reach out to my partner, get him in on this."

"You have a partner?" As soon as I asked, I wanted to take the question back. Of course he had a partner when out in the field. It was normal practice with the exception of assignments like this one.

"Chris is a good agent. I expect you'll meet him soon enough." There was a switch in his tone, and the formality was back.

I hated it, but it was the reminder I needed to stop

reading into any exchange we might have. Getting caught up with a colleague didn't seem Michaels's style at all. Remembering that would stop me from making a dick of myself and prevent me from getting caught up in fantasies of getting hot and dirty with the man between the sheets.

Cutting through the awkward tension, I confirmed, "So the unit will investigate Milton Technologies, and I'll wait for the next message, assuming I get one. We'll see what happens from there, right?"

"Yeah. I can't imagine them not reaching out. They'll be impressed with tonight's job. We just have to hope the next one will have a clearer link with Shadow-fall, somehow, to help confirm that your new employer is with the project. Kent's working on locating Hornell. Him being presumed dead for four years means she has her work cut out for her, but she's the best there is. If there's a single crumb, she'll find it, in time."

"Sounds good." A yawn ripped out of me, my brain beginning to settle after tonight's excitement.

"Come on. Let's head back. Get some sleep before you pass out in my car."

I snorted as he started the engine and headed the few blocks to campus. By the time we pulled into the corner of the car park, I was dead on my feet. At least it should mean that as soon as my head hit the pillow, I'd be unconscious.

We silently made our way around the buildings, sticking to the shadows as much as possible. The staff quarters were just up ahead, while my accommodation was a little past it.

The thud of a boot scraping concrete had us pausing. The sound was just around the corner. Fuck. Wide-eyed, I held my breath and stared at Michaels, who was half a step ahead of me.

He peered at me, his own "oh shit" expression frozen on his face.

We could not get caught together like this. Me in fatigues, and Michaels... well, me with Michaels in the dead of night. It screamed of dodgy dealings and stealth missions.

The thud of steps grew closer. There was little doubt that if the owner of the boots was a supe, they would have heard us by now. With nowhere to run, nowhere to hide, I hoped to hell Michaels had a cover story up his sleeve.

My brain was fuzzy from the adrenaline crash on the car journey, making it hard to come up with something that would get us out of this.

Less than fifteen metres from the corner of the

building came the sound of footsteps. They'd be on us before my next breath.

And Michaels moved. He twisted fully, one hand on the back of my neck, the other at my waist as he pushed me against the brick wall. His mouth captured my grunt, his lips finding purchase and pressing against my own, a smooth slide, a dip of his tongue, and my brain turned to mush.

Fire licked at my skin, and the grip of his hands threatened to turn the blood pulsing through my veins into molten lava. His mouth worked against mine, teasing out a reaction, urging me to respond in kind. I kissed him back, gladly, urgently, committing to memory his taste and the hitch of breath that followed my tongue touching his.

Wrapping my arms around him, I held him close, tight, not allowing an inch of space between us as he owned my mouth. I gripped his shirt, holding on for dear life, revelling in his touch and the connection. Blood rushed to my cock, filling it, turning it to steel.

I needed friction. Needed him to feel what he did to me. Shifting my hand to his arse, I grasped him and tugged until his groin brushed mine.

Hard steel.

There was no holding back my moan, no swallowing it down or controlling the desire urging me to drop to my knees to unfasten his pants and consume him. Fuck, to taste his cum, hear him call my name, feel him lose control—

The cough ripped through my lusty thoughts, bringing everything back into sharp focus.

We paused, our breaths heavy and mingling as Michaels removed his mouth from mine. Our gazes connected for a split second before he turned to confront who'd interrupted us.

Prescott's face was a picture of surprise as he stared at us. It took him a moment to control his expression, his focus on Michaels as he raised one brow. "Nice night for it." His lips twitched as he stepped around us, continuing on his way.

The interruption left me cold. Michaels's "Get some sleep" as he stepped away, leaving me gasping for breath, was a bucket of ice water and a punch of reality in the face.

Fuck it all to hell.

I waited until he was out of earshot before peeling myself from the wall and heading to my room. Making out as a distraction was one thing, but it felt crazy real to me. Did he really need to use tongue? Match my moans?

I shook my head, pissed off I'd been caught up in the moment. For a few seconds there, I'd imagined it was real. Talk about dangerous. All but forgetting the reason why Michaels had kissed me could have been catastrophic in another situation.

The fact that I had to keep reminding myself to stay focussed didn't bode well.

I had to stop half-arsing it. The consequences of losing sight of the mission were too terrifying to consider.

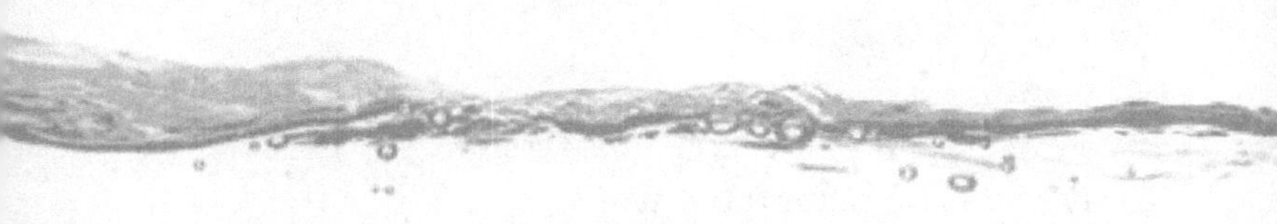

CHAPTER 5
MICHAELS

Unsurprisingly, I didn't sleep for shit. Again. My cock throbbed all damn night, but no chance would I give in and get off with the taste of Shaw still on my tongue. Which meant that this morning, tension strung my muscles tight, and I ended up in the gym to work through the knots in my shoulders.

"Interesting night."

The brief second pause was enough for Prescott to know I'd heard him, but I kept going anyway, pounding the reinforced punching bag, one hit after another.

His chuckle was low but closer than his first words. "And from the way you're pummelling that bag, I reckon I have an apology to make if it meant I cut your night short and you're *that* frustrated."

"Fuck off." I turned and rolled my eyes, taking away any sting behind the words.

I'd already decided how I had to play this—that Shaw was simply an easy lay. It made me feel shit, but infiltration rarely was clear cut.

Nor did it come without its fair share of casualties.

"You work fast, huh." He bounced his brows as I snagged a towel to wipe over my face. "Not even a week, and you're sharing your *special* talents." Prescott caught the sweaty towel I threw in his face and laughed. "Just be sure to let the poor kid down gently. I can't be dealing with broken hearts when you leave."

I grinned and swiped my bottle of water. Not having to confirm or deny anything made my job a whole lot easier. "What about you and Sandra?" I deflected.

A not-so-casual shrug lifted his shoulders. "What can I say? I'm still a ladies' man."

"I'm sure you are." I clapped him on the shoulder, keen to keep controlling the narrative and avoid talking about Shaw for the time being. "Is it serious?"

The smile lifting his lips didn't quite meet his eyes. "She's middle-aged."

Understanding had me nodding. He wasn't confirming her age to be callous, but the reality was, as a human, her life span was a hell of a lot shorter than a shifter's. Sure, there was a way to be turned, regardless of shifter species, but it wasn't pleasant, and it could also only be done on a shifter's deathbed, and if they chose to share their gift with a human.

Science had a whole explanation linked to cell transferal, but stories from elders stuck with the belief that the shifter gene was sacred and shouldn't be shared without thought of the consequences. Sure, shifters were also birthed, just like vamps, but it was the passing of memories that was a revered gift.

"Living a multitude of lives comes with its own trials, right?" I said sympathetically and squeezed his shoulder.

"It does that." A shadow crossed over his features. Before I could ask, he seemed to brush away the passing emotion, a smile splitting his cheeks. "Anyhow, you up for seeing one of the training sessions?"

I studied him a beat, giving him the out since he'd given me a free pass. "Sure thing. Just lead the way."

We headed towards the outside assault course. Surprised when we walked straight on past it, I side-eyed Prescott. An almost maniacal grin teased his lips, and when a holler and a cheer from up ahead reached us, it became even brighter.

"What the hell are they doing?"

Wide-eyed, I watched as two trainees grappled

while strapped in to abseiling ropes, probably nine metres in the air. Sure, I could see the merit, especially as they hovered over what I hoped was a plunge pool. "Uhm... do they have kni—?"

"Fuck!" The sound tore through the air a millisecond after Recruit Jordan Karten's rope was cut. She free fell at speed, spinning quickly, before manoeuvring into a dive.

"Jesus." I shook my head. "When did they start doing shit like this?" Not that anyone else seemed fazed. Hell, the rest of the small group were laughing, Williams, the victor, cheering.

A splash and a quiet inhale caught my attention as Karten broke through the surface. She came up, flipping Williams off before she swam to the side and pulled herself out.

Prescott chuckled at my side. "They didn't do this in our day, right?"

"Fuck no, they didn't." Not being a fan of swimming in my clothes, I was relieved as hell.

Trainer Peters called, "Anderson, you're up. Williams, back to the top."

We carried on walking, stopping once we reached Peters's side. He greeted me with a head bob before making his way over to the bottom of the twelve-metre tower, complete with foot- and handholds.

"Have you done this?" I side-eyed Prescott, who shook his head.

"Abseiled, sure, but not gone at it with knives."

A whistle blew, and Williams and Anderson started their descent. They'd barely made it two metres before Anderson launched with his knife at Williams's rope.

"Shit, I don't know if I'm impressed or appalled."

"Right. Well, no one's died, yet."

"Yet." I snorted and shook my head, watching in horror when Williams plummeted a couple of metres, then he released his rope before he snapped his cord tight. "How deep is that pool?" The water looked ink black and eerily still.

"Four metres."

The two recruits battled it out, showing impressive restraint at not cutting at anything but the rope. It didn't mean they would be bruise-free, though. My brows shot high when Anderson launched from the tower wall, somehow sprang high, and sliced Williams's rope in two.

"Okay, now I'm impressed." A thrill of excitement buzzed through my veins. On mission, adrenaline rushes were the norm. It was no secret that field agents, especially those in our elite unit, were adrenaline junkies. And me all but sitting on my arse for the past week—with the exception of the two hours a day I managed to spend with Shaw—was an unexpected drain.

Each session, he pushed my boundaries and my buttons. It was no wonder I'd made the idiotic move of fucking his mouth with my tongue in the middle of the night.

I shrugged off the lusty thoughts attempting to take up residence in my brain and focussed on the grappling wall. Did I want a go? Damn fucking straight I did.

"Shaw, you're up."

Peters's voice snapped my attention to the group.

While I'd surreptitiously searched the trainees when I'd arrived, I hadn't seen or sensed Shaw. But there he was, rising from a small wall, which he must have been sitting against, hidden from my view—and my nose—by those around him.

Awareness slammed into me. A tingle started in my chest before traveling through my limbs. Fuck, he was hot, especially with the confidence of his gait, the smirk at something one of the recruits said.

His flush had me pausing. His eyes connecting with mine had me holding my breath.

Appreciation flashed in his amber eyes before I lost his gaze, and he turned his back on me. Halfway up the tower, his shoulders turned rigid. Not that I only noticed because of the way his glutes turned taut or anything.

"Shit," Prescott said, his tone low. "This should be interesting."

"What do you mean?" I frowned, dragging my attention away from Shaw's arse to peer at Prescott.

"You not hear what Anderson said to him?"

I shook my head.

Surprise shot Prescott's brows high. "Hell, you must have it bad if you didn't hear the shit talk. What, did you see Shaw and hear cupid's wings or an angel singing or something?" His lips twitched, and my gaze narrowed as I lost all semblance of humour. When I didn't respond, he explained, "Shit talk about Shaw being your pretty cocksucker and that all it would take was one slip of a blade from Anderson for you to realise that you could get better head from a mutt."

By the time he stopped speaking, there was no sign of his amusement left. Whether he'd turned serious in response to what Anderson had said or the fury I struggled to contain, I didn't fucking know. But I needed to rein myself in before I tore the fucker Anderson's head clear off his shoulders.

Was it too late to swap places with Shaw and teach the kid a lesson?

"How'd they know?" The control in my voice told nothing of how pissed off I was. Prescott was the only person who'd seen us last night.

"Hey." Prescott raised his hands in surrender. "Not from me. But I'm not surprised. Nothing remains a secret in this place. Hell, it's gone noon, and I'm amazed this is the first time I've heard the gossip."

Controlling my breathing, I focussed on his words while peering up at the tower. Shaw was at the top, getting strapped in.

With no tells in his expression, no tension straining his limbs, I figured he had this.

There was no doubt Shaw could handle himself. Of that, I was sure.

But regardless of the source of the gossip, it struck me as odd that for the few days I'd been here, not once had I overheard, nor anyone discussed with me, thoughts about the missing chief or the dropouts.

That was weird for certain. Surely that would have been central to any gossip on campus.

The shrill whistle pierced the air, and try as I might to watch impassively, I held my breath, my muscles drawing taut.

The two shifters practically flew off the tower, slipping down their ropes. Not even making purchase on the wall, Shaw, knife in hand, twirled like he was in a circus act and went for the kill with a slash at the woven rope.

Anderson blocked him, the knife missing by a mere fraction.

Then it was on. Their swipes were brutal, fast, blocking and swiping with powerful thrusts. Mesmerised by Shaw's moves, his expression, I remained frozen in place, air still in my lungs.

If he'd been pissed off by what Anderson had said, there was no trace of it anywhere. Every movement was controlled, measured, fucking beautiful as he spun and struck. A flash of anger morphed on Anderson's face when Shaw's blade sliced through the edge of the rope, not quite deep enough to make it separate.

One more nick, and he'd be done for.

Shaw darted away with a grunt as Anderson slashed out at him, not the rope.

"The fuck." The words tore out of me, vibrating around the outside space.

"The hell you think you're doing, Anderson?" Roberts hollered up, but Anderson either wasn't listening or didn't give a damn. Another slash and the scent of Shaw's blood pierced the air. A third and Shaw's dagger spiralled through the air, landing in the pool with a splash.

And I was moving.

Charging forward, I leapt up the tower, reaching out to clutch one of the grips. I swung up, gripping and pushing, feet and hands never missing as I zeroed in on Shaw managing to punch Anderson square in the face.

The bastard sliced again, blood pouring from his nose, latching on to Shaw's shirt when he tried to shake the wolf off. I was less than three metres away, and time slowed as the blade made purchase, entering Shaw's flesh like it was made of fine silk.

I roared, lunging and grasping Anderson's back.

"The fuck. Get the fuck—"

My arm around Anderson's throat cut him off. He clawed at my arms, drawing blood with his partially shifted hands.

I couldn't speak. Couldn't do anything but hold on tight while staring wide-eyed at Shaw. Clutching his side, not dislodging the knife, Shaw raised his brows and released a hollowed laugh. "Jesus, what did he use, a hot poker? Burns like shit after a curry."

Startling a laugh from me, I eased off Anderson, his head no longer upright and his body slack. "Not quite like a pinprick, huh?" I grinned despite the galloping of my heart and the worry gnawing at me to make sure Shaw didn't lose too much blood.

"Not quite, no." He winced when he released one hand to move to the carabiner. "Good job there are no sharks in the plunge pool." With the steady drip doing a good job at sending ripples through the water, I had to agree.

"Let me help you down."

"What about him?"

"Figured I'd cut him loose and let him drop."

I shocked a snort out of Shaw, resulting in a pained grunt and a wince.

"How about I just take Anderson?" Roberts dropped down beside me, concern dipping his brows low.

"If you want to ruin my fun, have at it."

Roberts grabbed Anderson's prone form as I moved to Shaw. Once up close, I steadied my breathing, inhaled, and tried to cling to the fresh scent of rainforests I'd come to associate with him. I needed the gentle smell to calm my wolf, to help push away the sharp tang of blood.

Finding it, I relaxed my shoulders and reached out to steady him. On contact, Shaw sighed into me, the tremble in his limbs letting me know pain had a fierce hold on him. I expected he'd be dizzy from blood loss too.

"You want to do this by yourself?" I dipped my question low, sure only Roberts would be able to hear me.

"Yeah, but stick close."

I could respect that.

Keeping within touching distance, we made our descent, the journey painfully slow, all things considered. By the time we reached the ground, Anderson had been carried off somewhere, the trainees cleared out by Prescott, and Thatch stood waiting for us.

With no stretcher in sight, it seemed Thatch knew Shaw well. And between the two of us, we helped him to the infirmary in silence, relief warring with anger while confusion waited on the sidelines.

The whole situation was messed up and didn't make a lick of sense.

My heart beating with fierce intensity, determination bloomed in my chest, refusing to falter. Steely resolve formed. Nothing would deter me from getting answers.

AFTER A HUGE MEAL OF MORE STEAK THAN I'D ever seen a panther inhale, Shaw was on his feet. Exhaustion lightened his skin tone, but by the steel in his gaze, he wouldn't be heading to bed any time soon.

"Fine." Defeated, I shook my head. Since this whole investigation was going to shit anyway, it seemed like we were going for broke and sealing ourselves away in Thatch's office to talk this out.

The three of us. And Callen, apparently. At this point I wouldn't be surprised if Lucas showed up. If Kent was hot on his heels, I was out of here. The vampire rarely left the unit's base for work. If that ever happened, it would mean shit got seriously real.

"Thank you."

I nodded as we headed to the chief's secure office. Considering the attack, it made sense that Shaw would engage in some sort of confidential meeting with Thatch. Me joining him, though? I scrubbed a hand over my face. Beyond us claiming our being together was a ruse, and now rumours were flying, I had no idea.

It wasn't like my cover position in the Global Response Shifter Force warranted my attendance. Sure, I was a witness, but so were Roberts and Prescott, plus a group of trainees.

Moral support it was.

Jesus. The fuck had I gotten myself into?

I knocked loudly but didn't wait for an invite before I pushed open the office door. "If you kids aren't decent, I swear I'm going to share the pictures from your bonding ceremony...." I wrinkled my nose before I'd even finished. "Not as in the night, because fucking gross, but you know the photo I'm talking about."

I punctuated my words by closing the heavy door. The pop of my ears followed.

"Perhaps wait until the seal's activated before you start spouting shit, arsehole," Callen greeted, stepping into my space and tugging me into a hug. I grunted at the hard slap on my back, preparing myself to replace the wall that his over-affectionate neediness tended to tear down.

"There'd be no point in anyone following or trying to listen in. They know this room is rigged with privacy tech." I stepped away, eyeing the man before me. It really had been too long since I'd laid eyes on him, but fuck, every time I did, I was reminded of the op and losing Jenson.

The way he looked at me told me he felt it too. The whole mission had been a shitshow, starting with the death of his sister and ending with the rescue of his niece, who he and Thatch had since adopted.

Aware of eyes on us, I angled to peer at Shaw. A fresh thread of emotion unravelled from my chest when I saw the interest and questions in his gaze. "Shaw, meet Thatch's arsehole lesser half."

Retaliating with a flick to my ear, Callen shook his head. "Ignore him. I'm—"

"Agent Blackheath." Shaw reached out and shook Callen's hand. "It's an honour, sir."

Callen grinned and shot me a "fuck you, I'm important" look. I rolled my eyes and drifted towards the desk and sat.

"Good to meet you, Shaw. Please call me Agent Callen, not Blackheath."

"You know, you should have just taken Thatch's name and been done with it," I said helpfully, earning me a clear "shut the fuck up" stare from Callen.

He carried on speaking as if I hadn't spoken. "You've had an interesting morning. How're you feeling? Healed up okay?"

Shaw pressed a palm to his side, the move clearly unintentional, since on contact, he rapidly moved to stand at ease. "I'm healing just fine, thank you, sir."

"You see? A recruit who knows how to respect the chain of command." A smirk lifted his lips but fell as soon as Thatch snorted. "What?" He peered over at his husband, bonded, mate, whatever loved-up people were calling their better halves these days.

"Really? 'Respect the chain of command'? When have you ever respected the chain of command?"

Leaning back, I chuckled, slotting my fingers together and cupping the back of my head. When Thatch first met Callen, he'd been his boss. Callen barely followed his directives then, and he certainly didn't fall in line under the old division leader, the role he'd since been promoted to.

He'd been a loose cannon, a position I'd apparently adopted since losing Jenson.

Nobody was buying Callen's gasp of outrage. Not even Shaw, who stared on with wide-eyed amusement. I got it. Seeing your superiors for the loveable idiots they were was an eye-opener.

Before he could respond, Thatch told us all to sit. His voice was tired, strained, which was understandable, all things considered.

"What have you got on Anderson?" I got right to it, wanting answers and wondering if Anderson remained on site. If I paid him a visit to extract some intel, I could guarantee it wouldn't take long to get him to talk.

"You received a drop-off with coordinates and a mission via plain white envelope?" He addressed Shaw, who nodded. I'd checked in with Kent over a secure network this morning with an update. It made sense that Thatch already knew. "Same happened to Anderson."

"With what instructions exactly?" Fury tightened my voice.

"Injure without permanent damage."

"But why? And from the same people? For what purpose?" Shaw's composure was impressive. He angled to look at me, his gaze latching on to mine, searching. "When did he get the mission?" His focus shifted to Callen.

"This morning at 0800. The location of the attack was specific to that training session." Callen opened his comms with a click at his ear. "Come in, Kent. Over." He waited a beat before saying, "Results from the preliminaries? Over." He nodded at whatever Kent was saying, meanwhile I struggled to keep my knee from bouncing up and down.

When Shaw cleared his throat, his discomfort both obvious and surprising, all attention moved to him.

"I—"

Callen lifted a finger to pause him before saying, "Got it, Kent. Thanks, over and out. What is it?" he asked Shaw, whose neck flushed red.

Ah shit. There could only be one thing that got that reaction, and it wasn't from the heat in this room, since the air-com was pumping out cool air. My thoughts travelled to the kiss we'd shared this morning. Hell, did we share it, or did I launch myself at him, giving him no choice but to reciprocate?

It was no wonder I hadn't disclosed that ill-thought-out distraction in my morning report. It was a shit move of mine, but fuck, the man could kiss. And that low groan when his tongue had touched mine....

Sure, that could be faked, but his hard cock when—

"I was up at 0500, at breakfast for quarter past. Somehow the rumours had already started."

I held back my wince and looked pointedly at the wall behind Thatch's desk.

"What rumours?" Callen's tone was all business.

"When Agent Michaels"—my neck muscle flinched at the formality of my name—"and I arrived back on campus in the early hours this morning, Trainer Prescott was walking the campus. By the time we heard footsteps approach, there was no safe location to hide. It was also obvious by that point the person had heard us."

From my peripheral, I saw Callen angle towards me. Not a chance I was making eye contact. In my report, I'd included Prescott intercepting us but hadn't divulged specifics. "And what was your cover story?" he asked.

Damn it all to hell. I couldn't let Shaw deal with this, not when it had been my move.

"Hot agent comes in, sweeps the rookie off his feet, and makes out with him under the bleachers." Nonchalance that no one would buy filled my tone. I shrugged, finally looking around our small group. "It worked. Prescott took the piss this morning about me having all the smooth moves."

Silence met my words. Thatch's dark-brown gaze didn't waver as he scrutinised me. After years of working under the man, he knew me the best by far. He also knew I wasn't a player, nor would I hook up—be it fake or otherwise—if there wasn't something deeper.

I jerked my attention away, hating that he knew me so well.

"So you just, what, made out like a couple of horny teenagers and brushed it off as a bit of fun?" From the twinkle in Callen's eyes, the arsehole was enjoying my fuck-up a little too much. "Shit, do I need to worry about a sexual harassment charge?"

Heat spread across my chest, no doubt bleeding red into my cheeks if the wide-eyed expression appearing on Callen's face was anything to go by.

"No," Shaw said quickly. "It wasn't like that."

"Like what exactly?" Callen tilted his head, examining Shaw.

"Agent Michaels reacted in the best way he could considering the circumstances. It was a cover story that could work for us."

"Hmmm." Callen quirked his brow. "And people knew about your illicit affair by five thirty?"

"Jesus, Cal, give it a rest," I shot out.

Despite his obvious amusement, he raised a

placating hand. "Fine, but the question still remains: if Prescott was the only one who saw, how did everyone else find out?"

"I asked Prescott this morning. He said he hadn't told anyone," I said.

"And you believe him?" Callen turned to Thatch. "You trust Prescott?"

"I've not known him for that long," Thatch replied, "but his files check out. Injured a few years back."

"Got a prosthetic," I added, my brain ticking over.

"Cell regeneration." Shaw's words caught our attention. "That's more than skin and blood, right? What about bone... as in whole limbs?"

My stare was hard, assessing, and honest to God filled with awe that he'd drawn that conclusion at pretty much the same time the rest of our thoughts were aligning, I was guessing. "We were at the academy together."

"Damn, you remember all those years ago? Impressive." Shaw's sass was so unexpected that he tore an amused snort out of me. The sound had both Thatch and Callen jerking their heads in my direction.

"I'm not *that* old, arsehole." Unbidden, my lips tilted up. The smile he threw me eased something tight in my chest. Refocussing on Callen, whose brows were high, I lost my smile. "He was a decent guy back then.

Could be a bit competitive, but nothing new there in our field. Joined counterterrorism division straight out of the academy. The first I heard about his injury was a few days ago. He's also got something romantic going on with Sandra Olsen."

"Yeah. Neither have confirmed anything." Thatch rubbed a hand over his short hair. "They've kept it under the radar fairly well, but I've suspected it since the day I got here."

"The rest of the cadets know or at least think they know that something's going on between them," Shaw confirmed.

"Is it true that the academy is gossip central?" I looked at Shaw, then Thatch, wanting their take.

"Yes," they answered in unison.

"So someone finding out about this early-morning encounter," I said, trying to push away the discomfort in my chest, "confirms it's usual for something like that to spread quickly."

"I was a bit surprised someone asked me about it so early. Honestly, I expected it to take at least until this afternoon." The palest of pinks touched the apples of Shaw's cheeks.

"And how did you play it?" Callen asked, and by the fast spread of pink to bright red, there was no doubt Shaw had provided some sort of response.

A mild look of discomfort morphed his features, his gaze almost apologetic as he looked at me before he responded. "I thought it best to make out I'm cosying up to Michaels for a position in the Global Response Shifter Force."

Surprise jolted me into sitting upright. Rather than pissed, I was impressed as hell. "Smart move." I bobbed my head in admiration.

The red in his cheeks deepened at my praise. "Thanks. I didn't want our hooking up to threaten my mission. I thought if they, Shadowfall or whoever, believed I was playing Michaels and doing whatever it took to climb up the SICB ladder, they'd take my being power hungry as a positive trait."

"Makes sense." Callen nodded. "If they thought it was a legit romantic involvement, they'd be concerned that you were untrustworthy and would run to your agent boyfriend with news of the off-the-books ops."

I stilled as a thought slammed into me.

"What are you thinking?" Thatch asked, not missing a thing.

"So, when I was the first to react and charged up that fucking tower when Shaw was stabbed, that what, made his story bullshit?"

Nobody spoke for a few beats. I suspected all were thinking about how I'd fucked up.

"Well," Thatch said, "you're an active agent, so it makes sense you were the first to respond and react. Your reactions are more homed in, sharper."

I didn't have it in me to mock him or call him a has-been. Partly because he could in fact likely still take me down, but I wasn't sure anyone would believe that story. Considering my thoughts before we started the meeting, and me playing the lovesick fool card, I expected that was what everyone who'd witnessed the attack would think.

"You think anyone is going to buy that?" I asked.

Thatch was the master of not having tells, but given the level of control he was demonstrating, it was clear he knew something.

"Just tell me." Defeat coated my words. That I was embarrassed as hell didn't make this any easier.

"As you'd expect, the rumour mill is strong. You also haven't left Shaw's side since the incident."

"Obviously, in case another fucker tries to—"

Raising his hand, Thatch cut me off. "There're descriptions of growling and a whole story about your clear distress going around."

"You were growling, as in, *grrr, arrr*? Please tell me it's so."

Instead of looking at Callen and what I was sure was a shit-eating grin, I flipped him off. "I was worried that a cadet in my charge was attacked. Of course I was pissed off and went to help."

"Apparently there was fawning and gentle touches involved. Someone even said you did this whole tender kiss-on-the-head thing. A couple of the younger recruits had this whole swooning thing going on, saying your reaction was all romantic or some shit."

My mouth gaped, lips struggling to know whether to part or close. "There were no fucking gentle touches involved." Shit, were there? The few minutes I was up there were fuzzy in my memory.

"It's kind of sweet."

"Fuck you," I spat at Callen, who finally gave in and burst into laughter.

Taking a calming breath, I closed my eyes, wondering what the hell Shaw thought about all this. Risking a glance at him, I found his gaze on me. A tender smile was on his lips, and I all but melted under his attention. How the hell he managed to calm me from one sweet, simple smile was beyond me, but losing my shit wouldn't help anyone.

"Okay, so, damage control. What's the plan?"

CHAPTER 6
SHAW

Understandably, Michaels wasn't keen on the plan, but his reaction to Anderson's attack on me had been telling. Even the memory of him racing to me, the sound of his full-on roar that tore through the air was enough to get my heart picking up speed.

And that it was the memory of Michaels, his fear and anger, I recalled with ease rather than the attack itself should have raised all manner of alarm bells. In truth, it did. But it was also hot as hell. A possessive Michaels was a walking, talking wet dream come to life.

And this new more polished plan that we'd nailed down made sense, and honestly, it wasn't so different to the half-arsed one I'd already formed.

The most significant detail we'd agreed on was that

the nonlethal attack was another test. One I had to pass with flying colours, as it sure as hell wasn't about my ability to win a knife fight. Instead, we were working under the assumption that Shadowfall was testing my loyalty, my relationship. How genuine it was.

As it stood, I was a recruit not to be trusted. With Michaels reacting like a terrified lover—*which, holy shit, heart rate spike much*—the next couple of days was about damage control.

How I planned to achieve that was working the gossip mill in my favour.

The canteen was full, not surprising since it was dinnertime. A buzz of conversation filled the air, another given considering the events of today.

While Michaels hadn't wanted me to come to dinner, seeming genuinely concerned about my health and that I needed more rest, I was adamant it was for the best.

And if it meant I got to see Michaels in action, being possessive and in my space, well, that may have encouraged me not to skulk away to my room.

We entered hand in hand. The thrill of his touch wasn't one I locked down.

"Smells like barramundi is on the menu," I said. At his scrunched nose, I snickered. "What, you're not a fan of fish?"

"Not especially."

"Let me guess, you're a steak man."

He released my hand and settled his own on my waist, effectively hugging me to his side. "You know I like the taste of meat."

And that should not have sounded as dirty as my mind made it out to be.

I chuckled, heading towards the hot plates, aware gazes were on us.

Sure, when not in Michaels's company I had to play our relationship down, shrug it off, and pretend to be a bigger arsehole than anyone ever imagined, but for the time being, I eagerly embraced Michaels at my side. Him being attentive and playing the boyfriend card was no hardship.

"You want me to get you your food and you grab a seat?"

I turned, pressing a kiss to his shoulder. Our gazes met, and my heart thumped a little louder at what I saw there.

A good actor or not, Michaels's attention on me was something I liked a little too much.

"Thanks, baby," I said quietly, knowing those around us would be able to hear, "but I can manage."

I didn't miss the flare of heat in his eyes, and I

worked hard at tethering the very real desire I felt at being so close to him.

Silently, he passed me a tray, seeming reluctant to let me go, but I needn't have worried. As soon as we sat at an empty table, his hand latched on to mine, squeezing tenderly before it settled on my knee.

We'd barely taken a bite before the chairs scraped and my friends sat down. Wide-eyed, they stared at us, with zero subtlety whatsoever. It wasn't until I shot them a pointed look that they glanced away and set about eating.

"How are you feeling?" Henderson asked, cutting through the tension that surrounded the table.

"Yeah, I'm okay. Feeling better," I answered, fully aware Michaels had turned rigid beside me.

"Not quite okay," he said tersely.

I smiled and rolled my eyes, angling towards him when I saw him move. Not expecting his mouth to be so close to mine, my breath hitched. He closed the distance, eyes at half-mast and intense as hell as he pressed his lips to mine.

It was chaste, but still so not appropriate in the canteen.

"Uhm..." I cleared my throat as he pulled away, my cheeks heating.

"Sorry. Not the time," he said, voice rough with

gravel. "I'm still pissed." He shrugged, as if that was all the explanation he needed.

I bobbed my head and pulled my focus away and back to my friends. Henderson's lips were parted while Rickman's brow practically touched her hairline.

In response, I gave a "what you going to do" shrug and set about eating my food.

We continued to eat in virtual silence, Michaels a quiet force at my side. By the time we finished, genuine exhaustion slammed into me. With a full stomach and the impact of having to do so much healing, my body had been pushed to its limits.

"You really should head to bed," Michaels said at my side as he gathered my empty plate.

"I'll be okay. I could do with catching up with the guys." A jaw-cracking yawn made a mockery of my words and earned me a pointed arched brow.

"It can wait until tomorrow."

I nodded mutely, my heart bouncing around at his care. This would have been the ideal time to start with the shitty part of clarifying why Michaels and I were together.

When I didn't respond or make a move, he leaned into my space, dipping close to my neck. "Bed. I'll tuck you in."

He inhaled deeply, and fuck if it wasn't the sexiest thing he'd done so far.

"Yeah, okay. Sure." I shot a look at Henderson and Rickman, both looking far too amused. Jesus, I seriously had my work cut out for me tomorrow. Downplaying my reaction and interest in Michaels was going to be the hardest thing I'd ever do.

THE NEXT DAY, I FELT REFRESHED. THE EARLY night working its magic on my tired bones and exhaustion. And while I'd enjoyed Michaels's sweet kisses a little too much at my door, both last night and this morning, I wasn't lying about having to do some serious crisis management.

"Honestly, I'm fine." I squeezed Michaels's hand, smiling coyly. "I'll see you at lunch."

A frown drew his brows low. "Okay, but promise me that if you're worried—"

"Yes, yes, I know." I rolled my eyes for good measure and chuckled, more than aware we had an audience.

And then he kissed me, and just like last time, he drew the air from my lungs, making my head spin. Not the reaction I should be having, since I wasn't supposed to be really into the man, but when his lips were soft and his kiss owned me, pulling away and remembering my role was tricky.

Giving myself a mental smack up the head, I eased away. "You best go."

His gaze searched mine, and I wondered what he saw. Did he see a flush in my cheeks? The want in my gaze? "Yeah, okay." He cleared his throat, kissed my hand, then released me, turning on his heel and walking away.

I watched him go, tensed my muscles, spun, and did a whole-body shudder, forcing the slightest of sneers onto my mouth. The move felt so wrong, but to play the part of power-hungry user, I swallowed the emotion down.

"Holy shit. So it's true?"

"Hmm." I glanced at Rickman.

"Seriously, you and Agent Michaels.... How the hell did that happen? And holy shit, last night I thought I was going to have to put fires out."

That this was her first question, rather than how I was doing the morning after the attack, wasn't lost on me. In truth, I expected this gossip would bury the talk about Anderson attacking me and being taken into custody.

"Those extra sessions paid off."

"I'll say." She chuckled. "He seems like a decent guy. Hot as fuck too."

I shrugged noncommittedly. "He's all right."

Confusion morphed her features as we continued walking towards the gun range. "I don't get it. Last night—"

"What's there not to get?"

"If he's just all right, what's going on? It didn't seem that way at dinner."

I swallowed my nausea as I prepared to speak, more than aware there were several pairs of ears around us. "Bypassing the waitlist for Global Response Shifter Force."

"What?" She gripped my forearm, so I stopped beside her. "He can do that?"

"Apparently so."

"Shit, the GRSF has a two-year-minimum field experience prerequisite, right?"

I smirked. "That they do." I followed up with a wince and toned down my glee. Behaving out of character would already be raising so many questions. "I think I'm going to be okay with Dad's medical bills for the next four weeks, maybe, but once I leave here, you know how awful some departments' rookie wages are. No way will I be able to support my folks."

Sympathy clouded Rickman's features. "How is he?"

I shook my head, hating that I was lying to my friend, but relieved it distracted her about me getting hot and heavy with Michaels. The hard truth was, I couldn't trust anyone at the academy but Michaels and Thatch, not until we had answers and discovered who was working with Shadowfall. "I don't really want to talk about it."

She squeezed my arm. "I get it." She glanced around before lowering her voice even further. "Henderson mentioned you may have found something to help you out."

I searched her gaze, wondering what she thought and what she knew. Seeing nothing but concern and curiosity, I shot her a soft, almost defeated smile. "Maybe. I hope so. Time will tell."

The clattering of the door ahead dragged our attention in that direction. It was time to get moving. Head directed forward while reaching out with my senses, I tried to get a read on anyone who was paying extra-close attention.

Trainer Rogers stood in the open doorway, his attention on his device and not on me. Smythe stood just off to the side, his muscles rigid as Williams spoke to him in hushed tones.

When we were just a few metres away, Williams cut off abruptly, eyes darting at me before heading inside without another word to Smythe.

"You okay?" I asked once I reached his side.

He jolted into awareness, gaze connecting with mine. "Yeah, sure. Best get inside."

While Smythe could be a little shy, he wasn't usually this spaced out.

"What were you and Williams talking about?" I pushed.

His brows shot high before he seemed to pull himself together. "Just wondering what happened to Anderson. You heard anything different?"

"Other than him been taken in for questioning by headquarters, no."

"Wonder how long he'll last."

"What do you mean?" I indicated for Rickman to go on ahead. She did so after a curious glance between me and Smythe.

"Well, we're trained to survive interrogation, to not break."

It was curious his mind had gone there. "True," I said nonchalantly. "Honestly, he was probably pissed about some of his performance levels. You saw his last scores in war games. I just happened to be the guy who pushed him over the edge." I gave a half shrug.

"You really think that?"

"Well, what else could it be? It just blows my mind that he snapped so close to the end. Less than two months, and we're out of here."

Despite the bob of his head, he didn't seem convinced. "I suppose. It is weird as fuck, though, right? Him doing this. Gallagher dropping off the face of the earth not long ago. And where the fuck is the chief?"

Concentrating on my breathing and lowering my heart rate, I controlled each. This was the first time anyone had spoken about Gallagher or Chief Chambers to me directly. There had been gossip about both, though idle chatter died off really quickly. Honestly, while at the time I'd found it odd and talked out some theories with other cadets, training had taken over, and I'd pushed any thoughts to the back of my mind.

"Heard the chief was sick."

"He's a big-ass bear. The fuck is he going to get sick with?"

I shrugged. While it was possible for all species to get ill, bears were especially resilient. "Maybe a family emergency."

"And Kate? You don't think it's strange?"

I huffed out a breath. "I don't know, man. I've got

so much shit to deal with that I haven't really thought about it. But I suppose you're right."

Two lines appeared between Smythe's brows. "Yeah, heard about your dad. Sorry about that."

"Thanks."

"Keep me waiting much longer, and you're going to be doing laps until you pass out."

Smythe and I lurched towards the door. Without a doubt, Roberts would make good on his threat.

No matter how many times I pulled the trigger and hit my target, my mind remained in hyperdrive. Sure, when I exited the range, I remained on top of the unofficial leader board, but even the scent of sulphur and the distinct smell of metal after unloading so many rounds hadn't helped calm me.

Between the fake kisses I wished were real, the frustration of the case, and what Smythe had said, I needed something to happen.

Since making out for real was not going to be it, stepping up the investigation it was.

Someone in the academy was involved—possibly multiple people. No way they could be so thorough as to not leave some sort of clue behind.

"Hey, Smythe, wait up."

Smythe stopped in his tracks and peered back at me, brows high with surprise. Understandable, since beyond times we had to communicate, we didn't exchange pleasantries or hang out.

"Yeah?" he asked when I fell into step with him, heading towards the comms room for the couple of hours of training up next.

Keeping my voice quiet, I said, "I was thinking about what you mentioned earlier." There were too many people around to be more specific.

"O-kay?"

"You were friendly with Anderson, right?"

At my words, his spine straightened, and his features lost almost all expression. "I wouldn't say friendly. We were partnered up on a few exercise training excursions. Got on okay."

I bobbed my head, trying to get a read on him. I didn't think he was bullshitting me. "You want to team up in comms?"

Fresh surprise morphed his features before suspicion glinted in his gaze. "Any reason?"

My shrug was blasé. "Not long left before we transition into active duty. You're the guy in the know when it comes to comms. Thought it was about time I hit you up to share some of that skill set."

It took a couple of beats before he agreed. Without a doubt he knew I was full of crap, but he was smart enough to know that in the comms department, there were safe and soundproof work areas.

What I wasn't bullshitting about was his skills. Comms was more than call signs and using a two-way. It was secret coding, tech manipulation, and everything cyber related. All things he excelled in.

When we entered the comms area, Henderson approached me. We tended to team up.

"You want me to grab a folder?"

Shit. "Actually," I answered, flicking a quick look at Smythe, "Smythe and I are working together." Hell, why did it feel like I was back in high school? "I'll catch up with you later, though, yeah?"

Confusion was written all over Henderson, but rather than question me, he gave me an up-nod and left me to it.

"Booth E?" Smythe already held the manilla envelope with our exercise in it.

"Yeah." I indicated for him to lead the way, more than aware of the curious gazes being shot in our direction. Between the attack, my new love interest, and now teaming with Smythe, it was no wonder.

The door sealed shut behind us, a low hum sounding around the room once Smythe hit the sound-proofing switch. Smythe sat down at the large table in the stark white room that was kitted out with two chairs, two laptops, a CB, and a comms unit.

With his gaze on me, he opened up the folder. "You wanna tell me why we're here?"

There was something to be said about cutting through the small talk and getting to the real issue.

Sitting opposite him, I made quick work of separating the collection of papers containing our training exercise. "You and Kate were friends."

"We were."

"*Were* as in you no longer talk?"

"*Were* as in I can no longer get hold of her." Keeping his gaze steady, he switched on the laptops and the rest of the equipment. "Let me just do a quick check first."

Impressed he'd thought of it, I bobbed my head, renewed respect for the man forming.

"Okay. We're clear."

I raised my brows, indicating for him to carry on.

"I took this to Chief Chambers. That I can't get hold of her."

Shock reverberated along my skin. Information like that would have been shared with Thatch or Michaels. I locked down the buzz of energy at this new information. "What happened?"

I listened intently as he explained how he'd reported his concerns after two weeks with no contact, and the chief had said he'd investigate. Having received no follow-up, he'd gone back to the chief with some off-the-books intel just a few days before Michaels had come on board and I'd been read in by Thatch.

"What did you find out?" Holding back my excitement almost had me shaking him.

I understood his hesitation.

"Are you really dating Agent Michaels just to get a step ahead?"

Breath froze in my lungs.

Could I trust him? Not a chance I'd be sharing with him the truth of the investigation, but he knew something was off with me. Answering with a partial truth would either help this investigation or royally screw me over.

"No." My gaze remained steady, honesty resounding in that one word.

"So you really like him, then? Trust him?"

"I do." Honesty again.

He studied me harder, uncertainty and doubt still evident.

"You can trust me." I pushed all the honesty I could muster into my words. Still seeing his reluctance, I made a decision I hoped wouldn't bite me on the arse.

"I know Chief Chambers doesn't have a family emergency. I also know the SICB are actively looking for him."

Holding my breath, I waited for his reaction. If I'd fucked this up and revealed too much, I'd be in a world of trouble. But I had to trust my gut here, and Smythe, I had a good feeling about.

Pulling his attention away, Smythe focussed on one of the laptops. His fingers danced across the keyboard far too fast for me to keep up. Breathing a sigh of relief that he seemed to have made his own decision to share, I scooted my seat over to see what he was doing.

Letters and numbers glided across the screen. White digits flashing, moving, clearing before new ones formed.

"What are you doing?"

"Something illegal." Nonchalance poured off him, genuine and practically carefree.

Shock reverberated through me. This here was Smythe in his element. It was no secret his skills with tech and in comms were next level. What I'd never seen before was Smythe so focussed or dedicated.

Movement out of the corner of my eye caught my attention. I snapped my gaze through the large window. Michaels. Awareness slammed into me, along with his attention.

"Why did you just... oh." Smythe's breath hitched. "Fuck, I need to—"

"No." I jerked my head in his direction. "Please don't."

Looking paler than I'd ever seen him, Smythe swallowed hard. "What is it about illegal you don't get?" The words were spoken softly and through the side of his mouth.

"Do you trust me?" It was a big ask.

Smythe's nose scrunched, his uncertainty clear.

"I promise Michaels can help and will be interested in what you shared."

"And what about *how* I got the information?"

I shrugged, a little chuckle following. "Knowing Michaels, he'll be impressed as hell."

His fingers hesitated over the keyboard, and I willed him to believe me. Needed him to. When he gave a small nod, I exhaled and indicated Michaels should come in.

When he entered, his presence filling the room, he walked towards me. Curiosity shone in his gaze. Our ears popping with the hum of static had us both turning to an anxious-looking Smythe.

"We good in here?" A friendly smile tilted Michaels's lips, but the cord in his neck screamed of action. He was ready to pounce and make a move, depending on what I said. Who knew that would be such a heady feeling? Having his faith like that.

I smiled, throwing some flirtation into my expression should anyone be peering at us through the window. Well, that, and it was fun. "Smythe here is just going to do his computer whizz thing, and we're going to sit and wait patiently. You want to take a seat?"

Michaels eyeballed the chair like it was going to bite his arse. "And where are you going to sit?" He made no attempt to move.

"How hard are the muscles in your thighs?"

The widening of his eyes had me biting down on the inside of my cheek, and silence filled the small white room as Smythe stopped typing.

"Seriously?"

I angled to look at Smythe, his nose scrunched in disgust, maybe horror. Probably both.

"Please don't do that." Legit fear crossed his features.

"Jesus." Michaels huffed out a breath and shook his head. "He's not sitting on my lap. Don't let his frame fool you. He weighs a tonne."

"Hey," I complained with zero bite. Teasing Michaels like this, and him teasing me back, promised hours of entertainment I'd yet to really tap into.

"You want me to do this or not?" From Smythe's tone, it sounded like he had experience reining in kindergarteners or something.

I held up my palms in apology, dropping my guard a little to offer him a real smile.

He looked taken aback, completely unsure what my game was. Hell, maybe he thought I'd lost the plot. That, or I was simply a lovesick fool who was having far too much fun flirting and hanging out with my boyfriend.

My brain stuttered at the idea.

With a shake of his head, he turned back to the screen. Two neck cracks later, his fingers once again flew across the board.

Michaels perched on the table, his knee touching my arm. I concentrated on the sound of the keyboard rather than the welcome heat of his contact.

He was the best but most dangerous distraction.

With a surprising flourish, Smythe did an exaggerated final tap and expelled a loud sigh. "And done." He nudged the laptop in my direction.

I angled it back and the screen up so Michaels could see. "What are we loo—holy shit."

Screen grabs of video footage filled the screen. Ice inched along my veins as I took in each image. Kate

Gallagher's prone form being held by two men. Gallagher armed with a gun, two bodies at her feet.

There were more.

More bodies. More carnage. More horror.

The worst part was the occasional glimpse we got of her face. Devoid of emotion, her expression sent a fresh sliver of white-hot fear into my gut.

A complete lack of humanity.

That was what I was looking at.

None of these images, nor the couple of short five-second clips playing out, spoke of an agent in training doing their job. Not even a flinch when bullets rained down on three individuals wearing white lab coats.

"Where did you get these?"

Hardness leached into Michaels's tone, breaking my wide-eyed stare.

"Hours of digging and following a trail of bread-crumbs no supes, let alone humans, could see."

"Where?" The question was punched out, Smythe's half-arsed response not cutting it.

Smythe blanched, fear pouring off him. A sheen of sweat glistened on his forehead. "I suppose if you're the bad guy, I'd already be dead." A tight smile formed, and he huffed out air through his nose.

"I'm not the bad guy here." Tone softening,

Michaels unclenched his fists. "Do you trust Acting Chief Thatcher?"

"Yes."

That Smythe answered immediately had us both nodding. Tension evaporated, Smythe's shoulders relaxing a fraction.

"Why haven't you gone to him about this?"

"Look what happened to Chief Chambers. He left after I came to him with this." The click of his swallow seemed amplified in the small room. "I couldn't go to anyone. I've been trying to dig while staying under the radar with no fucking clue what to do with anything I've found."

My heart panged at the tremble of fear in his voice.

"You definitely stayed under the radar."

He had, but fuck if I didn't hate the jealousy bubbling in my chest at the praise and admiration there. So far I'd been little more than useless. In fact, I'd made this investigation unnecessarily more complicated by making out with Michaels.

Sure, he'd kissed me, but still, what had I brought to the table so far?

"And why did you tell me?" The thought had been playing around in my mind, especially as he hadn't held back his initial reluctance.

"There's no way you'd become compromised."

Surprise at his conviction had my brows shooting high. "No?"

"No. For almost two years I've watched you. In a non-stalkery way," he added on quickly, pink spreading up his neck. "But you're unmoveable. Dedicated. And honestly, I wasn't buying the whole using Agent Michaels here." He shrugged, and while I should have been mortified he'd read me so well, we wouldn't have this information without my shit acting abilities. "It meant I figured there was something real between you."

My chest warmed at the idea of something real. Apparently Michaels was a better actor than I was if he had Smythe convinced.

"What do you want to do?" I peered up at Michaels, shaking off my inner turmoil. Pity had no place here.

As always, Michaels's eyes on me took my breath away. Fuck that seeing into your soul bullshit. Michaels had the power to drag mine out for the world to see.

"We lock that down. You finish this comms task. Then we're going on a fun excursion." He spoke to the two of us, his voice almost jovial, like this wasn't a huge deal. "We do not split. From here on out, we stick together. Got it?"

"Got it." Without being told twice, Smythe shut down the intel, wiping it from the screen with the press of a few buttons.

Meanwhile I stared at Michaels as he pulled out his phone. After the press of a button, he put the mobile to his ear, and there must have been just one ring before he said, "Lair in three hours."

Lair?

When he ended the call, his attention was back on me. His brows shot high, no doubt reading my expression.

"Please tell me you have a Batman cave." For real, that would be freakin' amazing.

A devil-may-care smile formed on his mouth. The strength of it hit me in the solar plexus. "You'll have to wait and see." The wink that followed sent fresh bubbles of fizz to pop in my stomach.

What I wouldn't do to keep being gifted smiles like that.

***

THREE HOURS LATER ON THE DOT, AND SO MANY changes in direction and reroutes I wasn't sure if I'd even remember the way, we pulled into a warehouse district.

A couple of buildings were clearly operational businesses. We passed them by, and I took note of the names. The lot was a maze of brick and concrete buildings of varying sizes. Streetlights glowed on the main drag, but the smaller roads relied on individual buildings' lights.

We turned right. There was a small building on the narrower road that looked a little like an office block. No lights shone from it. We slowed as we passed it, then Michaels finally pulled alongside it before driving towards the rear and turning into an alleyway of sorts.

A concrete warehouse loomed at our side. Just two storeys high, and beyond the large square footage, there was nothing about it that indicated this was a place we'd be visiting.

But stop we did.

Michaels pulled into the building through a large garage door. The open space was like a plane hangar. He drove close to the outside wall, reaching another exit onto the street, where he pulled up and turned off the engine.

As we stepped out of the car, the garage doors sealed closed.

Before we'd left the academy, Michaels had instructed us to leave our phones in our rooms. So, empty-handed, feeling a little naked without my phone or even a service weapon—something we wouldn't be issued until we were on official assignment—I climbed out and followed Michaels to the back of the large space.

I watched in fascination as he punched in a code. A small flap opened, revealing a retina scanner.

"Holy shit, that's next-gen tech." Awe had Smythe angling around to see better.

An amused snort escaped Michaels. "And you're about to meet the man who designed it."

"Mathew Lucas?" An honest-to-God gasp fell from his mouth.

I'd spoken to Lucas a couple of times. Thatch had arranged the calls after seeing potential in me, figuring me as a good fit for the ITU.

The vampire was old, as in well over a hundred. And from the way Thatch told it, he was super smart and just as deadly.

While I hadn't met Lucas in the flesh, the two calls we'd exchanged had pretty much solidified that about him.

We entered a small concrete room. The light was already on. It was nondescript and void of, well, anything, beyond a second door. Another code, this one different, judging from the movement of Michaels's arm, and a room that I expected was Smythe's fantasy brought to life filled my vision.

"Holy fucking Batman lair."

Lucas stood from behind a gigantic desk, which looked like a high-tech spacecraft hub. He chuckled, the sound rich and warm. "Without the dankness and flying rodents." He stepped towards us, hand outstretched. "Good to finally meet you."

I shook his hand, an eager, slightly unhinged smile tilting my lips high. "You too. This place is incredible."

He gave a slight, almost bashful tilt of his head. "And completely mine."

I bobbed my head in understanding. Smythe didn't know the ITU special-ops division existed. Sharing this space was a huge risk, but revealing the location of an unofficial, SICB-funded unit without the right approval would have been a no go.

"Flynn Smythe." Lucas shot Smythe a charming smile and reached out to shake his hand.

"Holy shit, you know who I am?"

A jovial chuckle fell from Lucas's lips while I could practically hear Michaels's eyeroll. Me? I thought it was kinda sweet. Heck, I'd behaved in a pretty similar way when meeting Michaels.

I eyed the man at Lucas's side. Relaxed shoulders, a cocky smile, this here was Michaels truly at ease.

The shit brewing around us didn't matter. He was with his people, his team. I wanted to be counted too. Desperately wanted an in.

A metal door opened from our right, drawing my gaze.

The vampire was tall, slender, dark-skinned, and from the way she walked, the strength radiating from her, lethal.

Her gaze zeroed in on our group. Missing nothing and reading everything, I expected. Stopping before us, her focus snapped to Michaels. She looked pissed off.

"What did I do?" Humour lifted Michaels's words, and he shrugged, the gesture making his arm brush mine. When the heck had he moved so close to me? Or maybe I'd been the one to stand next to him.

It was like that, the pull, the desire to be close to him.

There was an inexplicable gravitational force between us. Holy shit. He was like my very own moon.

As soon as the thought entered my mind, I wanted to slap myself. Fuck, I was an idiot.

Whatever the expression was on my face was enough to snap the vampire's attention to me.

I fought hard not to squirm under her scrutiny. "Hi. Jett Shaw." I held back from shaking her hand.

Something told me the woman didn't do the whole polite greeting thing.

Silently, she studied me. Talk about intense.

"Kent, stop being an arsehole." Michaels shifted again, the skin on his arm below the hem of his T-shirt pressing against mine this time.

I couldn't stop the hitch in my breath.

Kent's brow quirked at the sound, and I shoved down my embarrassment, knowing full well everyone heard it. Even Smythe, I expected, despite his human hearing.

Lucas intervened, slicing through the weird intensity. "Ivy Kent." He indicated her. "Right, now formalities are out of the way. Shall we get started?"

"What about—"

"And the old crew are back together." Agent Callen's loud greeting cut through Michaels's question. "Bring it in, Kent."

In fascinated amusement, I watched as Callen made to hug Kent, receiving an alarmed shove from the woman followed by her middle finger lifting.

"Really, you haven't seen me in a month, and you don't want my love?" The division leader pouted.

"What the hell is happening?" Smythe whispered from behind me. "Is that Agent Blackheath? Did she just shove the division head?"

The shaking at my side grabbed my attention. Michaels was chuckling, shoulders trembling with his amusement.

"The fuck is that?" Kent's voice was mildly alarmed. She pointed in the general direction of Michaels's face. Wide-eyed, Callen and Kent both turned towards Michaels.

I couldn't look away, despite tingles shooting down my spine when I felt the presence of two more supes behind me, one of which I recognised as Thatch. The other, another panther.

"You heard it, right?" Callen side-whispered to Kent.

"Has hell frozen over?" Kent eyed Michaels with curiosity. It looked like she was a second away from poking him. "That must be it, because it's the only reason I'd accept being dragged away from my desk, making me late home. Jada's going to make me wash up as punishment."

Callen snapped his head around to look at Kent. "Washing up is a punishment?"

"Well, yeah. Chores suck."

"Is washing up really a chore, though?"

"Of course it is."

"Jesus." At my side, Michaels groaned. A mistake, probably, since both Callen and Kent refocussed on him. "We're meant to be working, not having front-row seats to the disaster of the two of you together."

"I should totally resent that." Callen's shrug spoke volumes. He didn't give a damn.

"More to the point, what was that thing you just did?" Kent waved her finger around again. "It wasn't just me, right? You saw it?"

Callen nodded solemnly. "I did."

Around me, I heard Lucas sigh, Thatch following suit, and the unknown panther chuckled.

The whole thing was as farcical as it was fascinating.

"He..." Kent raised a fist to her mouth, as though overcome. She was so not overcome. "...laughed."

"I thought it was more of a chuckle." Folding his arms, Callen eyeballed Michaels.

"You guys are fucking ridiculous." Michaels moved away, not that I felt his loss or anything. He headed to the large table with numerous chairs dotted around it. Did I hope he'd save a seat for me next to him? Maybe a little.

"Panic over. He's back," Kent deadpanned. This time, she scrutinised me rather than watching Michaels stride away. Without another word, she turned and went to the table, sitting directly opposite Michaels.

It was enough to get us all moving.

I didn't get to sit next to Michaels. Instead, the panther who introduced himself as Jamison took the seat I'd been eyeing. The other side of Michaels was taken by an agent called Chris, who entered just as we were about to settle at the table.

Chris, a lion shifter, was gargantuan. He also had a killer smile that riled me the fuck up when he directed it at Michaels and took him into a hug. They were also partners, effectively destroying my fantasy of me and Michaels being paired up when I officially joined the unit.

At my side, Smythe remained tense when they disclosed some of the investigation with him. But when he started to share what he'd found, hooking up to the large screens attached to the wall, his muscles finally loosened. The slight tremble in his voice eased.

This cyber stuff was his language.

And from the first genuine emotion flowing from Kent, it was hers too.

"What led you to this intel?" All jokes had been well and truly pushed aside when Callen spoke. Smythe getting the images and footage was as incredible as it was worrying.

No wonder the division leader was on high alert.

A surreptitious glance around the table told me everyone was.

As he rubbed a hand around his nape, discomfort oozed off Smythe. The pressure of so many intense pairs of eyes on you had that effect. "Angelica Gallagher."

"Kate's mum," Callen stated.

"Teri Hughes and Carla Smith," Smythe continued.

"Relatives of Martin Hughes and Paul Smith." Callen didn't tear his gaze from Smythe. From his stillness, I wasn't even sure he was breathing.

"They all work for AFX, which from the look of it, you already know." He didn't wait for anyone to respond before he said, "I put digital locators on their vehicles." Wariness held his voice tight. But credit to the guy, Smythe held it together.

None of the agents around the table reacted for a beat.

Jamison was the first to give. He barked out a loud laugh, one that shook his whole body. "Gotta hand it to the kid. He's got balls."

Smythe flushed.

"What system did you use?" I couldn't tell if Kent was impressed or not, but her stare held true, studying Smythe intently.

"Genesis VI with a Gatton add-on. I added some extra coding." Smythe's gaze darted to Thatch, no doubt wondering exactly how much trouble he could be in.

"That bypassed the Cornelius system?"

A slow nod from Smythe answered Kent's question.

With no idea what they were talking about, as a cyber geek I was not, I looked on and practically shit myself when Kent shot out a loud, "Holy shit. Jada's been talking about adoption. Would you consider being adopted? I could get on board having you as a kid."

A wave of reactions ranging between amused and bemused travelled around the table. The flush on Smythe's cheeks turned fire-engine red, and his shoulders sagged.

"Considering what arseholes my parents are, I can't see that being a problem. Twenty-five may be too old for adoption, though." A tentative smile stretched across his lips.

"Your parents are arseholes?" Kent's tone turned deadly, sucking the joy from the room.

"Nothing I can't handle or anything major," Smythe said quickly. "They don't need to be unalived or anything."

My lips twitched, liking Smythe more and more. It was a shame it had taken almost two years to see this different side to him.

"Shall we get back to it?" The voice of reason came from Lucas, and I expected it usually did.

With a nod, Smythe carried on. "I have a thing for patterns. Recognised the commonality with the cadets being AFX. From there, I hacked into calls they received by their vehicle's Bluetooth. Managed to trace that to a secure hub, and it took some work to pass through the firewalls that led to a maze of information, which led to this footage.

"This is static surveillance footage that had been wiped. I found the loop to their remote wipe system. Not even sure they know the storage exists."

"Fucking genius." Kent said what I was certain we were all thinking. "Lucas, I want him."

"Uhm...." Smythe froze in his seat.

Lucas's simple "Noted" had her smiling. From the looks of the reactions of those around her, it wasn't something that happened often.

Everything Smythe shared was incredible. Beyond anything we could have hoped for. Yet again, discomfort rattled around in my chest. Feeling insignificant was not something I was used to. After this, would Callen and Lucas change their minds, rescinding discussions about me joining ITU?

Hating that I was thinking about that when, in the

grand scheme of things, it didn't matter, I steadied my breathing. Focussing on this win and being proud of Smythe... that was what I needed to home in on.

Feeling the weight of a stare, I flicked my gaze around the table. Michaels's dark eyes peered into me, forcing their way inside and trying to read all my secrets. My insecurities.

Questions filled that one look. Was I okay? Was something wrong? Knowing that I could read the silence and understand his expressive eyes loosened something in my chest.

A kick of a smile lifted the corner of my mouth. He studied me for a beat before giving a barely perceptible nod, then glanced away.

The break of his attention brought the room back into sharp focus. If he knew the effect he had on me—how everything else all but disappeared when he had me in his sights—how would he react?

"Anything on Shadowfall?"

Callen's question put me on high alert.

"Not that I've seen."

Disappointment buzzed in the air.

"But there's so much in the hub left to go through."

"That's where we'll start." Callen glanced around the room. "All hands on deck sifting through the system. Kent, Lucas, work with Smythe on getting everyone access. With Gallagher apparently active, there's no telling how many more are or what their current mission is. Questions?"

Since nobody had any, we got to work, burying ourselves in pages of deleted files, searching through the proverbial haystack, just trying to find that damn needle that would burst this thing wide open.

The next three hours went by in much the same vein.

A few remarks were made here and there, someone stretching occasionally, shooting the shit and making an off-hand joke to cut through the tension and our exhaustion. Throw in a couple of smouldering glances between me and Michaels as well. Alongside all that, everything we'd discovered ticked around in my brain.

Just as I wondered if my system could handle another coffee, Callen called for our attention. "Thatch and I have to get back to Lucinda. Go do whatever it is you have to do. Be back here at 0600."

A collective sigh of relief went around the room. Thankfully it was Friday night, which would make it easy for Smythe and me to return without any drama.

We said our goodbyes, and Michaels drove us back to the academy. Fatigue beat at me, but even the movement of the car couldn't lull me to sleep. I was too wired for that.

Once we arrived, we parted ways after another scorching-hot kiss that made my knees weak. I headed to my room with only a sly second glance at Michaels's retreating form.

The kisses we shared were ridiculously delicious. The one we just exchanged did nothing to help me feel less edgy—a problem since tiredness made my limbs heavy.

As I unlocked my door, I paused with my hand on the door handle when I caught an unfamiliar scent.

Pushing the door slowly open, I hesitated in the doorway, scanning the room.

Nothing appeared to be moved or out of place, but the taint of something "other" drifted through the air. Someone had definitely been in my space.

The door had been locked, but any one of us in the academy could pick a door lock in our sleep. Latching on to the scent, I followed its route. It drifted to the right of the room, to my bed, my wardrobe, my small set of drawers. I tugged the top drawer open.

Everything was as I left it. Leaning down, I inhaled, jaw clenching when the same smell tickled my nostrils.

There was nothing to find in my room. Nothing confidential or compromising. Hell, I didn't even have a Fleshlight or a dildo here.

"There a reason why you're sniffing your undies?" Amusement coloured Michaels's words.

"Why, you want in?" I turned towards him, scent momentarily forgotten as I took my fill. He was a fine specimen of man. He had the whole chiselled jaw, intense gaze, and high cheekbone thing going on. "I've still got my laundry to do. Feel free to take it off my hands. Have a good whiff while you're at it."

Michaels being in my space dislodged a fission of tension I'd been carrying all day. Sure, the man was often serious, his dark-brown eyes often feeling like they had the power to penetrate my soul, but beneath all that, I sensed something more. A part of him he locked down. Something fun and light.

Every now and then, like the quirked brow and smirk he directed at me as he leaned against my doorframe, I got a hint of a different version of the agent Michaels seemed reluctant to let loose.

And that bright, bold laugh earlier... just the memory raised goose bumps on my arms. Hearing that sound again made me want to try harder to tease this other side of the man out of him.

I wanted it so desperately, I put my hands on my belt, pulling it open.

"Or maybe you want something fresher." Leather brushing against leather reverberated in the room as I teased him, the memory of his deep laughter making me bold. The clip sprang free, and my heart bounced when his gaze dropped, a flash of hunger appearing in his eyes.

Holy shit.

My cock twinged in my pants, eager for me to stop teasing and let him know I was more than okay with exploring this tension between us. Fake boyfriend or not, chemistry like this, you could not fake.

When he took a step into my room, my stomach fizzed, and my heart tripped over itself.

This was happening.

I held my breath, not willing to spook him or sabotage this moment.

Then something flipped. He frowned, brows dipping low. "What's that smell?"

Air whooshed out of me. There was no concealing my exhalation. No pretending I wasn't affected. Not when Michaels was already fully in my room and stalking the space.

"That's what I was checking out when you came. Someone's been in here, looking through my things. Not a single item is out of place, though."

"Not even a millimetre?"

He wasn't even teasing. "Nope." And neither was

I. Keeping an eye on my shit in such miniscule detail was one of the first assignments in the academy.

"You recognise the scent?"

"No." I shook my head, watching him move around my room. "I can't even tell the species." Which was honestly worrying. Each species had a distinct scent. "You?"

Our gazes connected, frustration evident in his. "No. They must have masked it."

"To either stop us from tracking them down—"

"Or preventing you from recognising a scent you know."

Shit.

I looked around my room, realising we shouldn't be discussing this here or anywhere in the vicinity of anyone who could overhear us. Change of tack it was. "Back to this open belt I have. You going to do anything about it?"

Wide-eyed, Michaels peered back at me. When the click of his hard swallow reached my ears, I smirked while willing my heart to calm the hell down.

His own lips lifted into a cocky smile. "I actually came here to see if you wanted to hit the gym. We didn't discuss plans this weekend. You don't have anything scheduled."

My smirk shifted into something warmer, despite

knowing he was setting up a cover for us being away together. "Have you been checking my schedule?"

"Maybe."

"The gym's locked."

He tugged keys out of his pocket. "Good thing I've got these, then."

"In that case, count me in. It's not a visit to the bar, you know, like how normal dates go...."

His smile slipped, and my teasing hollowed out in my stomach.

"A gym session sounds much better," I rushed to say.

A crease appeared between his brows. "Yeah?" It almost sounded like he cared, that this was more than an opportunity to keep our story going.

"Definitely." I smiled softly, meaning it, wanting him to see the warmth in my gaze.

The past few days had been nonstop crazy, filled with snooping and deception. Not that any of that wasn't a rush and didn't get my blood pumping.

But to switch off behind locked doors in a separate building away from the dorms and any other building sounded like heaven. This evening's findings still buzzed in my brain. No way would I switch off and be refreshed for more tomorrow unless I worked the noise out of my system.

"I may have some extra energy I need to burn off." Truth teased from within my words.

He snorted, his shoulders relaxing and his features morphing, losing some of the shadow usually there. "Something I can relate to."

"Meet you there in five?" I needed to get my sweats on, and no way could I do that with him here. I may have been playfully taunting Michaels before with a striptease, but me actually stripping down would be pushing it.

I had a suspicion I wasn't the only one feeling that way.

"Sounds good." He winked and left my room.

I closed the door and got changed. There was no telling what the intruder had been looking for or hoping to achieve.

Waiting games sucked.

But for now, at least I had an outlet. That included watching Michaels get hot and gloriously sweaty.

CHAPTER 7
MICHAELS

SLICK WITH SWEAT, I ARCHED MY BACK, FLEXING my loosened muscles, luxuriating in the pull. It had been too long since I'd pushed myself like this. The burn felt good, soothing my wolf.

That didn't mean awareness wasn't making my skin feel like it was attached to a live wire.

Each hit of the bag, each flex of the weights, every single move I made, his gaze trailed me.

There was no imagining it. That was unnecessary, since Shaw was never far from my thoughts, let alone my line of vision.

Whoever thought it was a good idea to train together, an attempt to work off some steam while his pheromones and tantalising forest scent invaded my senses, was a fool.

It wasn't lost on me this was my bright idea.

But between the investigation, the pretence, the lies and deception, there'd been so many kisses and touches that I was coming out of my skin with want.

The complicated story of fake dating, boyfriends, whatever, with Shaw's added layer of charade didn't make the faux kisses feel any less real.

"Fuck."

The clang of a weight being dropped pulled my attention, putting me on high alert. "What's wrong?" I asked, abandoning the rowing machine.

"Got distracted and whacked my leg."

Surprise had me pulling my brows high, but his attention was on his leg, and holy shit, he was undoing the knot on his sweatpants.

"What are you doing?" I barely recognised my voice, the question coming out shaky and high-pitched.

His attention snapped to me, brows drawn low. "Need to check my leg." Not even a breath later, his sweats were at his knees, revealing thighs muscular enough to snap timbre. The light brown hair covering his skin looked soft, tempting.

I followed the movement of his hands as he rubbed a section of his leg, trying and failing not to notice the substantial bulge in his grey boxer briefs. With my tongue feeling thick, I struggled to swallow and get moisture in my mouth.

Fuck knew where all my saliva had gone. Probably in a pool on the floor from the drool.

"It's fine." Realising Shaw was speaking to me, I dragged my gaze up his glistening abs and over his pecs before landing on his grinning face. Clocking his wide, self-satisfied smile, I clenched my jaw.

The arsehole had played me.

"Already healed. No harm, no foul." A twinkle danced in his eyes, the affect alluring and hinting at mischief.

Jesus, maybe this was what we needed—to break through this tension. Smile and laugh. Poke ridiculous fun at each other. Without it, I didn't know how much more I could take.

"You need me to look at it? Massage the sting out?"

The widening of his eyes warmed my chest. Yeah, flirting and testing boundaries was definitely what I needed. And from the dropping of his gaze and the heat bubbling to life in the depths of his eyes, I figured so did he.

"Well, if you're offering...." He let the words hang between us, an open challenge to the thrown gauntlet he'd triggered.

It was finally time to step up to see how this

panned out. Undoubtedly, Shaw had a pull over me that I struggled to fully comprehend. Maybe I didn't need to. Maybe all I needed to do was feel, touch, finally get a taste.

"What are you—"

I cut his snark off with my mouth, swallowing his words and holding him tight as I kissed him. It was the first kiss without an audience. The first touch of our lips, our tongues when all that mattered was us.

"Fuck." The word tore clear out of me as I leaned back to look at him, drink Shaw in. His mesmerising honey-coloured eyes connected with mine, pupils blown as his lips remained parted. Needing more, I pressed my mouth to his, lips moving, tongue seeking entry, kissing him with all the pent-up frustration and lust and longing shrouding us since the moment we'd met.

Grasping his hip, I hauled him close, seeking more contact. I didn't let up as our mouths connected, moving in tandem.

With nothing existing to me but the taste, the touch, the feel of Shaw, I threw myself into the sensation, welcomed how my mind quietened.

There was nothing but the two of us. In this room. In this feeling.

The shifting of his hand to the back of my head, his

blunt nails scraping my scalp, caused a fresh scattering of goose bumps to break free.

It had been so long since I had this, experienced the raw passion of a first kiss. Got lost in the excitement of the unknown.

But there was no room for overthinking. I didn't want to. Couldn't. Wouldn't. Not when he felt so good.

A groan was the precursor to him moving again. His strong hand landed at the small of my back, fingers flexing, effectively tugging us closer together.

Boneless, I went willingly, inhaling his strength and direction.

I may have been the first to take what I wanted, press my mouth to his, but Shaw owned this kiss. My mouth.

The way he tangled his tongue with mine shot a lightning bolt of awareness through every cell of my body. Spiralling, head filled with nothing but the sensation of him, I snaked my arms around him.

Capturing his soft grunt as our bodies pressed against each other fully, I didn't let up. Each gasp, each groan, each slide of our mouths felt stolen, important. Just for us.

But I craved more.

I eased out of the kiss, finding a semblance of

control. His soft whine was sweet, unexpected, causing my lips to curve upwards.

Making eye contact, I searched, looking for his reaction and any signs of regret.

"Don't stop." The words rushed out of him. Pink-cheeked, pupils blown, this version of Shaw was perfection, or at least a close second to the time nothing but adrenaline and joy radiated from him when we'd finished that exercise together, just the two of us acing a mission that he'd previously failed with a whole team.

That had been one heck of a rush.

"You've still stopped." Rather than uncertainty, challenge coloured his words. His confidence was hot and did things to me that no other man had ever managed before.

"You want my mouth?" The gravel of my voice sounded loud in the echoey gym.

"Yes."

I smirked, wondering if he knew what was coming.

From the speed his brows shot up when I dropped to my knees, I expected not. Taking him by surprise was fun, but hearing him moan was fast becoming my new favourite sound.

I worked swiftly at freeing him from his grey boxer briefs, swiping my thumb over the damp patch I found there. Recalling how he'd teased me earlier when we were in his room—when he'd tugged open his leather belt to get a reaction—I paused, my mouth a hairsbreadth from him. Exposed, thick, his balls heavy, even the scent of him called to me.

"Seriously." The strangled word gasped out of him.

I peered up. Already he looked debauched. With frantic eyes and kiss-swollen lips, he was the picture of desperation. "It's not nice to tease, is it?"

His brows scrunched in confusion, his gaze darting over my face. The moment he recalled what I was talking about, he slammed his mouth shut. While the need rode him hard—his legs trembling, his dick jerking with every other exhale—his eyes brightened with amusement.

"Next time you tease me with a belt, you'll find it being used as a restraint." I watched him carefully, taking in the way his breathing sped up and the flash of heat sparked in his eyes.

Jesus. I was not into the whole bondage thing, but teasing Shaw and seeing his reaction at the very idea of it was something I could totally get on board with.

"So I need to make sure I'm always wearing pants with a belt. That's what I'm hearing."

I shot him an amused smile before leaning in and finally getting a taste. I snaked my tongue around his slit, lapping up the pearl of precum just begging to be swallowed.

A loud groan rent the air, spurring me on.

Swollen and begging to be worshipped, Shaw's cock bobbed. Jesus, it was pretty. Long, with just the right amount of thickness to stretch my jaw.

There was no holding back as I tongued his dick, licking a long stripe down his length, burying my face against his soft pubes. The scent of forest was stronger here, filling my senses. I wanted to bottle it up, carry it with me wherever I went, the scent familiar, soothing, while simultaneously able to twist me up like a pretzel with need.

Meeting his gaze, I held eye contact as I pressed open-mouth kisses back to the tip. Sunlit gold peered back at me, his gaze wide open, emotions free to read and take as my own.

"Please." The whimpered plea was my undoing. I expected it always would be.

Holding on to the backs of his trembling thighs, I opened wide and took him in my mouth. I pushed forward, down, further, wanting him to leave his mark and hear the scratch and rasp in my throat come morning.

"Fuck, fuck, fuck." The sweetest of keens rolled

over me like a warm caress, his sounds wrapping directly around my cock.

With my nose nuzzling his groin, I held my breath, swallowed once, and pulled back. His legs shook, a loud grunt reaching me just as one of his hands latched on to my hair. With no strength in the hold, he let me lead. Let me take what I wanted.

And then I moved, up and down with strong sucks, each press going as far down as I was able. I wore each moan I pulled from him like a badge of honour, savouring each growl of my name like the most decadent chocolate.

But fuck if I wasn't close to unravelling.

I needed him to come. Needed him to let go so I could drink him down before I came in my sweats.

The trembles morphed into full-on quakes as his cries turned desperate. But, fuck, it was hearing "Vaughn" leave his lips that nearly pushed me over the edge.

I held on to his shaft, jerking him at the root. On every down swipe, I fondled his balls. The whole time I sucked hard and fast, not sure how I'd survived life so far without having this with him.

And then he shattered. A loud "Oh fuck, fuck, Vaughn" splintered the still air.

Warm and thick, his cum was an elixir I'd willingly

drink every damn day. I swallowed each drop, wrung every bead from him. He slumped. Quickly releasing him, I happily guided him to the ground before me.

Rather than collapsing, his mouth connected with mine. He chased his taste, his soft groan shooting tingles down my spine. I needed to release before I exploded.

Still kissing and drinking down his moans, savouring the combined taste of his mouth and his cum, I wrestled my cock free from my sweatpants. The relief of not being restrained was immediate, but my dick felt hot and angry and so close to—"Nngh."

His hand found my cock. Dry and rough was never my favourite feeling, but that it was Shaw's palm was all that mattered. Working me over with a firm grip, he twisted a little at the end. I rocked into him, barely able to accept his kisses.

"You're so fucking hot." His words hit my cheek as he kissed his way to my ear, down my neck, nuzzling in my collarbone. "Paint my hand."

A shudder ripped through me.

"Like that. Come on." Open-mouthed kisses slid against my exposed skin, and I groaned, tilting my head back.

"Fuck." The word tore out of me with the first stripe of cum.

"Holy shit." Shaw eased back, hand still working, attention on my aching cock.

I followed his gaze, watching each spurt of warm cream jetting out of me. It streamed over his hand. But it was the slow trickle travelling down his stomach, pooling in his belly button that held me captive.

Emptied and shaking, I dropped my head on his shoulder, shuddering when he released me. While still on my knees, my limbs turned to mush. I shifted, arse falling on the foam mat. Not letting go, I tugged him with me, smiling when he came with a grunt, landing in my arms.

"You okay?" It took a lot to make me breathless, or apparently not, since an amazing hand job did the trick.

"I could sleep for a week."

A low chuckle rumbled through me. I felt the same.

We were a mess. Sweats not fully off, covered in sweat and spunk. No way I was willing to move just yet. I didn't want to break the moment. Didn't want to give the real world and the frustrations awaiting us the chance to creep back in yet.

"We should wash up and get some sleep." The gruffness of his voice sounded like he was already halfway to snoozeville.

I sighed, hating he was right. It would be too easy to pass out. But with Shaw's weight on me and still feeling the high of my orgasm, I felt... safe. The sensation was alien, especially being in such a public, open space.

There were less than a handful of places in the world I felt truly able to drop my guard. As well as my home, the lair, and the ITU headquarters, the only other place had been Jenson's house.

But here, in a locked gym that plenty of others had a key to, it felt like Shaw wrapped a blanket of safety around me. The shift of something in my chest caught my breath. He would have felt that. Rather than calling me out, he nuzzled against me, placing gentle kisses across my chest, ending up on my collarbone.

"You want to come back to my room?" Hesitancy sat just below the surface of his question. He was expecting me to say no. Maybe he expected me to blow him off and dash out of here like my arse was on fire and this was an incredible, mind-blowing mistake. "Please."

And there it was. The soft request that would continue to be my undoing.

Agreeing now, saying yes, would change everything.

Was it wise?

Fuck no and for so many reasons.

"How about you come to mine?"

I felt his smile against my skin, and a soft purr that was all panther vibrated up my cheek, pulling a ridiculously sappy smile from me.

Fuck it all to hell.

There was no turning back now.

WAKING UP IN SHAW'S ARMS WAS MY NEW favourite thing. Being wrapped up in his scent calmed something inside me I hadn't realised had been so restless.

By the time we got out of bed when the first rays of light filtered through the blinds in the room, I was sated. That didn't mean ease settled fully on my shoulders.

I wanted this case over, for all the obvious reasons. The sooner it was closed, the better. But that would mean not seeing Shaw every day—an event I was coming alarmingly attached to.

"We're going to be late."

In response, I pressed another kiss to the back of his neck, preventing him from putting his T-shirt on. The sound of his chuckle pulled a smile to my lips.

"I'm not doing anything. It's your fault." It seriously was. The man smelled divine.

He attempted to shrug me off, and even got as far as reaching the door and tugging it open.

"Just one more kiss before we have to enter the land of the living."

When he turned in my arms to face me, my heart flipped, loving that I'd won and I'd get his mouth on mine.

"Never imagined you'd be this needy."

He could tease all he wanted. I could take it. I quirked my brow, saying, "There's something about shooting my load so—"

An exaggerated clearing of a throat had me jolting. Fuck. I hadn't realised we weren't alone. The reality was a bucket of ice-cold water in my face.

We stepped fully out of my room, Prescott's scent already registering.

"Morning." A smug grin sat on his face, but it didn't quite reach his eyes. Instead, his attention was assessing as he studied us.

Shaw quickly tugged on his tee, now that I wasn't groping him.

"You're up bright and early," Prescott said.

"Weekend date," I offered, aiming for a casual smile. "How about you?"

"Just off out for a run, then I'm away from campus for the weekend."

I bobbed my head. "In that case, I'll leave you to it."

He offered me a wink, gaze lingering on Shaw for a second longer than I liked before he said goodbye and headed towards the exit.

Once we were alone, Shaw angled to look at me, his expression careful, controlled.

I didn't like it at all.

"You good?" I stepped into his space, gripping his waist.

At the contact, emotion flickered to life, pulling a small smile from him and loosening his muscles. "Yeah, but we really need to get going if we're going to get our weekend date started."

After this, I hoped I could make that actually happen. Take him out on a real date. I sent the wish into the universe as we headed to the car hand in hand. The gesture—his hand in mine—was becoming more and more natural. And after the night we'd shared, fuck if I didn't like his touch a hell of a lot.

By the time we arrived at the lair, I was worked up with the level of teasing Shaw threw my way. But at least we were on time.

We passed through security, and I watched Shaw head to Smythe, my stare not so subtly on his arse.

Today was going to be busy, which meant I needed to focus on the case.

With just a little spring in my step, I made my way to the same workspace I'd set up yesterday and got to work.

Bleary-eyed, the words on the coffee jar wavered before me like black lines shimmering in desert heat.

"You look like shit."

Flipping off Kent took more energy than I had, but I managed to, just the same.

"So what gives with you and the kid?"

She shoved the chair near the small kitchen table back a little before smoothly sitting down. For all her shit talk and her foul mouth, the woman was grace personified.

I glanced around, noticing the door was closed between us and the rest of the team. I'd taken another trip to the kitchen in the lair to scrounge coffee. Unsurprisingly, I hadn't slept for shit last night.

The exchange of lazy hand jobs once we'd made it to my room was partially responsible. But rather than knocking me unconscious, which to be fair, usually happened after wringing not one but two blissful orgasms from me, I'd stayed awake, staring at the ceiling.

When I wasn't staring down at the man who'd wrapped himself around me like a giant koala bear, that was.

"Michaels." She kicked out the chair beside her. "Seriously, sit before you collapse." While the usual snark was evident, the concern in her gaze pierced me. I should have run, but it took energy I simply didn't have.

When I finally sat, fresh coffee in hand, I held her stare.

With escape impossible, it made sense to let her get on with it.

"So?"

"He's not a kid." I sounded petulant at best, like a dickhead at worst.

Her brows arched pointedly at me.

"Fine, compared to most people, he's not a kid. You're close to celebrating your second century, so you don't count." She waited me out, something she was great at. The difference was, ever since I'd lost Jenson, she'd given me free pass after free pass.

She'd taken all my foul moods. Covered for me when I went off radar. Didn't even kick my arse from here to kingdom come when I had a close call or seven.

"Why are you asking?" Legit question. What had changed for her to push? For her to pin me down, tease me mercilessly, something had to be different.

"You laughed yesterday, kicked back, and I swear that weird vein in your neck that's usually throbbing gave up the ghost."

I slapped my hand on my neck. "I do not have a weird throbbing vein on my neck. I don't have any weird throbbing veins, thank you very much."

Her eyes widened, comically so, her lips pursed.

Fucking hell. "Fuck off."

Her laugh was loud, abrupt, dragging my own from me. It filled my chest, pouring out of me, glee rippling through the air between us.

Her gaze softened, an expression she rarely shared. "It looks good on you. I've missed it." *Missed you.* Her unspoken words were loud and clear, snatching emotion from thin air and practically cramming it down my throat where it lodged. "Just keep it up, okay? Whatever you're doing. I know Jenson wo—"

"Please don't." That damn crushing emotion broke free, shredding through the last of my amusement. Her face fell, compassion lasering into me. "I'm just not ready."

A silent nod and a squeeze of my arm, and then she stood. "Right. Inhale the coffee and get your tired arse out of here. That panther of yours thinks he's got something."

"Shit, why didn't you say anything?" I stood abruptly, sloshing my coffee.

"Easy, wolf boy. It's not urgent, well, not yet. Thatch is double-checking something with Chris and Jamison before we know if the intel is good."

While Jamison wasn't in our unit, he'd worked with Thatch a lot over the years and was one of the few people who knew who we were and what we did. I'd itched to go out with Chris and Jamison, who'd partnered up to be our gofers. Funnily, they didn't appreciate the name Callen assigned to them. I'd been eager to put my boots to the ground, but there were Shaw and Smythe to consider.

Yesterday I'd told them we'd stick together. After the unknown invader had been in Shaw's room—Smythe's had not been infiltrated—I wouldn't compromise their safety or my promise to them.

In a handful of weeks, they'd be assigned to full-time positions and sworn in as agents. It didn't matter they were in spitting distance of that. They were still cadets and were now in the thick of this.

I nodded and wiped up my mess. Lucas would be a

grouchy sod if we didn't clean up after ourselves. "Okay. Coming."

I stepped to the sink, turning when she called my name. "Don't think I didn't notice you didn't deny he was your panther."

Narrowing my gaze at her did nothing but earn me a middle finger. I shook my head, finished my coffee, and tried not to think too long and hard about why the thought of Shaw being mine made my heart race and teased an emotion I'd buried deep last year to the surface.

Hope.

It was a fuck of an emotion, especially when it meant you had so much to live for.

By the time I entered the main war room—named by Callen and vetoed by Lucas—Thatch was pacing, finishing off his call, by the sound of it.

I wasn't even three steps in before I sought out Shaw. Already, his focus was on me. Concern shimmered in his eyes.

With the kitchen door closed, he wouldn't have heard anything, but he'd have seen that Kent and I laughed, talked about something that had me frowning, and now, I had no clue what he could read from my expression.

The slight tilt of his head asked a silent question,

Are you okay? Reading me, us reading each other, became easier the more time we spent together. And after worshipping his body the best I could in the twenty minutes we spent in the shower together this morning, his body was a map I could read with my eyes closed.

Was I okay?

Peering at Shaw, absorbing his sweet smile, his dazzling eyes, letting his unique rainforest scent wrap around me, I knew I was. Or at least was going to be.

Shoulders relaxing, I smiled, just for him. A smile that told him I was okay. A smile that told him if I could steal him away and bury my tongue between his arse cheeks, I totally would.

A flush of colour spread up his neck. Message received and understood loud and clear, apparently.

Good. As soon as possible, I'd make that a reality. There was still so much left to explore and do with my amber-eyed panther.

"Got him." Thatch's deep voice sliced through with satisfaction. All eyes were on him as he explained, "It's official. Hornell is alive." While we'd all suspected as much, considering the activation of Shadowfall, to know for sure tied up another thread. "There's evidence he was at Gore Cove just yesterday. Chris and Jamison took the mobile AFIS, managed to get a fingerprint match."

"That he's on the move and out in public has to mean something, right?" I said, taking the open seat next to Shaw.

"That's what I'm thinking." Lucas inputted something into his computer, his attention still firmly on the conversation despite his flying fingers. "Hornell doesn't make mistakes."

"Not technically true, since his op was taken down four years ago." As soon as Callen spoke, he grimaced. "Which clearly wasn't shut *all* the way down, and he faked his own death." He clenched his jaw. "Fucking hell."

"I've got something."

We all snapped our attention to Smythe.

"You've received a text." He glanced at Shaw, and I frowned, my gut clenching.

"I don't have my—"

When Smythe arched his brow, Shaw stopped, colour rising in his cheeks.

"Please, carry on."

Smythe's lips twitched. He'd activated traces on Shaw's phone, distorting the GPS to make it seem like Shaw and I were having a cosy time at Lunar Park. We were still waiting tentatively for a call for another job, hoping for an additional bite and another way in.

Another fake invoice had also been sent from the hospital this morning, complete with an email from his mum and her concerns.

"Coordinates and a time." He studied his screen. "Glebe Bay."

"Another port," I stated. "What time?"

"Four hours. 2200."

"You'll need to split our GPS locations, make it seem like we head in separate directions. Any way of tracing the location of—"

"Already on it," Kent interrupted. She sounded pissed off. "The signal is bouncing around like a fucking kangaroo on acid."

"Meet many roos on acid in your very, very long life, Kent?"

Kent extended her arm and flipped Callen off.

"Right, let's get to work." Lucas stared hard at Shaw, who sat up straighter when he realised he was under scrutiny. "You up for this, Shaw?"

"Absolutely, sir." Confidence wrapped around his response, sure and steady.

I had to believe he had this. Plus, regardless of what anyone said, I would be on the ground, waiting in the wings. Nobody knew that yet, but I was unmove-able in my decision.

I'd let a man I cared about go off by himself once before. Like it or not, I'd be stuck to Shaw's arse like superglue.

CHAPTER 8

SHAW

"I don't like this."

I tightened my jaw, back molars grinding. It should be sweet, Michaels's worry. His desire to protect me.

It wasn't.

It was annoying as fuck.

"This is my job."

"Technically, no, it's not. You're an academy trainee. You're not an employee of the SICB. This is so fucking wrong." Tension wired Michaels's words tight as he white-knuckled the steering wheel.

I took a calming breath, trying to see this from his point of view. Would I be worried if he was going off on assignment by himself? Most definitely. But what I wouldn't do is lay my concern on him, especially not just before he'd be leaving the vehicle to walk into who knew what.

Jesus, as much as I'd like him to be, he wasn't even my boyfriend. I had no idea what we were exactly, but we'd spent literally one night together. Shared three mind-blowing orgasms.

"Just pull over here. I can run the rest of the way."

I didn't need to look at his face to see his shock. His tension shifted into something different. I just hoped it was remorse, and he'd back off.

"I'll take you to the drop-off point."

I waited him out, hoping for more.

The heavy sigh following was as loud as it was frustrated. "And I'll keep my mouth shut."

"Thank you."

"It's not that I don't think you can do this."

Wide-eyed, I stared at him. "This is you keeping your mouth shut?" Humour mixed with incredulity as I spoke.

When his lips twitched, I grabbed on to the expression with both hands.

"I can do this. I'm prepared. I also have you as backup."

His gaze roamed my face, and I tilted my lips. Reaching out and taking his free hand, I pulled it to my mouth, dotting a kiss there. The gesture felt right, a moment of intimacy within the unknown waiting for us.

"I'm sorry."

"It's okay, but we need to trust each other."

"I do trust you." Conviction fired his words, giving them the trajectory to pierce my heart.

He trusted me? Jesus. I squeezed his hand. There was still so much left to discover about Michaels, but earning his trust seemed monumental.

"Thank you. I trust you too." My lips quirked, and heat zipped across my skin as I committed this moment to memory.

He pulled over a short while later. "We're here." For the first time, my heart stumbled, hitting my ribcage with an almighty thump. The sound caught his attention. He unbuckled his seatbelt, and I did the same, the space between us crackling.

Cradling my nape with his palm, Michaels squeezed lightly. Our gazes didn't waver as we drank each other in, our breathing synching. A few breaths later, my pulse steadied, matching his beat for beat.

"You need me, I'm there."

His words sped up my pulse. I loved that he wasn't offering last words of advice. Liked too much that the intensity in his stare spoke of his absolute trust.

Conviction, deep in the depths of his brown eyes, fired back at me.

"If I need you, you'll be there."

A small smirk angled his lips at my words. Wanting it for my own, I captured it with a kiss. Drawing him towards me, stealing his breath and his gravelly groan.

Wanting so much more but aware of the clock counting down, I tore away. Unable to speak, I simply bobbed my head and left his SUV.

I didn't look back.

There were four kilometres between me and my destination. I ran the whole way, using the momentum of my legs to centre myself. I passed by dark streets, closed stores, and a handful of older houses.

This area was dedicated to the port. Allotments with large cranes and trucks were closed up for the night. Dark warehouses lined the route, the occasional smattering of bushed area dividing the sections.

The steady thud of my heartbeat helped me control my breathing.

Calm flowed through me, adrenaline just within reaching distance, ready for me to tap into it.

The city skyline glowed in the distance, creating a bold spray of colour and brightness. At this time of night, the city would be full of life. Clubs would be opening, supes and humans alike spilling out of restaurants and bars, most oblivious to the dangers surrounding them.

Sure, most supes had the strength and speed to protect themselves, but they weren't trained to withstand the level of crazy the SICB faced. It wasn't hard to imagine the horror and contagious panic if they knew a former agent, a captain at that, had created genetically enhanced super soldiers as lapdogs.

That was totally what we were dealing with.

The problem of not knowing his endgame remained.

Why target the academy? Why turn a potentially life-changing research project into one so harrowing and terrifying, it turned my stomach?

And why did they even take the bait and pull me into the fold?

With my dad no longer working for a medical research lab, I didn't have an in like the other three missing recruits. And from the audio and tracking files Smythe had ripped from the AFX employees' vehicles, access to confidential research and samples had been the clear purpose.

But with at least one recruit already having been genetically modified, whatever they were doing clearly worked. It begged the question of why they needed more research or meds or samples or whatever the hell it was they were chasing.

What the fuck were they doing and why?

My phone vibrated in my hand.

Unknown: SP34526

I studied the numbers before glancing around as I stepped further into the docking bay. Containers littered the large space. Stacked four high in some rows, they cast deep shadows, turning the narrow walkways between containers pitch-black. Not even the low lighting of the sporadic spotlights dotted around the port could bleed into those areas. The darkness was impenetrable—for human eyes at least.

The hair on my neck rose. My panther pushed to the surface.

Predators by nature, we didn't do well being hunted. That was our job. Seek and, on occasion, destroy. Or as much as we could in this not-so-civilised world we lived in.

But here in the shadowed darkness, this was my world. Night was my friend.

Sticking closer to the walls of the metal containers, I wove my way through the maze, looking for the container with the same numbers as the message. The sense of being watched didn't fade.

Michaels was out there, far enough away to remain undetected, with no chance of a strong breeze picking up his scent. Not only did I know that, but I also knew this—whoever had eyes on me—wasn't him. The sensation of Michaels's gaze on me drew a whole different type of reaction from me.

This felt off. Wrong.

Screw this.

I eyed a container to my right, on the opposite side of the narrow laneway. Here, I was a sitting duck, so up I'd go.

Sprinting with long strides, I angled towards the rusty blue container. A giant leap, a push of my foot, and my fingers found purchase. I hung on, walking my fingers until I reached the end, knowing on this side, I could lever myself up, one container after another.

With a final pull, my boots connected with the metal roof, the scrape of steel louder than I liked. I crouched, counted to ten, then stood, scanning the area.

From up here, the metropolis stretched out further. I turned my back to the CBD, focussing on the city of containers. The moon, covered by thick clouds, provided little light. That was more than okay with me.

I called my panther forward into a partial shift. My eyes morphed. They'd be brighter, more piercing, slightly larger, but more than that, the inky night practically melted away, bringing my vision into almost crystal-clear focus.

I could make out where the containers started and ended, the numbers attached to the sides, bright like a spotlight, was shining on them. The pattern, the numbers, came into sharp focus, making sense.

Another scan didn't show me any movement. Shadows remained still. No hunched figures. No scent in the air. While something still felt off, the prickle of sensation on my neck eased.

It was time to move.

Sprinting and jumping from container rooftop to rooftop, I headed towards the one with the right number. With my senses on high alert, each touch of metal made me wince. The sound wouldn't reach human ears, but something told me that if there was anything lying in wait for me, it wouldn't be human.

One container away. "What the—"

A flash of movement. A whistling in the air.

Instinct made me crouch. Self-preservation had me tearing off my boots, ready to shift.

It was too late.

With a thunderous growl, fire roared, metal creaked, and a deafening pop had me ducking and slamming my hands over my ears. The container exploded. White-hot heat and fragments of metal spiralled through the air, shooting through the darkness like panther-seeking missiles.

A stab on my leg made me wince. A slice on my back had me shifting.

Black fur sprouted over my body, my bones realigning and morphing. To stay was to die. *Screw that.*

Paws bracing on heated metal, I launched across container roofs, needing to hit the ground. With my feet on concrete, I could push myself far faster than springing from roof to roof.

A crack sounded, and I jolted, spinning just short of receiving a bullet in my chest. A roar split the air.

Not mine.

Michaels's.

Another crack, multiple this time. Bullets peppered metal, spearing holes where my paws had just been. I jumped, arced, needing cover.

In midair, I grunted, the force of the hit changing my trajectory. Flesh tore, bone split, and I fell. With my head spinning and molten agony rushing through my chest, there'd be no landing on my paws.

Consciousness wavering at the crunch of impact, I parted my lips to call out, to scream, to keep Michaels out of harm's way. But darkness descended, cutting off my cry and pulling me away.

Blood and pain flooded my senses. The scent of sharp metallic and acrid smoke clung to my skin, so thick I could probably scrape it off.

A jolt of fear shot through me. I felt steel around my ankle, but it wasn't a chain or a cuff.

Debris split my skin, the cuts searing as they mangled my flesh. A cry tore from my lips, but it didn't stop the movement. The hand clamped on my ankle in a vice grip didn't relent, even though I was conscious. The sure and steady footsteps continued, marching through the wreckage.

I had to open my eyes. Had to at least try to cling to the concrete I felt under my back as I was dragged by my ankle. One eye, then the other one, and I blinked rapidly, trying to clear the grit and blood.

Vision blurry, it was hard to see beyond basic shapes. The smoke didn't help, nor did the raging fire behind me and to my right. I zeroed in on the figure before me.

A man.

A shifter.

At some point, I'd shifted back. Another scrape of metal against my naked form had me moving. I dragged myself towards my captured foot, fighting for strength. The shifter jolted. While he didn't stumble, he did stop.

Ignoring the pain eating at me, I kicked out. My unrestrained bare foot made contact with the man's back, loosening his grip on me so I could tear free.

He turned fast, his arms outstretched, ready to make another grab for me.

Scrambling to my feet, I considered my next move. The water was close by, clearly the direction I was being dragged. Fire was behind me, but somewhere in all that was Michaels.

Between the roaring of the fire and the sirens growing closer, I couldn't hear him. But he'd be coming.

The man lurched forward, swinging out. I spun, finding my momentum to angle out of the way.

He was fast. I was faster.

I landed a punch in his ribs. The shock reverberated up my arm. He didn't flinch, didn't grunt.

I stepped away, my brows shooting high when I realised who the shifter was.

Paul Smith.

"Paul?"

Nothing but a feral snarl stretched his lips. Beyond that, his face was devoid of emotion. Emptiness swirled in the depths of his almost black eyes, traces of red in the whites.

"Pa—"

His clawed hand slashed out, the tip just grazing my chest.

"Fuck." *Fight or flight. Fight or flight.*

The decision was taken from me when he pounced, the move all lion.

The twist of my body didn't soften the impact, but it did mean he couldn't find purchase. I needed my fangs, my claws.

In a blink, I transformed. By the time black fur covered my body, my fangs had already sunk into the juncture of his neck. Blood, thick and tainted, seeped into my mouth. I tore away, unable to spit in this form. Instead, I shook my head, flicking away the blood as I dug my claws into his chest and shoved, my rear legs joining the strain.

He was heavy, out of control as he struggled.

Pushing harder, I managed to fling him away, freeing myself.

Healing but weak, and aware that at least one bullet remained wedged in my body, my head spun.

Blood loss made my brain slow and fuzzy. But I had to move.

I charged before he could fully regain his footing, sharp teeth making contact with his neck once again.

Thick bands of steel around my chest had me breaking free with a snarl.

Agony shot fire into me as I heard the sound of a rib cracking.

Fuck, he was strong. Stronger than he should be. Stronger than I was.

Sinking my fangs in once more, I tore away flesh. More syrupy blood filled my mouth. I shook it out, gaze landing on the deep red pumping out of his body with fast spurts. A severed artery. Relief punched into my chest, but it was short-lived under his crushing grip.

Paul didn't waver. Didn't sag.

I bit again, barely able to breathe.

A growl tore through the air. Blessed reinforcement, and one angry wolf.

I would have smiled if I wasn't hovering in the white space between being awake and passing out.

Falling to the hard concrete, I pushed myself up, head lifting off the floor.

The large grey wolf, speckled already in blood and soot, tore through Paul like he was a rag doll. The fight was over before I collapsed, Paul's prone form almost unrecognisable.

Michaels changed back into biped form. "Fucking hell." Distress whipped through him as he checked me over. "Don't shift." Gentle fingers scoured my body, and I whimpered when his tender touch over my ribs shot raw agony through my veins, whiting my vision and making me sag.

"I've got you."

For the second time, darkness played in my vision, colouring over the white-hot pain in my head, beckoning me. With Michaels at my side, I slipped willingly into unconsciousness.

MY MUSCLES PROTESTED AS I MOVED, TUGGING THE last remnants of sleep from me. The dull pain suggested my bones had healed and only bruising remained.

I'd take it.

Anything was better than the sharp sting of agony from having my bones broken.

That and bullets tearing through my flesh.

"Go steady."

The words, spoken close to my ear, jolted me. My eyes sprang open, heart slamming against my chest.

"That *is* *not* steady." A reprimand if ever I heard one.

I pressed a hand to my sheet-covered chest. "I thought I was alone." My gaze connected with Thatch's. Concern beat down at me, a furrow between his brows as his eyes roamed my face.

"Your senses won't take long to go back to normal. Your ribs were a mess. Two were crushed rather than just broken."

Shock reverberated in my chest, a tremble quickly following. "You had to operate?"

"Well, not me, but yeah. We had to bring you to ITU headquarters and call in one of the surgeons we work closely with. You're in our small infirmary now."

"Okay." I thought that through, my pulse calming at the knowledge I was in good hands. Safe. "Well, I did want to visit the headquarters." Ideally before I joined the team. I aimed for a smile, but I wasn't sure it reached my eyes, judging from the frown staring back at me.

"How's your pain?"

I shrugged, only wincing a little. "Sore rather than in pain. Can I get up?" I was naked under this cotton gown. Getting some fatigues back on sounded mighty fine.

"Let's try sitting up first. You might still be woozy, so we'll take it from there."

I nodded and took his help, becoming more and more aware of the gaping hole spreading in my chest. Michaels wasn't here. Not that I expected him to be playing sentinel exactly, sitting here mopping my brow, but fuck, I wanted it just the same.

"How long have I been out?" Warm sunlight spilled through the window, but beyond that, I had no idea of the time or even day.

"It's a little past nine. You were rushed into theatre just after midnight."

So ten hours give or take.

"And what's happening with the investigation? Any idea why the explosion happened?"

When he hesitated, I frowned.

"What is it?"

"It may be best if you're off this investigation." While his voice held steady, there was more he wasn't saying. He carried an undertone of reluctance in his shoulders, in the slight shift of his features.

Turning rigid, I stared at him, shock and anger bubbling in my gut. "Who made that call? Who thought it was best?" Proud as hell I kept the tremble out of my voice, I fought hard to maintain eye contact.

Thatch was an excellent instructor. I'd heard enough to believe he was an incredible unit leader too. That he came to me about this investigation meant he saw something in me. Getting my arse handed to me last night was far from spectacular, sure, but I'd battled tooth and nail. Literally. Being kicked off the team was not an option.

He studied me, his focus so intense, I held my breath. I didn't take the man for someone to spout bull-shit, so when he parted his lips, saying, "Michaels," I knew he told the truth.

It sucked. Fucking hurt. Fresh pain ripped through me before settling in my chest, playing havoc with my heart.

"Do you think it's best?" This time I didn't quite catch the wobble. The hurt of Michaels speaking out against me was a pain I was unprepared for. "What about the rest of the team?"

Another intense stare followed. "We think you've earned your place."

Relief barrelled into me. I sucked in air, holding it down, calming myself before exhaling. "Thank you." I bobbed my head. "I won't let you down."

"Of that I have no doubt." He stood and moved

over to a side table. "Doc's orders. You need to eat, and then we can get you moving." When he removed the metal cover, the scent of beef called to me. My stomach rumbled, and despite the ache clasping my heart, I set about inhaling calories.

Within an hour, we were back at the lair. Despite all that had happened, Smythe hadn't been cleared for information about the existence of the ITU.

That didn't stop surprise from slamming into me when I entered the war room and was pulled into a hug.

"Holy shit, you're okay. Thank fuck." Smythe eased away, his face flushed.

I smiled, a little overwhelmed with his greeting as well as his untypical display of affection. He cleared his throat and stepped back, rubbing the back of his neck.

"It's good to see you too, Smythe."

His shoulders relaxed, a half smirk forming. "Everyone freaked the crap out. I swear, my heart stopped for a minute or two there," he rushed to say. I'd never seen him so animated.

"Have you been here all night?"

His nods were fast, somewhat manic. "All night. So much has happened."

I latched on to that titbit and would circle back to

it. For the moment, I was too concerned about Smythe and how close he was to overloading. "Have you slept?"

"Kent frogmarched me to the sofa a few hours ago, but I couldn't sleep." He shrugged, his whole body jittery.

"Jesus, how much coffee have you had?"

He scrunched his nose. "I don't drink coffee."

An unimpressed cough caught my attention. Kent sat at her station, arms folded, and looked pointedly at the chaos of Smythe's workspace he'd claimed. It was littered with bright green cans. I winced. Energy drinks. The guy was going to crash so damn hard.

"If you've finished conversing with the Energizer Bunny, we'll get you caught up to speed."

My gaze flicked to Callen, who smiled at me. "Good to see you back."

Some of the tension between my shoulders uncoiled. "Good to be back, sir."

He bobbed his head and indicated for me to sit. As soon as my butt touched plastic, the rest of the team followed suit. Everyone except for Michaels and Jamison.

A weird energy zipped around the table. It crawled over my skin, settling as a lump in my throat.

"Where're Michaels and Jamison?" It wasn't like I could simply ignore the fact they weren't here.

"Jamison's following a lead." Callen's voice was tight.

"And Michaels?" I prompted. Goose bumps fired up, spreading over me with the speed of wildfire.

The tick of the muscle in Callen's jaw told me whatever he was going to share, I wouldn't like. "We don't know."

I startled, completely nonplussed by his answer. "How can you not know?" I stared at Kent. She was the whizziest of tech wizards or some shit. How could she not know where Michaels was?

Ice-cold and with the sharpness of a blade, Kent answered, "No phone. No vehicle tracking. No weapons with digital support. He's a ghost."

"After we got you to the infirmary," Lucas started, his skin almost ashen with what I was guessing to be barely contained fury, "we had a few moments to regroup, talked out some theories." He cut a glance at Thatch, who nodded. "He wanted you off the team. We all balked. He said he was going to clean up. We believed him. He was still fresh from the fight. After an hour, Kent went to track him."

"He'd been back to his house. Jamison's been there."

Callen's words were clipped. "Soiled clothes in the bathroom. Not sure if a bag's been taken or not. The weapons we know about are gone, except the AKR53 and T97."

The firearms with built-in software. Ones that could be tracked.

"So are you searching for him? Where have you looked?"

"We find Hornell—"

"We find Michaels." I finished for Callen.

He nodded in approval, but there was no glow in the praise. No basking in knowing we were on the same wavelength. How could there be when the man who had me tied up in knots had gone rogue?

Before we got back to work, they told me about some of the progress they'd made.

Thanks to Smythe's hidden database find, the unit had discovered movement approximately thirty minutes after last night's attack. The information had since turned cold, though.

Listening to the call found in the database had hurt my stomach. It was Hornell telling Paul's wife about his death. The facts were loose on accuracy, unsurprisingly. But the truth remained that I was responsible for taking a life.

While Michaels had been the one to finish Paul off, the tear I'd put in a main artery would have killed him a few minutes later either way. I'd taken a former trainee agent's life. The reality made my vision swim. The memory of Paul's expression remained burned in my retinas. I expected it would for many years to come.

"We're sending someone to get you." Those words had been spoken too many hours ago by a voice we presumed was Hornell. And since then, Carla was officially MIA. Her vehicle was abandoned not far from last night's ambush. There'd been no fresh leads, which included the couple of hours I'd been searching through data.

"Hey, Kent." Smythe's voice split through the frustrated sighs and the tapping of keys. "Have you ever seen anything like this before?"

She rolled over on her chair, stopping at his side, peering at the large screen. A frown slid across her features. "Is that Mirrormat coding?"

"You think that too?" Shock pitched his voice high. "I've only heard rumours about it, but this has the workings of theories I've read."

"Can you get it all? Get it to work?"

Excitement zipped between them. Their faces alight, eyes shining like they'd discovered the secrets to making the best meat pie or possibly establishing world peace. *Tomay-to, tomah-to.*

"What have you got?" Lucas was beside them in a

heartbeat, catching on to their eagerness while the rest of us stared on. I was relieved for the break, welcoming the distraction from feeling so butt sore with Michaels abandoning me and the team the way he had.

With his intent on the screen as Smythe's fingers sped across the keyboard, Lucas's brows shot so high, they almost touched his hairline. "Where did you find this? In Hornell's database?" Worry bled loud and clear into his question.

"Anyone want to clue the rest of us into what this code is that's giving you all a hard-on?"

Smythe flushed, Lucas sighed, and Kent flipped Callen off.

"In layman's terms, if you will," he tagged on.

Lucas answered, eagerness widening his eyes. "The Mirrormat coding is the stuff of fantasy. Think of it a bit like the Pandora's box of the cyber world. A unicorn finally appearing amongst a field of horses." My lips twitched at the analogies. "It's code that could potentially unlock all other coding."

"Unlock, as in...?" Thatch folded his arms, his expression turning serious.

"In theory, it's possible to create coding to unlock literally every other type of coding in the world. Firewalls, antivirus software, system security—"

"Encrypted files?" Uncrossing his arms, Thatch sat

forward. "Could it break through those without damaging them?"

Kent chimed in, "It can literally unravel anything. Nothing is impenetrable. If a vulnerability doesn't exist, it makes one."

This was huge. Terrifying but freaking colossal. The ramifications for the world were harrowing. The possibility it offered us, though, could change everything.

"Smythe." Lucas's voice cut through the buzz of renewed energy. "Where did you find this?"

"That's the thing." He rubbed at his face, looking perplexed. "When I was in Shadowfall's remote wipe-system drive, something new was there."

Confused, I asked, "But isn't that normal? Won't they delete stuff all the time, and then it appears there?"

"Well, yeah, but it was the date of this that got my attention. It was my date of birth. The year and everything."

That could not have been a coincidence.

"Someone left it for you. Knew you had access." The reality of what Thatch's words meant to us all, to the investigation, was like a load of bricks freefalling with no end in sight.

Heavy with tension, the atmosphere pushed down on the room.

"They wanted me to find it."

I happened to agree with Smythe, and from the nods around the room, so did everyone else.

Lucas took charge. "Okay, let's take a breath. There are so many cogs turning at the moment, so many players. Let's focus on what we can control."

While his quiet determination helped me breathe more easily, I wished like hell Michaels was by my side.

"Kent and Smythe, pull the coding, make sure it works, and run it through the files Chambers left. We'll get to who and why someone is helping when we have the capacity to deal with it."

I kept my mouth shut. If this coding was as big of a deal as they said it was—and I had no reason to doubt them—whoever this mystery unicorn-code creator was would never be found, unless of course they wanted to be.

"Thatch, Callen, pay a visit to Angelica Gallagher and Teri Hughes. Based on Smith, it's clear we dropped the ball and didn't push hard enough. They're involved somehow. Find out what exactly their part is."

Lucas's gaze shifted to me. I pulled my shoulders back, waiting for instructions, and hoping like hell it wasn't something lame like going on a coffee run.

"Shaw, strap up. We're going to pay Anderson a visit."

Alrighty then. This I could get on board with.

ARMED WITH A SERVICE PISTOL AND CREDENTIALS Kent had handed to me with a wink, I took careful breaths as I waited for the green light to activate. A beat later, it did, and I passed through the first scanner. At the second, I handed over my SICB-issued weapon and walked through the second security checkpoint.

After a fingerprint check, Lucas and I walked into an interview room of the SICB detention centre. It was a small holding centre, not intended for a long stay, yet despite that, Anderson remained here.

We sat on the welded-down stools, the sharp, cool air of the pumping air conditioner too cold to be comfortable. Magnolia-white walls, reinforced doors, and windows I expected were defensive-strength glazed as opposed to glass.

A buzz sounded before the second door opened, revealing Anderson.

He blanched and tried to step away, but the guard behind him forced him in, shoving him to the stool and connecting his reinforced cuffs to the floor. I studied

Anderson as he looked everywhere but at us. Fear, thick and rancid, seeped out of his pores while his one leg bounced.

This was not the Anderson I knew.

Gone was the cocky mouth, the confident swagger. The shit talk he could so freely dish out.

Broken. Terrified. Combined, they made for a disturbing image.

What the hell had happened to him?

"Derek Anderson, I'm here from the SICB domestic counterterrorism—"

"No, no, no. I didn't say anything." Trembles racked his limbs so damn hard, his teeth rattled.

"The hell? Anderson, no one's going to hurt you." My words fell on deaf ears. He continued to shake his head.

"I'm just here to discuss with you the events that led to the attack of Jett Shaw."

"I didn't say anything."

"We know, Anderson," Lucas continued. "It's why we're here. We need to know. No one is going to hurt you. We just want answers."

Nothing but the rattling of teeth reverberated around the room.

My brain ticked over, assessing his reaction,

thinking about why, after a handful of words, Anderson would crumble like this.

I dropped my voice low, almost whisper soft. "Whoever got you to hurt me didn't send us."

From the slight tilt of his head, he'd heard me.

"Think about it," I continued. "Why would I be with anyone who tried to hurt me?"

Just one movement, one slight shift, and I made eye contact. Just one eye from this position, but it was something.

"You're smarter than this. The last thing I believe is that you woke up one morning and decided to take a stab at me. Something happened, some*one* forced your hand with this. I need to know who. The why doesn't even matter at this point."

Lucas remained a silent, steady presence at my side, holding back and letting me take the lead. Anderson stopped bouncing his knee, though small trembles still shuddered through his body.

"Please, Anderson, let me help you."

"Why would you want to help me after what I did?"

"Because even though we've never been friends, I thought of you as a comrade. You would have made a good agent. You attacking me the way you did makes no sense, which means someone forced your hand. While there's going to be consequences to you following through, you don't deserve to take the brunt of the punishment."

"But what do you think you can even do?" Finally, he glanced up and looked at me head-on. Desperate hope swirled in his gaze.

"I can find out who did this and make them pay."

Anderson's gaze flicked to Lucas's. "What division did you say you're from?"

Lucas surprised me by saying, "I work for the SICB and have the ear of Director Durrant. I'm also close friends with Acting Chief Thatcher. The department I'm based in is inconsequential."

I thought back to Anderson's reaction when Lucas had started to say the domestic counterterrorism division. Had he freaked out when he'd heard the name? Based on Lucas's response, he clearly thought so.

Lucas undid his shirt cuff, revealing his watch. Both Anderson and I looked on, wondering what he was doing. Hitting a couple of keys on the digital watch, Lucas then glanced at the two cameras.

The green lights were off. They were on when we'd entered. I'd checked.

"The cameras are off. They'll remain off for approximately two minutes. It's all we have before security comes knocking. What you share with us now will make a difference. It will help to put dangerous people away. From your file and what Recruit Shaw has said, it's clear you would have made an excellent agent. Do not let the person who did this to you get away with changing the course of your life scot-free. We need these people, this organisation off the street. Help us do our job."

As Lucas spoke, Anderson sat up straighter. A glimmer of the former version of the man began to form. His shaking calmed, a fleck of hardness, of determination sparking in his gaze. "If I tell you, before you do anything, will you make sure my dad and sister are protected?"

"You have my word," Lucas immediately said, solemnly. "As soon as I have my phone, I'll make the call to get them in protective custody."

Emotion flushed Anderson's cheeks, and his eyes turned watery. "Okay." He nodded and sniffed before clearing his throat. "I didn't receive an envelope like I said I did. It was Trainer Prescott."

White noise filled my head as I processed the name. How was it possible to feel both hot and cold at the same time?

"Take him down, and I'll give you anything you need."

CHAPTER 9
MICHAELS

What I wouldn't give to be able to knock back two fingers of Royal Salute right now. Whiskey burning through my veins would help numb the helplessness trying to take hold.

Since the moment I'd gone off radar, dread had been my companion. That and regret.

What I should have done was turn around with my tail between my legs.

Asking for forgiveness wasn't a new thing between me and my team. But it was the thought of abandoning Shaw that curdled my stomach. Guilt sat like a heavy weight on my chest.

I hadn't been there for him when he woke. Hell, I didn't even know if he'd fully recovered or not. Running off and breaking my promise to have his back

—and Smythe's—was a shit of a thing. But as far as I was concerned, I'd obliterated that promise the moment I'd let him walk into the port without me and with too much distance between us.

I'd failed him. Failed my unit.

My word was worth shit.

Shame threatened to keep me rooted; if not that, it tempted me to seek out whiskey and bury myself in self-loathing.

Knowing Shaw would keep on battling, continue working on the investigation—despite me being a coward and telling the team he needed to be removed—was the only thing stopping me from spiralling completely.

I had to make this right.

I turned off the tap, my hands finally clean of the fresh blood I'd spilled.

Xander, an ex-con who'd previously been put away for large-scale theft of medical supplies and equipment, didn't know shit about Shadowfall. Though the hits he took hadn't been completely in vain. I had a lead on black-market dealings of medical equipment that sounded promising. Plus, he'd ratted out Kingston for something completely unrelated, but the vampire had already been on the SICB's radar, so I'd feed in the intel.

Probably by a tip-off if I was fired, or a prison cell if I carried on the way I was.

Two hours later, the medical equipment info was a bust, but it led me to something else that held promise —a warehouse in Mosman. The first thing I noticed was the collection of cameras. While most of the warehouses in the area had security, the equipment was government grade.

That and they were positioned with precision.

Two security personnel also walked the perimeter, crossing paths at seven minutes and sixteen seconds, give or take five seconds. No guns were on display— only SICB and the specialist armed human police division could openly carry in Australia.

It didn't mean they couldn't be carrying a concealed weapon, though.

A truck being unloaded blocked the view of what appeared to be the main entrance to the building. Several loading areas lined the front and the rear, but currently only one was accessed.

Five men systematically unloaded large boxes. A woman stood to the side with a clipboard, hollering orders and demanding the crew be careful. One thing was clear, she was stressed. The pink of her cheeks was visible through the high-powered binoculars I aimed her way.

While a tip led me here, it was my gut that kept me watching and waiting. My instinct screamed at me to stay, find a way in. Ignoring it would be a mistake. And as I'd learned over the years, the times I'd shoved my instinct down—whether to follow orders or having a difficulty in following through for one reason or another—I'd lived to regret it.

At the sound of a car heading towards the warehouse, I repositioned myself, ensuring I was well out of sight. From this angle, and the late morning sun reflecting on the window screen, the occupiers remained in the shadows.

When the vehicle pulled up, a man stepped out of the driver side. With wide shoulders and a straight back, it was clear he was former service. At least I hoped the former was accurate and he wasn't active.

A second later, the passenger door opened. A woman stepped out, short and slender, clutching a bag to her chest. She angled, turned to say something to the driver, and my breath caught in my throat.

Carla Smith. The file we had on her had a slightly outdated photograph, but it was most definitely her.

Holy shit.

Adrenaline fired through me, and I reached for my ear, stopping short. No comm. No phone—beyond the basic burner I'd pulled out of my safe.

Clenching my jaw, I fought off my frustration. I'd made the decision to do this. It meant I'd follow through. This way, no one else would be getting hurt. Not on my watch.

But what if someone gets hurt because you're not around, dickhead?

I shook my head, shaking off my traitorous thoughts. Calling in to check on things was a temptation I didn't need distracting me.

Instead, I focussed on Carla.

Surprise had me doing a double take.

The woman may be small and on first glance appear to be out of her depth, but she could pack a punch. The man who'd exited the warehouse and stopped before her, hand bobbing around as though attempting to placate, now rolled around on the floor, clutching his nose.

Too far away to hear, it didn't take a genius to realise he was complaining and cussing up a storm. He gesticulated wildly as he stood up, only to scurry back when Carla stepped forward, hand fisted at her side.

Interesting.

After another ten minutes, the truck left and the outside area cleared, the three people, including Carla, heading inside.

I eased closer, ready to make my move.

Broad daylight was never an ideal time for breaking and entering. I figured—hoped—it meant that anyone inside observing the cameras wouldn't be too diligent, as who in their right mind would be trying to break into a place with an indeterminable number of people inside, solid security, and potentially armed guards?

Me, apparently. Though, the jury was out on whether or not I technically qualified, as I clearly wasn't in my right mind.

The guards passed with barely perceptible up-nods.

Three, two, one, and I ran low, sprinting towards the metal dumpster to the side of the building. Momentum carried me, jumping, foot connecting on the lower roof until I sprang up high. Once my fingers found purchase, I hauled my arse up to the main rooftop.

Scanning the area, I stayed low, relieved to not discover any additional cameras up here. Skylights and solar panels littered the roof. The space was clean, debris free.

Towards the back of the rooftop was my target, a two-by-five raised area that gave access to the roof. Glass windows lined the side, a door at one end.

Up close, I grinned. The windows here were an older style.

After checking for cameras and alarm wiring, I prised a window open, opting for this route rather than the door. It released without even a squeak, and I sent a grateful salute into the universe.

Another two minutes passed by as I listened intently, relying on my enhanced hearing.

Clattering of metal, voices, wooden crates scraping across the concrete floor. A grunt, a shout, a thump. All were music to my ears. Whatever was happening down there provided me with the sound cover and distraction I needed.

Brightness flooded the upper area of the warehouse. A single open walkway circled the walls, the path metal and solid. Three wider sections—two landing areas for metal staircases, one for small storage —formed part of the circuit.

The storage area was my target, offering me some semblance of cover. It took but a few moments to squat between crates. I shuffled in, lay flat on my stomach, and peered down.

A wide space took up most of the warehouse floor. It was cluttered with stacked boxes of various shapes and sizes. To the far left was an office space, large with a strip of windows, and an open door. To the side of that was a cordoned-off area. Additional storage perhaps, though with no windows and a closed metal door, I couldn't tell for sure.

In the corner sat another room. Floor-to-ceiling windows and a closed glass door. Monitors filled the one wall. A woman sat at the desk, eating a yoghurt, her gaze intent on her spoon scraping out the contents rather than the screens.

The ground floor was a hive of activity.

I counted twenty people. Four were in forklifts. Two stood on guard on opposite ends of the space. Armed with rifles, they looked bored rather than fierce.

It was the three individuals wearing lab coats who caught my attention. My heart wanted to pick up speed, the possibility I'd discovered something important pushing eagerness into my veins. But with at least six supes below me, I couldn't give myself away.

As it was, I was relying on the constant sounds, the flutter of the engines on the forklifts, and the heavy scent of diesel to disguise any trace of me.

"We have to move tonight."

My gaze snapped to Carla. Her voice was tight, as was her stance.

"That's impossible." The man who she'd previously sucker-punched stood before her, dried blood on his nose that he hadn't managed to clear away. "We've been given direct or—"

"We've been compromised. Martin and Angelica are on the move. The captain told us—"

The ring of a phone cut her off. *Captain.* A slow smirk formed on my lips. Fucking finally.

"John," Carla said into her phone. I listened intently, trying to hear the other side of the call, but to no avail. She nodded. "I know. I'm just here now." A pause followed, her eyes widening a fraction. "Are you sure it's not compromised?" Worry coloured her words. "Okay. I can be there in a little over an hour." Another pause. "Fine, I'll wait instead. I'll let him know." Her gaze flicked over to the closed door. "I'm just going to check now. The sample wasn't right. Degeneration within nine days." A frustrated sigh followed. "Yes, I'm more than aware that's two days longer, but it's hardly ideal. I'll see you soon."

She shoved her phone in her handbag, indicating for the man she'd punched to go with her. I tracked their progress to the door, angling a little and tugging out my binoculars.

A key followed by punched in numbers, and the bloody-nosed guy turned the handle. Lights flickered on automatically as soon as the door opened, revealing a clinical white room complete with stark white curtains and a metal table, but it was the scent of disinfectant that had me arching further and wishing I could see through walls.

The door closed, Carla and the man no longer visible.

I'd have to wait it out and hope for another glimpse or another scent. Anything that could clue me in about what was hidden inside.

With the workers on the ground floor going about their business, I melted into the shadows of the crates around me. Reaching the crate furthest away from the front, I tugged out my flip knife. The crate was open. Inside were cardboard boxes.

Cutting open one, I frowned, seeing only basic medical supplies. The second box revealed the same. On the third, I paused, a pulse of adrenaline trying to find purchase.

Passports.

I tugged out a handful. The navy blue of the Australian passport, complete with motif. A dark blue with a gold royal crest indicated a British one. The photos showed a mix of men and women, all supes in the ones I examined.

Rubbing my fingers over the pages, I felt for the chips. They felt real. The Aussie one in my hand appeared no different to mine locked safely in a security deposit box. I had no doubt these were counterfeit.

I tucked the five passports into my inside pocket, fastening the zip afterwards. The barely audible sound of an opening door alerted me to movement.

Darting back to the front, I caught another glimpse of the inside of the room. The curtain had been shifted, revealing a surgical trolley. My view was cut off by the closing and locking of the door. I struggled to hold back my growl of frustration.

A clang of metal had me stilling and holding my breath. Boots on the steel staircase.

Stashing my binoculars to free my hands, I angled to locate the person. One of the security guards had reached the seventh step. I mentally chided myself for taking my eye off the ball, too focussed on what lay beyond the locked door and inside the boxes.

Three more steps, and I had to act.

Should I try to fade into the limited shadows of the box of crates, or make a run for it? Hiding would mean being penned in. My gut screamed at me not to get trapped.

Run it was.

I darted out of the space. There was no being subtle. No hiding.

I relied on my speed to get me back to the short staircase that would lead me to the roof.

"Hey!" The voice sounded startled. Panicked.

I kept on running, pumping my arms, hearing a holler. The static of a two-way reached my ears, but I kept going. Foot on the first step, I bounded up, shoving through the window, hearing a smash as I did so.

The pounding of footsteps echoed behind me.

"Stop!"

Thank Christ it wasn't an active agent. By now, I would have been shot at, likely killed. There'd been plenty of time to receive a hit to my back.

Out on the roof, I squinted against the bright sun, finding my bearings quickly. I heard a second set of footsteps. These were lighter, no doubt going to pass the first security guard who'd spotted me.

With no time to check, I headed in the direction I'd come from while trying to listen to the outside security on patrol and hoping like hell I lucked out and didn't land on top of them. I jumped, landing in a crouch, and scanned around me.

One security guard was just rounding the corner. The other wouldn't be far behind.

Launching myself off the entrance roof, I hit the ground in a roll, popping to my feet in a sprint.

A shot fired, a warning or a shit shot, I wasn't sure. In the near distance, a car was heading into the yard. *Fuck my luck.* Another shot, and I jerked to my right, sure as hell I was going to hit gravel at any second.

The car screeched to a stop, and I pulled out my weapon, ready to turn and fire. The door opened, the sound reaching my ears and spurring me on.

"Leave him."

The order almost made me stumble, the voice like a punch to my skull as it ricocheted around my brain. But with the only sound of footsteps being my own, I figured the security had listened. Once I was over the fence, I turned, gun ready, and focussed on the man who'd called out.

Prescott.

As clear as day before me, my old friend's gaze was on me. Staring intently, I read his message loud and clear. He'd saved my arse, and he expected me to back off.

I gritted my teeth, feeling the weight of what abandoning the unit had done.

They should have been with me. If they had, we would have taken the whole warehouse down, had every single person in cuffs, including Prescott, and got all the answers we needed. But the fuckhead I was had screwed that up for everyone.

Still standing there, staring, he shook his head.

It was my only warning. Stick around, and go under fire. Leave, and by the time I got back with reinforcements, they'd be cleared out.

I backed away, sending him a silent promise that this wasn't over. Whatever he'd gotten himself into, I'd tear it down around him. And if I discovered he was responsible for the attack on Shaw, I'd take blood in payment, just before I dumped his arse in a prison cell to rot.

Jogging away, I pulled out my disposable cell, calling one of the few numbers I'd committed to memory. I didn't know what I was going to walk into, how much of an arse-kicking I was going to get, but on the bright side, it had been less than sixteen hours since I went MIA. It wasn't like I'd disappeared for days.

That had to count for something, right?

Apparently it didn't count for shit.

I came in bearing the gift of telling them about Prescott and Smith's involvement. They'd already known.

I told them about the warehouse. Lucas had a drone above it within half an hour of me telling them. The place had already been cleared out.

Sure, there were still some boxes and shit lying around, but we didn't need to search it to know there was nothing of value. Not that we wouldn't send someone in anyway, just in case there was a trace of useful evidence left behind.

What it meant was, we were back to square one.

That I'd been discovered and identified by Prescott meant the whole of Shadowfall would know the SICB were onto them. When I'd made the killing blow to Paul Smith, there had been the small possibility of playing the overprotective boyfriend, effectively keeping me undercover until I'd been spotted. But now that cover had been well and truly blown.

The worst thing was Shaw's reaction. He wouldn't even look at me.

I'd expected the cussing out from Kent and Callen, the stern, disappointed looks and talking-to from Thatch and Lucas. I could even handle the frustration from Chris.

But not one single glance from Shaw beyond the wide-eyed shock when I'd first entered the lair.

The hurt rolled off him. I'd fucked up majorly.

"I'm sorry. I thought—"

"That's the thing, you didn't think—well, beyond anyone but yourself."

"That's not true," I said, defending myself against Lucas's words. What made it worse was, there was no anger fired at me. No spite. Just well-aimed disappointment.

"Isn't it?" He tilted his head, quirking his brow in challenge. I parted my lips to answer, but he shook his head, cutting me off. "I want you to really think about what I'm about to say and how to respond, okay?"

I bobbed my head and peered over his shoulder, watching the unit working, talking, sharing a few chuckles. He'd pulled me away for this conversation, ordering me into a small meeting space complete with thick soundproof Perspex.

"Losing Jenson changed something in you." He ignored my wince, his gaze remaining steady. "I understand all too well the devastation and pain of losing someone you care for. It's why I stepped back, allowed you free range to try to grieve and deal, but maybe I was wrong." Sorrow dipped his voice low. "Maybe you lost your way and forgot what it means to be in a unit, have a team who is at your back but willing to step in front and take a bullet for you. Because out there"—he angled and pointed to my friends, my comrades—"each and every person in your unit, Callen and Thatch included, and Shaw"—I squeezed my eyes shut, not able to bear the thought of losing any of them, let alone him—"they're your shields, your armour, your strength. Every time you walk away, you're all vulnerable, weaker."

I jumped, snapping my eyes open when he gripped

my shoulder. Fear spread its icy, cruel fingers into my chest, digging deep. How could I ever break free from such a thing? When terror and doubt were my constant companions, what good was I to anyone?

"This is it. Today. Now. You make a decision. You're either in, all the way in, standing shoulder to shoulder with your unit, making sure you're there, no matter the outcome, or you leave. You walk out that door for good."

"Fuck." Lifting my arm, I buried my face in the crook of my elbow before tugging at my hair. The pain did nothing to dull the agony of his words. It didn't distract from knowing how right he was.

"Jenson was more than your teammate."

I froze, angling my arm away to see his face. "What?" My stomach bottomed out.

"Jenson was in love with you."

Unable to hear it, I shook my head. "No." I backed away, head going back and forth. "No, he wasn't."

Sadness, so stark and gutting, spread on his face. "I'm sorry you lost him."

"We weren't—"

"I know you weren't. It doesn't mean he loved you less, or you him."

Struggling to swallow against the lump in my throat, I shook my head again. "I wasn't in love with him." Fuck. Jenson had deserved my love so much, and how I wished I could have loved him back the way he'd wanted. I loved him, more than my blood, more than anyone else, but like a brother.

"It's okay. He knew how you felt. Your love was still enough for him."

Tears blurred my vision, and try as I might to shake the emotion away, I couldn't do it. The heartache refused to go, the tears holding strong and steady as the first drop spilled and trickled down my cheek.

"What if I lose someone else? What if I get close to Chris, and he gets killed? You and Kent." I shook my head. Kent was the pain-in-the-arse sister I'd never wanted, but hell if I didn't love the woman. "And fuck, Shaw." The memory of his scream at the container yard was etched in deep. "If I lost him...." I trailed off, unable to verbalise my thoughts.

It didn't matter that we'd only known each other for less than a month. Our connection, our chemistry was undeniable. Already I cared for him more than made sense, got tingles in my stomach like a giddy teen at the possibility of a future together.

He could be it for me.

The man who got me tongue-tied with excitement and need while understanding me in a way that seemed almost instinctive.

That combination was heady and filled with promise.

He calmed me as much as he riled me up. Pushed me as much as he tried to hold me close.

I wanted to try, to explore. Wanted something more for me. But fuck if it didn't make me feel guilty.

"Shaw's a capable agent." Lucas hauled me out of my tangled thoughts. "But if you don't think he's right for the unit, and you decide to stay, to step up and make promises you won't break, then I'll talk to Thatch and Callen about getting him reassigned."

I balked, tears stopping in their tracks. Shoulders literally jerking at the idea of Shaw being anywhere but here. With me.

Fuck. I dropped my head, knowing my answer. And I had no doubt Lucas did, too, the wily fucker.

Peering at him, at his carefully controlled expression, I narrowed my gaze. The man knew what he was doing. Knew just what to say to get me to pull my head out of my arse.

"You also need to have at least five sessions with Dr Novak."

"Hell no."

"Nonnegotiable." The barest of pauses followed before he reached out and squeezed my shoulder again, saying, "I'm sorry I let you down."

"What?" I frowned. "You didn't let me down."

"I did." He dropped his arm. "When I took over Thatch's position, that became the focus of the unit. It meant I didn't do right by you to make sure you had the support you needed. But I'm doing so now."

My face soured, not keen about the idea of talking to Novak. The woman was good at her job, I was sure, but sitting down and talking about feelings and trauma wasn't my idea of a good time. It's why I'd bailed so spectacularly the first time.

"You need to do this, for you and the unit. And for Shaw."

"Jesus, Lucas, really?"

A smirk finally formed. "I think this is the point where you simply say thank you for me not having an issue with you dating someone in the same unit."

"To be fair, Thatch and Callen kinda destroyed the rulebook with that one."

He arched a brow at me.

"But you're right. Thank you." I huffed out a heavy breath. Not even denying the possibility of dating Shaw for real, I rubbed a hand over my face, clearing away the tracks of tears. By the time I looked at Lucas again, he was quietly contemplating me. "I promise I'm in this for good. The ITU is my family. I don't want to hurt anyone or let anyone down again," I said solemnly, meaning every word.

"Or yourself. Don't hurt yourself either."

I nodded. "Or myself."

"Okay." He reached out for my hand. When he got a good grip, he tugged me into a hard hug. "You need to sort things out with Shaw," he said next to my ear before easing back and meeting my eyes.

"You trying to add matchmaker to your list of skills?" I asked, injecting humour I didn't really feel.

"More like wanting a promising young agent to have his head in the game and to not be walking around like someone kicked his puppy, but you never heard me say that."

I snorted despite the stab of anger at myself for hurting Shaw so badly. "I'll fix this. Even if he doesn't forgive me, I'll make sure we can work together." The words tasted bitter on my tongue, because fuck, what would I do if he told me to piss off? What if he didn't think I was worth it?

"Good. Everyone could do with a break, so let's all take an hour. When we reconvene, I'm hoping Kent and Smythe will have cracked the files from Chambers."

Adrenaline punched into me. "What? How? When?"

Lucas chuckled. "Sucks to not be in the know when you do a vanishing act, right?"

I groaned and rolled my eyes. I deserved his dig.

"We'll talk about it in an hour. Now go and set things straight."

"Thanks, Lucas. For everything." With emotion still so close to the surface, I expelled a slow breath, worried about losing it again.

"No worries. I know there won't be a next time, so it's all good." He turned on his heel and left the room, Shaw's laughter filtering in through the opened door.

A moment later, it cut off, and the room quietened, all attention on me inside the office and Lucas in front of the door. Not surprising, since I expected they'd all been chewing at the bit, wanting to know what Lucas said to me.

My gaze connected with Shaw's. I held my breath, just waiting for him to look away. But he held my gaze, staying present, his brows dipping as he searched my face.

I let him take his fill. He deserved to see my red eyes, the glaze still there, the guilt and fear that swaddled me like a second skin, threatening to suffocate me. But I also needed him to know I'd try hard to shed it, let him and the unit see me. They all deserved so much more.

"—one hour exactly. Go stretch your legs, have a nap. If you leave the premises, be secure, go in pairs." As Lucas spoke, Shaw didn't turn away. Concern etched his features, sparking a flame of hope in my gut.

Maybe he'd forgive me. Just maybe he'd be willing to give me... *us* a chance. I might not deserve it, but if he did, I promised myself I'd never let him regret it.

Knowing they were relationship-defining words should have come with a hit of panic. Just a month ago, they definitely would have done. Meeting Shaw, opening myself to him, mattered. And what I was absolutely certain of was, whether he gave me a chance or not, I couldn't afford to close myself off again.

CHAPTER 10

SHAW

IT WAS HIS LOOK OF DESPONDENCY THAT HAD ME agreeing to leave with Michaels. The stricken expression, the pink eyes, the roughness of his voice, all had been impossible to ignore.

He called to me—his hurt and pain wrapping around me in a way that made me want nothing more than to hold him close and kiss away the distress pouring off him.

With my own hurt pressing down like a suffocating weight, I followed him to his house when he invited me to, trying not to be curious about what I'd find.

This thing between us was new, undefined. In truth, we didn't owe each other anything. But a secret part of me called bullshit.

The man already had a fierce grip on my heart.

Chemistry like we had couldn't be imagined, let alone forced into existence. Being with Michaels was as natural as breathing.

Every smile, laugh, story we'd shared, every training session he'd pushed and tutored me in, each moment shone a big, bright spotlight at how well we fit.

The beeping of his alarm system cut off, pulling my attention to him.

"So, this is my place." He gestured around him.

I gave myself permission to take a glance. The front door led directly into the open-plan living space. It was bigger than I expected, more modern too. High ceilings and open space, with each area—sitting, dining, and kitchen—flowing seamlessly.

The tones were neutral with a bright splash of coordinated colour in each section. A deep jade accented the sitting area. Throw cushions on the large comfy-looking couches, a patterned vase in the same splash of green on a small side table. A bold painting on an antique-white wall, an abstract forest of some sort. Reds dominated the dining area, and bright yellows in the kitchen.

While tidy, it looked lived in. The collection of printed photographs on a bookcase with titles I was curious about checking out. A magazine on a leather armchair, open and ready to be picked back up. A throw on the back of the couch that appeared soft. I wondered if he snuggled up in it during winter. While wolves ran a little warmer than humans, it still could get miserably cold in Sydney.

"Would you like a drink?" His voice didn't contain the usual confidence I was used to. A flicker of hesitation in his face, and it was clear he was uncomfortable. Nervous.

Did he think I was going to bolt? Wasn't he used to people in his space? The latter had my heart picking up speed a little. Perhaps I should have controlled it, knowing he'd be able to hear, but my emotions were in a constant state of turmoil around Michaels.

They had been ever since he'd rocked up to the lair earlier, his usually bright eyes a little dimmer.

"No, I'm good."

He'd asked to talk. Asked me to go with him—his house being just an eight-minute drive away. Now that I was here, I didn't know what to say, how I felt.

Pissed? Sure.

Confused? Very.

Hopeful? I didn't want to admit the truth of that even to myself.

"Okay. Uhm... you want to sit? We don't have much time."

I nodded, veering over to one of the two couches. It

was comfortable. It was easy to imagine being snuggled up to Michaels on an evening, watching a movie, wrapped up in each other. While it would be snug, that would just make it even more perfect.

Swallowing hard and forcing my fantasies as far away as possible, I watched Michaels edge closer. The hesitation about where to sit was clear, almost making my lips twitch. Finally, he sat on the armchair opposite me.

"You're important to me."

Shock coursed through me, widening my eyes and hitching my breath.

"I should have been there when you woke up. I'm sorry I wasn't."

Swallowing heavily against the tightness in my throat, I tried to marshal the sadness in my tone when I asked, "Why did you leave?"

"I reacted to you getting hurt, let my fear rule me. Got it in my head that if I could just get this case closed, you'd be safe and wouldn't get hurt again."

While I'd expected as much, hearing his apology didn't dull the hurt clinging to my very being. No words formed. I couldn't tell him it was okay or even that I could forgive him.

Emptiness clawed at my chest, trying to create a hollowness where it could set up sentinel.

Regret morphed his features, pulling his brows low and tightening his mouth. "I was wrong."

"About?"

"Saying you shouldn't be in the unit. I panicked, which wasn't fair on you."

"It was... low, what you did."

"I know. The thought of losing you had me spinning out."

A humourless laugh spilled out of me. "So your intention was to cover me in bubble wrap and force me into a desk job? What exactly was the plan?"

A wince and a shake of his head, and he looked defeated. "I didn't have one. My reaction was ludicrous and about me being a dick and freaking the fuck out. You are going to be an incredible agent. I'd be lucky to work with you."

At some point my breathing had picked up speed. My heart snagged on his fear of losing me, that he cared for me so much. "You want to work with me in the ITU?"

"More than anything."

"Even if it means you're not my partner, and I could get injured or killed, and you're not there watching my back?" The words tasted wrong, bitter and ashy on my tongue. But I needed to say them.

Agents put themselves in the line of fire every

single day, and some units more than others. From what I'd learned, the ITU was right up there with high-risk operations.

"Yes." He clenched his jaw, the word coming out hard, but he held my gaze.

For the first time, I allowed his response to hit home and find its mark. The thought of Michaels being in a similar situation, being hurt, killed, while I stood on the sidelines, possibly listening in on comms but out of reach, sent icy fingers down my spine.

"I get it. I do," I admitted, my tone losing some of its tightness. "I feel the same way about you, but this can't exist between us."

Every muscle tensed at my words. "What do you mean?"

The barely contained sorrow of his words slammed into me, constricting my chest. Fuck, I was exhausted. I'd been so damn worried about Michaels being AWOL. Terror had been my constant companion since I'd woken up.

I'd rallied, kept going, and stayed on mission. But the crippling sense of loss and fear had nearly brought me to my knees every time I'd given myself even a moment to think about where Michaels was and if he was okay.

"This panic of wondering if you're going to question me or run or even be there if I get hurt. If we're going to be toge—work together, I have to be able to trust you."

"And if we're going to *be* together too?"

I swallowed hard, not at all surprised he'd caught my words. That he'd called me out had to be good, right? Mean something.

"The same thing applies for both." My words escaped with a sigh.

I wanted to kiss him and punch him and get him to make promises while making him mine.

It was foolish. I knew it.

The last thing I should have been thinking about was my heart, let alone my cock, but Michaels was completely, irrevocably embedded in my soul.

It was fucking ludicrous.

That didn't make it any less real.

"Forgive me." Getting off the chair, he got to his knees. Seeing him before me, gaze peering up at me with naked vulnerability, my heart stuttered, the protective shields surrounding me wavering. "I want to work this out."

"For the team?" It was easier to push and make him say the words than come right out and ask him to be mine.

"For the team, sure. But I meant us, you and me. I

want to spend time with you. You matter to me. I made all the wrong moves, but if you let me, I promise to never let you down again." A tender smile tilted his lips. "It doesn't mean I'm perfect and won't make mistakes, but I trust you and hope you'll trust me back."

"I want to." With Michael so close, I could no longer hold back. I cupped his jaw, brushing my thumb over his cheek.

He sighed into my touch, leaning into my palm. "Let me prove it to you. Forgive me."

I drank him in. The pink around his eyes from earlier was no longer visible. Whatever he and Lucas discussed, I hoped one day soon he'd feel able to share. Trust wasn't about spilling all our secrets right now. To make this work, we needed to give each other grace and time.

"You came back," I whispered, holding on to his face.

He bobbed his head and placed his hands on my thighs. "I finally saw sense and knew I couldn't do it alone. I *don't* want to do any of this alone. Not anymore."

Questions buzzed in my head, and I wondered what he was referring to. More things to learn and discover, and that was okay. His behaviour had been a blip, right? A knee-jerk reaction he made in fear. The thing was, objectively, I understood his reaction. Felt his worry.

"How long do we have before we need to leave?"

A quick glance away, and he said, "Thirty-five minutes."

"Okay." My pulse picked up speed, galloping through my veins. He tilted his head, gaze drawing me in.

"Okay as in...?" The tremble in his voice shot a thrill through me.

"Okay, I want you. It's never been about not wa—"

His mouth cut me off as he captured my lips and drank in my groan.

How could I have missed this... *him* so much in such a short amount of time with so few moments spent together? There was no understanding or rationalising it.

Instead, I wanted to luxuriate in the way his mouth dominated mine. Get lost in how his strong palms roamed my thighs, my arms, my back as he dragged me closer, spreading my legs as he did so.

When he shifted his attention to my arse, he cupped me, tugging me so our groins, hard and throbbing, pressed together. Pleasure zipped up my spine, tearing a deep groan from me.

"Fuck, I missed you," Michaels said on a gasp, not giving me the chance to respond before he sucked my bottom lip, then captured my mouth in a searing kiss.

Those words fractured the last of my walls.

There was no holding back. No villain, no fear, not even a nuclear bomb could stop me from taking what I needed.

And I needed Michaels more than I needed my next breath.

I pulled away, needing his gaze. "I want you inside me."

The words barely escaped before he was on me, tugging me up, dragging me into what I hoped was his bedroom. "Clothes off," he shot out.

A chuckle spilled out of me, melting away the distant threads of my uncertainty. "In a rush?" I teased, struggling with my T-shirt and having to let go of him to take it off.

"I want you naked as quickly as possible so I don't have to rush." He snatched back my hand, spinning me around and backing me up to his bed. I went willingly, desire sparking in my veins, awareness fluttering across my skin as his fingers roamed my body.

They landed on my combat trousers.

Our gazes caught, his Adam's apple bobbed, and

we all but tore the rest of our clothes off, scrambling to be free of them and naked.

By the time I was on the bed, Michaels's weight, delicious and perfect, holding me down, I was all but panting. "Minimum prep," I gasped out, hearing the click of the tube of lube he'd pulled out of his bedside drawer.

"I don't want to hurt you." Gruff and full of gravel, his voice pitched the lowest I'd ever heard it.

"You won't." Slick fingers parted my cheeks, and I shivered in anticipation. "I just need to feel you."

At my words, he shifted to hold my gaze. He searched my face, drinking in my expression while I silently told him how much I needed to feel him long after this moment.

Less than twenty-four hours ago was the closest I'd ever been to dying.

Less than twenty-four hours ago, I'd thought Michaels had abandoned me, quite possibly forever.

I'd been a kite in the breeze, set free with no one holding the strings. And I needed him to be the one to ground me, help guide me, be the man at my side as well as at my back.

But right now, I needed him buried inside me so deep, I could lose myself in his warmth, his fierce protection.

"Okay." A whisper-soft kiss punctuated his response as a single digit entered me.

I smiled even as a gasp burst free. "Yes, that, and another."

He nodded, focussed on me as he gave me exactly what I wanted.

Two and three and then a fourth that had me clawing at his arms, begging him to hurry the fuck up.

Michaels's smirk was short-lived when I took hold of his cock. He groaned at the contact, sucked in a breath when I squeezed.

"Now, Vaughn."

With the speed of his wolf, he pulled his fingers out, slicked his cock, and pressed against my opening. I parted my lips to tell him to sink inside when he pushed in hard, with one sure stroke.

My back arched, mouth opening in a silent cry. There was no time to speak, to do more than breathe and hang on for the ride as he pulled out and slammed back in.

Thrusting hard and fast, he railed me, each nudge of my prostate hauling a needy mewl from my parted lips.

"This what you need?" Sweat dripped down his temple. I followed the trail with my tongue, lapping it up.

"Fuck yes. Just like that."

I burned and ached. It was bliss and agony and exactly what I craved.

"I think we can do better." He slammed his lips against mine, searing his taste into my memory. Before I could get comfortable and devour his mouth, he pulled away and out, flipping me over onto my knees.

I groaned at his show of strength, loving that he had the moves to manhandle me. My smile was cut off with a deep groan as he rammed into me, pounding into me hard, tucking his hands under my armpits so he could tug me back.

Going willingly wherever he led, I leaned into him, feeling the caress of his chest hairs rubbing against my back as he drove into me with slow, sure strokes.

His cock hit deep. Stars danced before my closed eyes, my dick throbbing, thick and heavy as it smacked against my stomach with every powerful drive.

"Holy fuck." My world spun, head dipped as I gasped for breath. "I want this forever."

In response, he clasped my neck lightly, turned my head, and speared his tongue into my mouth. The kiss was all tongue, messy and dirty as fuck. Fresh need bloomed in my stomach, tingled my balls, and danced at the edges of my vision.

I pressed back against him, riding his cock, slamming down harder and harder.

Each tap edged me closer to spiralling, tugged me nearer to the precipice where I would fly.

Grasping my aching cock, his hand was a vice, punishing and perfect. White-hot heat spread like wildfire, setting me alight, and had me coming as he captured my cry in his mouth, my cum in his hand.

Sin was on his lips as he released my mouth and stared down at my face, saying, "Fuck, that's it. Give me everything."

And I did.

Two more spurts and my body trembled.

He thrust once, twice into my body, and cried out, "Fuck, Jett." Curses, garbled and spliced together, followed, but I could barely focus on catching my breath, let alone hear his words over the loud pulse in my ears.

And then he slumped, holding me tightly and easing me down on our sides.

Spent and dazed, I forced my eyes open and turned my head, aware a lazy, contented smile stretched my lips. Already staring at me, Michaels was a thing of beauty, all hard edges and intense eyes, but here, with a tender smile pulling at his mouth, a new softness filled his gaze.

He trailed his finger down my side, and as much as I liked his cock in me, could feel his cum beginning to trickle out, I wanted the closeness his soft smile promised.

Easing off him with a hitch of my breath, I chuckled lightly at his whole-body shiver. As I turned, I luxuriated in the ache of my muscles. Bone-tired yet feeling more alive than I ever had before, my panther agreed, basking in the combined scent of us.

"That was...." I placed a chaste kiss on his lips.

A ghost of a smile played on his lips, that cocky brow of his arching as he said, "It really was."

Not needing to say anything else, I pressed against him and darted a kiss to his neck when he embraced me.

We lay in silence for a couple of minutes, my mind at peace, my arse sore, and my heart doing a giddy, happy dance.

The buzz of his phone cut through the comfortable quiet.

"That's my alarm."

I eased back. "Do we have enough time for a shower, because, you know, cum...." My lips twitched, and Michaels groaned, his head falling back. "You all right there?"

"Next time, I need to look." The depth of his tone rippled across my skin.

"As in...?" My heart picked up at what he was saying.

"Seeing my cum dripping out of your hole, fuck." He groaned again, indecision crossing his features.

"Nuh-uh. *That* is definitely not what we have time for. We had one hour, and we will not be late."

Scowling had never looked so hot, or ridiculous, considering I knew the reason for his frown and his grumbly expression.

"Five-minute shower, then we leave."

"I could put the sirens on my car so we can—"

An abrupt laugh jolted out of me, so carefree and what I needed that I couldn't help but fall against Michaels, capturing his mouth, inhaling his laughter and wishing on every star I'd ever seen for us to have so many more moments like this.

***

WE PRACTICALLY FELL INTO THE LAIR AFTER having to race for the doors, making it with not even a full minute to spare.

Multiple eyebrows were arched high, wide eyes staring in our direction as we jerked upright from our mad dash. I cleared my throat, patting down my tee. Admittedly, it was a little creased from being scrunched up on Michaels's bedroom floor, but beggars couldn't be choosers.

"Pay up." Kent held out her hand, opening and closing her palm, a shit-eating grin aimed at Callen.

"Bloody hell." With a grumble, Callen tugged out his wallet, shoving a fifty-dollar note in Kent's hand.

"You bet against me." At my side, Michaels sounded thoroughly unimpressed. He pressed his hand to my waist, squeezed once, then walked into the main room ahead of me while I stood there, a little shell-shocked.

A glance around showed me the whole unit was here. Smythe and Jamison included.

Jamison sat on one of the couches, hands behind his head and sporting an amused grin as he took us all in. "You know, just the entertainment value alone could make me consider coming to the dark side and joining your unit permanently."

"As if you're badass enough to be hanging out with us permanently." Kent rolled her eyes, smirking when he blew her a kiss.

"Hey," I said quietly next to Smythe. Like so many times since all this started, he looked a mixture of horrified and amused. I got it. I really did. The agents around us were arguably the best of the best, yet they cussed each other out, took bets against each other, and scattered sarcasm like punctuation marks.

I freaking loved it and couldn't wait to take on an official post.

"Hey." He turned his attention from the group and offered me a smile, side-eyeing Michaels as he walked past us. Smythe gave an unsubtle nod towards him and bobbed his brows up and down, saying, "All okay?"

My lips twitched. "It is."

"As in *okay,* okay or fucking amazing, okay?"

Not for the first time, Smythe's teasing shocked a laugh from me. The drag of a chair caught my attention, my gaze connecting with Michaels, who lifted his brows, apparently waiting for my response as well.

Being surrounded by so many people with incredible hearing could be a serious pain in the arse.

"The latter," I answered, still looking at Michaels. A self-satisfied smirk formed quickly on his ridiculously handsome face, and I somehow managed to drag my attention away. In the office and surrounded by my team, I had to at least pretend to be professional.

"That's cool, Shaw. I'm pleased you figured things out."

Taking the seat next to him, I asked, "What have you been up to this past hour?"

"Chilled out on Lucas's sofa. He's got a killer gaming setup."

"Yeah?'"

"He's a bit pissed, though. I took the high score on *Blood, Punch, Kill.*"

"Only because you're a tricky son of a bitch who figured out where the secret stash of tranq darts were," Lucas hollered across the room. The rest of us snorted, and I found it hard to believe that Lucas, an almost hundred-and-fifty-year-old vampire, who also happened to be the team leader of a highly classified unit, was not only a gamer, but got into shit-talking too.

That this was now my life boggled my brain, but hell if it didn't feel like I was made for this. Made for hanging with these guys, shooting the shit, while trying to take down a bunch of bad guys.

"If you couldn't figure out the secret code that was right there for anyone to work out, that's on you, old man."

My brows shot high, and I choked on my spit at Smythe's smartarse response.

Yesterday, Kent had hinted that she was keen for Smythe to join the team. Seventy hours ago, I wouldn't have had much of an opinion on that. Now, I was seriously hoping Lucas could make it happen and that Smythe would consider it. It amazed me how much could change, opinions included, in such a short amount of time.

I also had the sore arsehole to prove it. Something that every time I moved, let alone sat, reminded me of that fact with an intense twinge. That I was still feeling it considering the time and my accelerated healing went to show just how good and hard a pounding he gave me.

I didn't know whether I loved the reminder more or if Michaels did. Anytime he saw me squirm, the smallest of smirks quirked his lips.

The laughter petered off, and Callen gathered us around. He and Lucas appeared to be tag-teaming running this mission.

"Kent, talk to us." With just those four words from Callen, we settled, practically holding our breaths, hoping they'd finally cracked the code.

"It's working."

A collective exhale rippled around the room.

"What's working exactly?" Michaels asked someone shiftily.

Kent shot him a death glare before finally saying, "Smythe found unicorn coding."

"Unicorn what now?" Nonplussed, a frown appeared between his impossibly sexy brows. Eyebrows weren't meant to be sexy, right?

A heavy sigh preceded Kent explaining, "Coding that's the stuff of fantasy. That coders dream about while governments have nightmares about the possibility that such a code exists. The code can break into anything with a digital pathway."

"Kent and Smythe have pulled the coding together to use on the documents sent by Chief Chambers," Lucas clarified. "What's been discovered so far?"

Kent typed on her laptop, and the two large screens on either side of the wall switched on, mirroring her screen. "So far, schematics for a facility. No address or coordinates, but it's a super distinctive pattern. I'm about to run it through satellite software to see if we can get a match." The information changed to what looked to be official documentation. Not government from the looks of it, but business oriented. "There's pages and pages of these," she said, indicating the screen. "Smythe?"

"I've been running the pages through intelligent software. They'll need to be read, too, as we all know the issues with AI—nothing can really beat the brain for deciphering—but to speed things up, I used the software to gather the initial findings. Shadowfall has been liaising with shadow agencies in Beijing and Mauritia. It looks like they're trying to fine-tune the drug and procedure that started off as cell regrowth to market it to anyone who's willing to buy."

"So this is just about money?" Distaste bled through Jamison's words.

Kent took over, saying, "Since the results are showing the degeneration of the cells as well as significant impact to the brain after seven—"

"Nine." All our attention turned to Michaels. "That's outdated information. Carla Smith said nine. The description was too close to what you're saying for it to be referring to anything else."

"Which means they're still fine-tuning the procedure," Callum said. He looked around the table. "How are they marketing this? If the degeneration has disastrous consequences—I'm assuming the final result is death—why are there interested parties?"

"Expendable mercenaries."

My head jerked towards Michaels.

"Fuck." Callen's already serious face darkened into a furious scowl.

"Kent, when previously looking at former agents going dark, what did you find?" Michaels asked, his tone more serious than I'd ever heard it. Even frustrated, the man was beautiful, and as much as I hated hearing him say the words "expendable mercenaries"—

and was sure he was right—a flutter of awareness for the man came alive in my chest.

He was smart and fierce, and so doggedly determined. I couldn't wait to keep getting to know him better, especially when there wasn't so much hanging in the balance.

"Hold on." She clicked around on her keyboard, finally pulling up a spreadsheet of names, complete with a wealth of other information, including injuries, reasons for leaving the SICB, and dates missing.

We all focussed on the findings. The commonality had me widening my eyes, but it was Michaels who said, "Fuck. All physically injured or suffering acute PTSD."

"And all with at least one report on their records indicating they were on the antiestablishment watch-list. Plus more than 78 percent had substantial financial debt." Kent flicked through some of the material for us to scan over.

"And all of this was in the files Chambers sent?" Michaels asked.

Kent nodded.

"So where the hell is he?" Strain held his voice taut.

"I'm hoping the last two files we're running through the coding software will give us an answer to that." Kent displayed the coding wriggling around the screen. "Based on what Smythe told us about his discussions with Chambers, it's safe to say he went deep and had some outside help."

"The same mystery someone who left the unicorn coding for you to find?" Callen asked.

"It's not actually called unicorn c...." Smythe petered off, a reaction to Callen's deadpan look. "Uhm... yes, that's what we're thinking. The genius behind the coding helped Chief Chambers. What we don't know yet is whether the chief went off-grid to protect himself or dig deeper, or"—he winced—"he was discovered by Shadowfall, and they've taken him."

That we didn't know if he was dead or alive was left unsaid.

"So, we're saying there's a possibility that the former agents gone dark are involved, and what, offering themselves up as mercenaries, despite it being a death sentence?"

"It's more than a possibility," Kent said, looking at Callen. "The passports Michaels brought in were obviously all aliases, but facial recognition identified them as former agents."

Five profiles appeared on the screens around us. Seeing their faces, knowing they were former SICB, bottomed out my stomach. Had the SICB let them down so badly, they were willing to give their lives, for what... money? To give the bureau the middle finger? Nothing we'd discovered indicated any plans against SICB or any other government agency in Australia, so it wasn't like they were attacking.

"We don't know if they've volunteered or not. But we've traced money to accounts and debt settled for all five," Kent explained. "As for the three recruits that we started off with, it now makes sense why there were no financial red flags concerning them."

"Because of their connection to AFX and the three employees' involvement."

"Exactly that." Kent nodded at Callen. "It also meant we alerted them earlier than we thought to the fact that we were investigating, as we never expected the three individuals to be complicit in anything Shadowfall related."

It was true. Even with the footage of Kate Gallagher, we'd assumed it was against her will.

Pissed-off grumblings echoed around the table. Understandable. Nobody liked missing shit, especially anything that tipped our hand.

"But all this intel gives us the upper hand." Venom, ice-cold and sharp, dripped from Kent's voice.

A ping from Smythe's laptop had him reacting and us looking at him in expectation.

"We've got a location." While Smythe spoke, his fingers flew, eyes darting all over the screen. "Are we surprised that it's close by one of the Sydney ports?"

I smirked at his amusement.

"Any idea what it is?" Callen stared hard at the information popping up on the large wall screens.

"Kent, let's get a drone in the air. This place is important." Lucas folded his arms, staring intently at the image of the large warehouse. The building had a helipad, a boat slipway, and multiple layers of roof space with long rectangular spaces reaching out like spokes.

I felt it too, the significance of this place.

The spoke-like rectangles almost looked like cold storage, perfect for storing medical equipment, I expected.

"You want us on the ground, a couple of clicks out?" Michaels asked, his body almost vibrating with energy.

We all wanted this over with. The past few weeks had been a breeze of stealth and not-so pretend kisses compared to the chaos of the past forty-eight hours. While my body had healed, exhaustion hovered around me, tempting me to find a quiet room, ideally with Michaels, and pass out for hours.

Soon. I had to help end this. No amount of wishing

or hoping would work. We, our unit, needed to do what we did best, and fuck if I didn't get a surge of adrenaline thinking of myself as a fully fledged member.

This team was everything I wanted to be a part of, even if I'd never been able to put a name to it until a few months ago when Thatch spoke to me in both confidence and official capacity.

There was no looking back now.

Lucas and Callen continued to have some sort of silent exchange while I peered over at Michaels. His attention was on me. The zip of awareness, chemistry, whatever it was between us, sparked to life.

I studied him, wondering if this was the point when he'd freak. Attempt to demand I stayed put. For his sake, and for any chance of a possible relationship, I hoped to hell not.

And then his lips curled, barely a fraction, but it happened and was just for me. His faith, the untamed excitement that I knew bubbled under the surface, slammed into me. I drew it in, wrapped myself up in it, and smiled back.

"Okay. Here's the plan," Lucas started, drawing our attention as we all sat up, prepared to suit up, and hopefully get to Hornell and Prescott.

CHAPTER 11
MICHAELS

I ANGLED TO SEE AROUND THE SHIPPING container, because of course the surrounding area was littered with the damn things. Just the sight of them made my skin crawl. I expected they always would. The memory of seeing Shaw passing out, enclosed by metal debris, wounds flowing red, would stay with me for a while longer.

Streaks of clouds passed over the silver moon, limiting visibility. That was more than okay. The extra shadows clinging to the ground were our friends, and with our exceptional night vision, I was grateful for the thickening clouds.

"Callen, are you in position? Over." Kent's voice whispered in my ear, the sound familiar and reassuring.

"In position. Over," he answered.

Despite Thatch's protests, Callen had joined us. For a while there, I'd expected them to throw down, Thatch having no issues about reminding him of his responsibilities for their niece and about his promises to Thatch himself.

It had been hard to look away. My feelings for Shaw were no doubt barely a fraction of what Thatch felt for Callen, yet my heart galloped every time I considered the possibility of the panther, who I couldn't get out of my mind, being hurt, let alone losing him.

I'd wondered if it would get worse or easier, the deeper I got, the more he burrowed into my heart.

But still, Thatch had let Callen go when he'd promised to stay safe and not to "fuck around," and sealed it with a heated kiss and declarations of love that everyone had witnessed.

Callen peered over at our small unit, gaze connecting with each of us before he nodded and pointed at us to take formation.

Shaw was to stick to my arse like glue. It helped me breathe easier. We'd found our rhythm from our first unplanned training session together, and our ability to read each other had been even more on point since then.

I ran over the plan in my head.

En route to the site, we'd heard from Lucas with news from Kent and the drone.

We'd hoped the warehouse would be a hive of activity. It was. The drone had picked up as much. The implication that Shadowfall was active, ready for us to swoop in and shut them down, had already buzzed in our veins. Learning that trucks had been in and out, transferring boxes into the warehouse, had spiked our adrenaline even higher.

Whether Hornell would be on site, we'd have to wait and see, but if he was, he wouldn't go quietly. Nor were we going in completely blind or gung-ho.

Director Durrant had been looped in and had called in Jamison's unit. While I didn't know the rest of his team well, I trusted Jamison, even though he could be a cocky arsehole—a prerequisite of the ITU, apparently. He'd fit right in.

As we shifted into position, Shaw's exhale shook. The sound prickled my skin, but I caught myself from making a move that would piss him off. Instead, in our second location, still too many metres to be within scenting distance, I pressed my back to the warm steel of the container.

Shaw followed suit, his shoulder brushing against mine. On contact, I inhaled slowly, carefully, quietly, before counting to four and exhaling as steadily as if all was well in my world.

On the next breath, relief brushed across me, hearing Shaw match my breathing.

Thirty seconds passed before we moved again.

The pounding of footsteps about a hundred metres northwest of us filled the air. Crouching lower, holding my breath, I waited on high alert.

A loud snicker burst through the air from the same area, easing the tension pulling my neck muscles taut. I relaxed, confident that we hadn't been made. Shaw's hard triceps against mine followed suit.

Before I moved to the next position, Kent's voice crackled in my earpiece, saying, "Something's happening on the northeast quadrant. Hold. Over."

I scanned the area, focussing on the direction she'd indicated. Smoke, light grey and barely a trickle. Only visible in the darkness because of the floodlights lighting the area around the warehouse. "Come in, Callen. I've got a visual on smoke. Over."

"I see it. Flank the right as soon as we hear from Kent. Over."

"Copy that. Over." I held steady, waiting for the all clear.

"Copy, Red Team." Kent's use of our call name cut through our preparation, letting us know shit was about to hit the fan. Immediately vigilant, I prepared to move. "I've got air control giving permission for a helo to fly into your airspace in fifteen minutes. Fifteen minutes. Over."

"Copy that," Callen responded. While I couldn't see him, since he and Jamison were approximately forty metres west of us, it wasn't hard to picture his frustration.

A ticking clock was better than a ticking bomb, though, right?

I didn't peer behind myself to look at Shaw or Chris. Any second we would be given the go.

Feet prepared to launch, legs ready to propel me forward, my limbs vibrated expectantly.

I leaned to my side a fraction, bumping Shaw's shoulder, a silent cue. *I've got your back.* The barest of pressure against mine let me know he understood loud and clear.

"Red Team, move out." The order came from Callen and had us moving.

I raised two fingers, giving my signal to Shaw and Chris. *Time to go.*

With adrenaline coursing through my veins, my heart remained steady, years of training my body's reaction going a long way to keep me undetectable for as long as possible.

We ran towards our point of entry, aware that once we rounded the corner, we'd be running into their first line of defence. Moving fast and low, I kept my eyes on the target, trusting my team to watch my back.

Five metres out, we slowed, giving Chris the two seconds he needed to place a smoke mine on the ground—sometimes having added protection for an escape if things went wrong was necessary.

At our entry point, we paused. Chris crouched, stringing a tripwire into place. Preventing someone from creeping up on our arses was standard preventive procedure. The two cans were armed with tear gas.

They packed a hell of a punch.

With no instruction or all clears, we pushed forward.

Steady steps had me rounding the corner. One wolf appeared to my left, and then he was on the ground, tranq dart in his neck, before Shaw was at my back.

IH tranquiliser rounds were our ammo of choice. Quiet and not quite deadly, they could take down any supe in 1.2 seconds flat. Though that didn't mean we weren't strapped with Glocks and live ammo. Not a chance we'd go into a situation without being fully prepared or able to defend ourselves.

We kept moving. A whoosh of Shaw's tranq gun

alerted me to him taking out another perp. I didn't look back. Didn't check.

The aim was to get into the central warehouse, locate Hornell, and shove a tranq dart so far up his arse, he'd be crying tears of the stuff for months to come.

The space between us and the next entry point was clear. Smoke still hovered in the distance, but it looked to be outside and not getting worse.

Maybe it should. If the smoke got too bad, a helo couldn't land. That could buy us some time. Something I'd make happen if it became necessary.

Darting forward, I hit the wall next to our entry point in the warehouse. This was where we'd be going in blind.

"Michaels in position. Over," I whispered into comms.

Three seconds later, a crackle, then: "Callen in position. Over."

We'd be entering at the same time but through different entry points.

Five.

Four.

Three.

Two.

An explosion somewhere at the north of the

building shook the foundation. We ducked for cover. Fuck if it would stop us, though.

Hand on the door handle, I tugged. The door swung open, and we raced inside.

Alarms blared. The area was in disarray. Whatever the explosion had been was also clearly unexpected. The few armed guards in this section looked frazzled. Wide-eyed, they darted towards the impacted part of the building, letting us slip on in unnoticed.

Other people, humans and supes, some dressed in workwear, some in lab coats, dashed around in panic, heading directly towards us and the exits.

Fuck. We couldn't just let them escape, but whatever the hell was going on inside meant they couldn't stay either.

"Blue Team, come in, over." Reaching out to Jamison's team it was.

"Blue Team, copy."

"South entrance is going to be swarmed in four seconds. Contain staff. Over."

"Copy that," the team leader responded to my request.

Indicating for my team to step out of the way to prevent the escaping bodies freaking when they saw us, we raced to the left, well away from the exit and the stampeding group.

"The hell was that explosion?" Chris grumbled from behind. With so much noise from the alarm and panicked cries, there was no longer the same level of need for stealth.

"Distraction or destroying of evidence. Both I expect," Shaw answered, an edge in his tone that told me he was wired and on high alert.

"We thinking Hornell is towards the explosion or elsewhere?" Chris asked.

"West of the building." Certainty ran through my veins. "That's where the stairwell is to the roof." Scanning the area, I saw there were just two more people racing past us. Clocking their faces, I dismissed them, not recognising them as individuals on our watchlist.

With no more security in sight, I snorted. Shadowfall must have scraped the bottom of the barrel to hire these guys. That they'd abandoned their posts so easily didn't speak highly of their training or their commitment.

Dicks.

The space was clear—our cue to get moving.

With steady breaths, I pushed out my senses, listening, scenting for anything beyond the smoke. Relying on my skills, we bolted forward, preparing to enter the next room.

I stopped short, hand up in a fist. Three fingers, then go, and we swarmed the room.

Charging, I sprinted, my team hot on my heels. A lion appeared at my right. Springing forward, I was out of his line of fire, hitting the ground with a roll just as the lion hit the deck with a direct hit from Shaw.

Shifting my raised gun, I fired, the second shifter falling to the ground like a sack of potatoes. Not even a blink later, the third shifter, a female wolf, went down hard.

"Come in, base. Three down in entrance B, copy," I said into comms.

"Copy that. Blue Team will be on site shortly. Over," Kent responded. "Smoke in outside area is clearing, and helo nine minutes out. Over."

For the first time, my pulse picked up speed, loud enough for anyone in hearing distance to detect. We needed to get this done. "Copy that. Over."

Practically flying through the rooms, clearing them out, we reached a central area complete with staircases leading to multiple rooms above. What we hadn't reached yet was the epicentre of where the explosion had taken place.

I had a decision to make. "Copy, Callen."

"What you got for me? Over."

"Heading up a central staircase now. Over." It

wasn't the staircase I'd intended, but with approximately eight minutes left, I didn't expect Hornell to be hanging out in the open, just waiting for his ride out of here.

Plus, we had a drone in the sky. Any movement, and Kent would have checked in.

"Roger that. We'll head to the north stairwell. Check out the explosion first, see what's going on. Over."

"Copy that. Over." I turned to Shaw and Chris. Both stood on guard, weapons in hand, gazes scanning our surroundings. "Up sound good?"

"Not the east stairwell?" Chris met my gaze before continuing his scan.

I shook my head, focussing up above and on the rooms I saw there. "Something doesn't feel right."

"Your gut's saying we go up here?" Shaw's question tugged my attention to him. Nothing but trust filled his features as he waited for my direction.

"My instinct's screaming at me that this is the way we go." Even the thought of bypassing this staircase made the hairs on my nape rise in wrongness.

"In that case, we go up."

Jesus, his conviction, his absolute belief that I'd do right by him shot fire into my veins. It was as heady as it was terrifying.

"Up we go, then." Amusement tinged Chris's words. For all the shit I'd given him since we'd partnered up, the man took understanding to the next level. I sure as shit didn't think I'd be as tolerant.

Our gazes met, and I nodded in his direction, hoping he heard without words my thanks and silent apology.

At his up-nod, I readied myself and took point.

With time not on our side, we charged up the stairs. Our footsteps were too noisy, but with all that had happened since infiltrating, there wasn't a shred of doubt they already knew we were here.

One office space was clear. An empty lab, contents looking destroyed, which would piss Kent off. A third room had us pausing.

The sound of a struggle. A grunt, a smash, metal hitting wood.

I stepped to the side as Chris shoved open the door, immediately there, my weapon raised, ready to fire.

On his knees, Jack Chambers jerked his attention to us. Fresh blood spilled from his nose, a slight swelling taking shape to the right of his eye. At his side a prone form sprawled, dressed in the same fatigues as the other security personnel we'd taken down.

"Fuck." His hands shot in the air, a zip tie secured to just one wrist. Wide-eyed, he took us in. Panic filled his expression, only morphing when his attention landed behind me. "Shaw?" The word was a relieved gasp. His shoulders sagged, and he fell forward.

Head bent, one palm pressed to the floor, his breathing became laboured, loud.

"Chief Chambers." Surprise shot through Shaw's tone, but he didn't move, knowing his job at this moment was to have my six.

"Are there any more threats in this room?" I asked, voice low and steady, eyes on the man breathing raggedly before me. A door to the right could be a storage area or lead to another room.

"No." Chambers shook his head, leaning back on his haunches, making eye contact. "About four minutes ago, they cleared out. Left the last guard to take me down." His breathing stuttered as he appeared to be trying to pull himself together.

He was a big guy, a bear, and easily had thirty kilos on me. He packed muscle too, not quite as firm as I expected it would have been twenty-five years ago, but at sixty-three, the man was in good shape and hadn't let his administration job at the academy fatten him up.

Without a doubt he could take a guard out by himself.

"Can you stand?" I asked, taking him in.

"Yeah. Took a slice to my arm, not my leg."

I didn't check, instead watching as he pulled himself up, all six foot five of him. He staggered, and I sensed Shaw tense behind me, yet he stayed in formation.

"Who held you here?" With the countdown still on, we didn't have much time. I needed answers. Needed to know who I was racing to the rooftop to stop.

Thunder twisted his features. "John Prescott. The bastard got the drop on me at the academy. Shot off a bullshit email about emergency leave before a unit came in and dragged me away practically hogtied."

For the barest of moments, I held my breath, the weight of the stares at my back itching my skin. My body threatened to vibrate under the force of my team's unspoken words. But I held strong, remained visibly unaffected despite the churning of my stomach.

Not reacting in any way, my gaze held steady as I took in the man before me.

The man with an impressive service history.

A family man.

A man who relied on a metal tube in his heart to keep his blood pumping, damage he'd received on assignment eleven years ago.

Aware the pause edged towards too long, I bobbed my head. "Who else, beyond Prescott?" At my words,

Shaw, already in touching distance, pressed his fingers against my back. The contact was featherlight and gone in an instant but steadying all the same.

"A guy named Hornell. Calls himself Captain Hornell. I expect that title was stripped from him long ago." He grimaced as he wiped his nose, wincing slightly.

"It looks broken, but we've got to move."

He waved me off. "You go. I'll be okay. I can make my own way out."

Like hell he would.

"Prescott and Hornell, they heading to the roof?" I asked, indicating with a barely there shift of my head for my guys to back away.

"Yeah." Exhaustion seemed to cling to his body— the droop of his shoulders, the rasp in his breaths. But it was there. That something. Not even a glint or a flicker, though, but something at the edge of my senses that made my instincts scream.

I bobbed my head, saying, "Chris, give Chief Chambers here a weapon."

I didn't pause or hesitate in my instruction, trusting Chris to have picked up on all that had been left unsaid.

We also needed to hurry the fuck up.

Unease permeated the air. It burnt my nostrils. But I had no choice but to turn my back to Chambers.

Giving Chris a curt nod, I angled, betting on myself that I'd read this situation right.

The itch between my shoulder blades grew stronger. My gaze flickered to Shaw. He stood statue still before he backed away, focus returning to over my shoulder. He moved to the side, back to the wall so both Chambers and I would have to pass him.

Meanwhile, Chris had stepped out of the way, doing a visual inspection of his weapon, checking the magazine, before he handed it over to Chambers with a brisk nod.

"Red Team, helo three minutes out. Over."

I had to bolt. Had to reach the rooftop.

Uncertainty threatened to snatch the air from my lungs. But I had no choice. I needed to move. I also needed someone on Chambers.

Fear tried to lock me down, keep my legs immobile and my words frozen. Knowing what I had to do and following through sat like boulders on my chest.

"Chris, with me. Shaw, eyes on Chambers until he's safe."

I didn't meet his gaze. Couldn't.

"Amber Team," I started, giving the code letting

everyone on comms know something was wrong. "Shaw's got Chambers. He's bringing him out. Over."

I didn't wait for anyone's reaction. Instead, I ran.

As I sprinted down the landing, shoving speed into my legs, my heart beat an erratic rhythm. Palms slick with sweat, I couldn't shake the wrongness of leaving him behind.

It didn't matter that I was trying to reach two perps who needed to go down. Not when Shaw was with Chambers. I just hoped like fuck Chambers's plan was to walk out of here at Shaw's side.

With each step, my legs trembled. First foot on the metal staircase to the rooftop didn't feel right.

It wasn't just the images of Shaw being hurt that were mocking me. But I couldn't put my finger on the dread growing infinitely worse as every second passed.

"Fuck," I growled, three steps from the rooftop door.

"Jesus, this stinks of something rotten," Chris said at my back. He wasn't talking about the scent of the ocean and fresh air growing stronger as we reached the top.

Desperation smacked into me a second before I gripped the door handle.

"Turn back." Steel threaded my order. "Now. Move."

We spun, bolting down the staircase, jumping the last ten steps. I hit comms as I arched through the air. "Shaw, if you copy, buzz your wrist comm."

When the faint buzz came through, I almost collapsed in relief.

"Are you heading to the exit we came in? Buzz if yes."

Nothing. "Fuck."

Urgency punched into me, forcing me to push harder. "Callen, you catch that? Over."

"Roger that. Heading to the south exit now. Jamison's heading north. Over."

My mind raced as worst-case scenarios pummelled my brain. We were running out of time.

"Kent, what's happening with the helo?" I hollered, barely managing to keep my shit together, let alone remember comms protocol.

"It's coming in to land now."

"Any movement on the roof?" My question escaped on a ragged gasp.

"Negative. No movement on the roof."

"It was a fucking trap," Chris all but snarled, saying exactly what I was thinking.

Kent's "The helo's pulled back up and is travelling due north, no passengers or pick up" confirmed it.

"You thinking bomb?"

I nodded at Chris's question. No doubt C4 or some other kind of explosive had been rigged to the door. Considering the time that had passed, it should have gone up by now, which meant that Chambers knew something had gone amiss.

With every second of Shaw being out of my sight, an expanding ball of fear formed in my throat. I pushed harder, feeling the burn in my legs, the ache in my chest.

Being too late to intervene was not acceptable. Today or ever.

"Give us an update, over." Chris's words were a welcome relief tearing my thoughts away from my churning stomach.

"Nothing at the south. There's no sign." Tightness filled Callen's voice.

A few seconds later, Jamison said, "North's empty and all clear."

"Fuck," I roared, slamming on my brakes and stopping in my tracks.

Chris veered to my right, just stopping himself from taking me out. He staggered and turned to face me, eyes alert. "What are you thinking?" Unlike my ragged breaths, his held steady and in control.

Hands on hips, I lowered my head and closed my eyes. I forced the sound of my breaths away, shoved out the frantic beating of my heart. Finding my centre, I exhaled, slow and deep, before pushing out with my senses.

Movement outside. I brushed that aside, sure it was our unit.

The soft hiss of gas coming from the direction of the explosion—that made sense.

Come on. There has to be something.

A clatter. Metal on metal. Again, the same pitch. A third before a louder clang. Then a gunshot.

Popping my eyes open, I surged forward, calling on all my energy while my heart lodged in my throat. "They're underground," I hollered, leaving it to Chris to call it in and gather the troops.

The sound of his steady footing followed me, his voice filling my ear, shouting out orders to look again at the schematics and find out where an exit point was.

I jolted over the door hanging off its hinges, courtesy of the explosion. The bomb had done more than vacate the premises and distract us. It covered up the exit Chambers had been planning to use the whole time.

We found the basement entrance behind a table. Gun in hand, I tugged it open, charging down, Chris hot on my heels.

I almost staggered, seeing a body facedown on the

ground. The hesitation had Chris passing me, dropping to his knees and reaching out.

"Prescott." His voice then filled the comms as he stood back up. "Prescott's down. Over." His palm then went to my forearm, squeezing tightly. "Shaw's going to be okay."

I couldn't nod. Couldn't agree.

"If Chambers took Prescott out, it means he has live ammo." A quick search didn't come up with Prescott's service weapon. It wasn't hard to imagine some sort of struggle and Chambers using Prescott's own gun on him.

Wide-eyed as my words sank in, his jaw clenched, a fierceness taking over him I'd never seen before. "You are not going to lose Shaw. Now, get your arse moving."

Hit with gratitude at the determination and reassurance I needed from him to keep grounded, I let him take point, following him step for step.

Shaw, I'm coming for you.

I sent the message into the universe, refusing to be a liar. Refusing to lose anyone else.

A sound, a scrape of a boot in the distance. At the noise, Chris and I pushed on, pressing closer to either side of the long stretch of tunnel the large basement had revealed. Concrete covered the walls, the finish rough. But it wasn't brand-new. There was no lingering scent of fresh materials.

"...what you hope to achieve."

Shaw.

There was no response.

"Everyone knows you're involved, so what, you expect to get out of here and disappear into the sunset?" This time snark filled Shaw's tone. That there wasn't a trace of fear evident warmed my chest, pride blooming. But fuck, I didn't want him to push Chambers over the edge.

"Where's Hornell?" he pressed. This time a shuffle of movement followed, as if Shaw had been shoved. It didn't deter him as Shaw continued, "He sure as shit wasn't on that rooftop. You stealing Prescott's Glock and putting a hole in his head made that story stink like bullshit."

Shaw knew we were in pursuit. The certainty of that helped to tame the wildfire of panic in my chest.

"He was a decent trainer, seemed content, so what did you do to persuade him to join the whole cyborg-zombie shit you've got going on here?" This time he grunted, and my muscles tensed.

"Shut the hell up."

Chambers was rattled. Good. Rattled meant loss of focus. Mistakes. I just hoped to hell it didn't mean a bullet in Shaw's head. There'd be no coming back from that.

Not shutting the hell up, Shaw said, "But seriously, did he think you could magic him a new limb before he realised how fucked everything was and that if you gave him anything, he'd turn into a brainless zombie? That's what happens, right? Is that why you killed him? Because he was having doubts?" Another shuffle of feet, but the voices were louder.

We were closing in, and I'd never been more relieved that while bear shifters were strong as fuck and had incredible eyesight, especially in the dark, their hearing was practically the same as a human's.

"Maybe he just realised there was no getting out of this without shackles on his wrists. Is that why you shot him? Because you knew he'd squeal and tell us all his secrets?"

"For fuck's sake, Shaw, shut your mouth before I figure you're more of a liability than any potential help." The thread of panic in Chambers's voice turned my warm blood to ice. He was on the edge and close to losing his shit—something else bear shifters were known for.

The fact he'd made it to chief of staff meant he must have had the control of a saint at some point.

That he was unravelling didn't bode well.

"You think I'm going to help you, you're stupider than you look. You know the cadets had a nickname for you, right?"

We edged closer, maybe ten metres from where they were around a bend. We paused, knowing that as soon as we rounded the curve, there'd be no more hiding.

Without a doubt, Shaw knew that too.

A scuff of a foot and Shaw's voice changed direction. He'd stopped walking and turned on him.

Fuck.

I didn't look at Chris. Didn't dare breathe.

This was it.

Do or fucking die. And no fucking way was Shaw taking a bullet.

"You know, chamber pots are to do with shit, right? Well—"

A grunt of pain, a smack of flesh, and we were moving.

Wide-eyed, I took in the scene just as Chambers angled his head, gaze connecting with mine. Fury distorted his features as he took a step to the side, weapon pointed at Shaw, who was on his knees.

The copper scent of Shaw's blood slammed into me. The hairs on my arms spiked, and I was sure my eyes blazed with the intense fire of resolve. With the muscles in my jaw clenching as I came to an abrupt stop, my left hand cupped my Glock, my right pointer finger on the trigger.

"By the time you pull, he'll already be dead." The lack of panic in his tone sliced fresh fear into my chest, threatening to seize my lungs.

The air crackled with tension, hovering, just waiting for the opportunity to explode.

Chambers was beyond reason. There'd be no talking him down. No trying to suggest he came in quietly.

"You must know how this is going to go down," I said, my voice steady, gaze unwavering. My heart pleaded with me to check on Shaw, make sure he was healing and okay.

"The way I see it, you either let me on my way down this here tunnel, or the kid dies. The call's yours."

"A bullet goes anywhere near him, and you're dead before your gun even smokes. You willing to die for this shitshow?"

"Die or spend my days in a cell?" A humourless snort shot out of him. His arm tensed.

Fuck. He was going to fire.

A slow, unhinged smile tilted his lips. "I think—"

Red bloomed between his brows, a perfect circle as

he dropped to the ground, Shaw shuffling out of the way. The echo of the shot vibrated the walls and my head.

Breath in my throat, I snapped my gaze to Chris.

"What?" He shrugged. "He was going for the trigger."

My lips parted, not sure what to say. Every single one of us knew Chambers had been holding Chris's unit-assigned gun—only different from our own because of a tiny wolf insignia assigned to his team. The one he'd loaded with a blank bullet in the first space of the magazine.

A protocol Thatch had brought in about four years back when in hostage situations.

But fuck if I hadn't been nervous he'd switched out the bullets. Plus there was Prescott's missing gun.

"He was," I agreed, not pushing it.

Dead meant Chambers couldn't manipulate or attempt any type of plea bargain. What he'd done to the recruits and former soldiers we knew about was evil. Pure and simple.

He didn't deserve the opportunity to plead his case.

The scrape of a boot on the ground had me moving.

"You're okay?" I reached out, gripped Shaw's hand,

and tugged, needing him close and in my arms. I didn't give a shit about Chris looking on. It was something he'd have to get used to—seeing me gone for Shaw.

"Other than the ringing in my ears, I'm good." He wiped at his temple, stemming the flow of blood. From the cut, I expected Chambers's meaty fist had done the damage.

I examined his face, tilting his head with my fingers on his chin. Sweaty, a bit ruffled, and smeared with traces of blood, he'd never looked more fucking beautiful. My gut clenched at the surge of feelings crashing into me.

Whatever he saw on my expression had his brows dipping and him stepping more fully into my space. "I'm okay," he said softly, hand squeezing my hip.

"When I had to leave you—" Fuck. I needed to keep my shit together. He was fine. I knew that. Saw it with my own eyes. So why the hell was it becoming difficult to breathe?

Softness flickered to life in his gaze, his head angling slightly. The ends of his boots pressed against mine.

"That was the hardest thing I've ever done." Fierce emotion clung to my words.

"And the smartest. It meant I stuck with him, so there was no chance of him getting away." He palmed my cheek, his own emotion appearing, raw and wide open for me to see. "I heard what he said about the email. No mention of a second one to Thatch, let alone it being Prescott who sent it, which was obviously bullshit." I nodded as he spoke, relieved he was so smart and a quick study. "And that bullshit zip tie." He rolled his eyes. "There wasn't a single mark on his other wrist."

I couldn't help my smirk at his tone.

"What fucking terrified me, though, was how fast he was moving to leave the first floor. It was clear he was getting as far away from the rooftop as possible." Shaw shook his head, awe brightening his incredible eyes. "How did you know not to open the door?"

I huffed out a breath. Pressing my face against the crook of his neck, I inhaled deeply, searching for the welcoming forest scent. It rolled over me, fresh and reassuring. "Listened to my gut," I said, pulling away, more than aware Chris was talking into his comms— selecting a channel that wasn't feeding to us. Any second now, this tunnel was going to get super busy.

Shaw searched my gaze, reading my expression. Hell, he may have been trying to work out if I was bullshitting him or not.

I wasn't.

"Everything is weaker than instinct," I said. "I don't

give a shit about how much training, how many qualifications, how much time in the field anyone has, we always trust our gut."

"And if my gut's telling me we have ten seconds before the team descends on us, and I need you to shut up and kis—"

Swallowing his words with my mouth, I kissed him with need, with hunger, with the desperation of knowing he really was okay.

A wave of heat surged to life, igniting wings in my stomach. Our tongues danced, stroked, tasting each other's desire with every flicker and tease.

Hearing voices, I reluctantly pulled away, committing his flushed cheeks and ragged breaths to memory.

It was going to be a long afternoon, probably long night too.

Between reports to fill in, the warehouse to take apart, and Hornell in the wind, we'd be lucky to be in bed before midnight. And I planned for Shaw to be tucked in tightly at my side in my home.

Tomorrow, he'd be expected back at the academy, as would Thatch. Being so close to the end of his training, Shaw wouldn't want to screw with that. While I'd also need to head to the academy, I didn't know if it would be to gather my belongings, or to complete the last few days of my placement.

Lucas would already be preparing for our next move, so would he be expecting me to cut my time short and return to headquarters? Finishing up early, even if it was by just a few days, didn't sit well.

Training with Shaw, spending so much time with him, had reminded me how I lived for this job. Enjoyed my role. But it was more than that. He'd broken down the hard crust trapping my heart. And I wanted to start living for me too. That included spending as much time with Shaw as possible, chasing every bit of joy I could.

Fucking Lucas.

Even though this wasn't the outcome we'd planned for, he'd known what he was doing when he'd sent me to the academy. His "getting to the roots" comment rang in my mind. I snorted internally. I wasn't so sure if his hope that I'd inspire a recruit meant I'd be claiming one as my own.

As that was so what I was doing.

But it was okay. In a few weeks, Shaw would be joining the unit. Of that I had no doubt.

"What are you grinning at?" Shaw whispered just as the tunnel lit up with extra light from bright torches and filled with loud voices.

"Just thinking about the future."

He seemed surprised by my answer, maybe by my

honesty. His brows shot high. "And how's your future looking?"

"On April 5th, I imagine a whole lot brighter."

His eyes widened comically. I didn't doubt he made the connection, considering it was a date he'd been working so hard to reach—his graduation.

But there was no time to answer. No time to tease. No time to worry about the hope flooding my system.

"Michaels, talk to me."

With the smallest of winks, I smirked at Shaw, hoping he could read the promise in my eyes. I then turned around, reining myself in and cracking my neck before responding, "You got it, Callen."

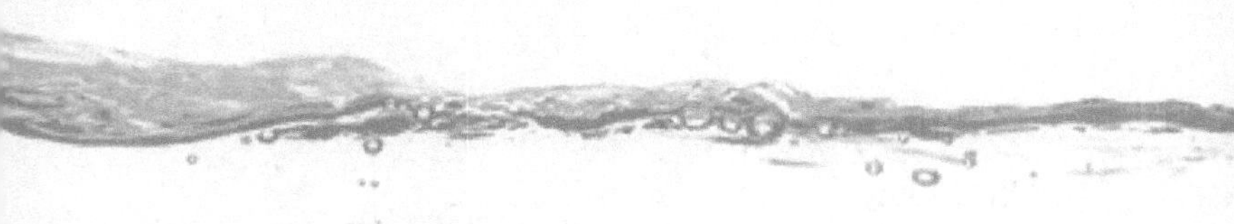

CHAPTER 12

SHAW

It had been close to one in the morning by the time Michaels and I crawled into bed together. We'd managed a sloppy mutual hand job before passing out, his alarm waking us up at 6:00 a.m.

With Thatch as interim academy chief, I'd been given grace to return to the academy by 9:00 a.m. My final assignment was coming up fast—a weeklong test mission into parts not disclosed until the first day. No way was I missing training time, especially when so close to taking my oath and becoming an active agent.

The morning had been filled with long glances, whispers, and more curious stares than I could count. Gossip at the academy seriously did spread like wildfire, but since we'd not had time to catch our breath between today's tasks, nobody had yet approached to ask what I knew.

Not that I could disclose anything or even confirm or deny some of the bullshit stories I'd heard mumbled.

On the surface, barely anything was out of the ordinary. Thatch was in residence, doing his rounds and whatever else kept him busy during the day. Michaels was here, having led a session earlier with the first-year recruits this morning.

Not on site were Prescott—for obvious reasons—and Trainer Hurley, who I knew had been taken in for questioning late last night. I didn't know whether she'd known about Prescott's involvement. For all anyone knew, she was an innocent girlfriend who'd remained clueless.

For her sake, I hope that proved to be true.

I took hold of a plate, about to join the line in the canteen, but was stopped by an arm looping through mine. While I'd heard Rickman heading in my direction, the contact surprised me.

"You doing all right there?" I asked with a chuckle.

"Yup. Henderson's got our lunch to go," she responded matter-of-factly, already tugging on my arm, her demand for me to join her. "It's a nice day for a picnic."

I pursed my lips, both relieved and entertained that

they were hustling me away from peering eyes and ears that would listen far too intently. "Sounds good," I said, my gaze snagging on Michaels's as he stepped into the canteen.

His brow quirked in question. Reading the twitch of my lips and the take-no-shit shifter leading me away, he smirked, throwing me a wink that made my heart flutter.

Every damn time I was near the man, he got a reaction from me. I needed to do better about controlling myself.

Well, not all the time. Where would the fun be in that?

Rickman snorted. I peered at her, catching the roll of her eyes.

"That's one answer to a question everyone's been wondering about, loud and clear for everyone to interpret."

Denying my reaction was pointless. The rumours I'd started about not being truly into Michaels would have been squashed from those traitorous fluttering wings. Not that I could be sad about that. Everyone and his dog could know how hard I was crushing on Vaughn Michaels, as far as I was concerned.

Hell, "crushing" wasn't the half of it. Gone. I was ridiculously gone for the man.

Once outside, I welcomed the early afternoon sun. Rays tickled my skin, the touch comforting, easing some of the tightness of my muscles.

"Oh, hey." I tugged Rickman to a stop as Smythe approached, clearly intending to walk on past me with barely a side glance.

"Oh, Shaw, hey." He bobbed his head, a slightly awkward smile lifting the one corner of his mouth. "You not going in for food?"

"Apparently we're eating outside, away from prying eyes and ears."

I felt Rickman's curious gaze at my side. Nobody knew where I'd been this weekend, let alone where Smythe had been. And as far as I could tell, nobody expected we'd been together.

"Makes sense." He bobbed his head in understanding. Casting a quick glance at Rickman, he nodded again. "So, I'll see—"

"Come join us." The hand on my arm tightened. Rickman would be confused as hell. "I know how Henderson stacks up food rations. There'll be plenty."

Uncertainty flashed in his gaze. I shot him what I hoped was a reassuring smile. So much had happened and changed this weekend. My respect for Smythe being one thing. More than that, I liked the guy.

He could be dry and witty. Was obviously next-level smart. And, if Kent had her way, I expected we'd be working alongside each other super soon. Already, he'd proven trustworthy, and after this weekend, out of all the recruits on campus, it was safe to say I trusted him even more than Henderson and Rickman.

Not that I distrusted my friends at all.

But going through what Smythe and I had together formed a bond I'd never expected. A new friendship I wanted to continue to explore.

"You sure?" He didn't hide away the hope in his tone, and immediately I knew I was doing the right thing—continuing to build our friendship before we were let loose in the SICB.

"Absolutely. Come on. Knowing Henderson, the arsehole will have started without us. We'll be lucky if there's anything left."

Rickman's death grip slacked off and she chuckled, peering over at Smythe as we headed towards the outside tables in the distance. "He's right. Henderson once told me about the time he competed in a pie-eating contest. Won a tacky trophy and everything."

We chuckled, discussing what other food-eating contests we'd heard of, moving on to what the worst type of food would be. Smiling at my friends as I plonked myself down on the picnic bench, I revelled in the moment of calm, grasping on to every quiet moment I could get.

The next few weeks were going to be manic, and after that? Well, I held on to the hope that we'd be able to finalise my contract to join the ITU, and that my test scores would be epic enough that Lucas wouldn't change his mind.

PRIDE. BIG AND BLATANT. THERE WAS NO HOLDING it back as I stood at ease while accepting my official SICB badge from Director Durrant.

She shook my hand firmly, her keen eye letting me know she knew full and well the part I had to play in shutting down Shadowfall. She'd thanked me in person four weeks ago in a full debrief, but this quiet gratitude felt more poignant.

Following protocol, I nodded at her, shook the official new chief of staff Thatch's hand, and made my way across the staging area.

On cue, the applause started, but it was the booming cheers of my parents and Michaels that had me grinning and seeking them out. They stood in the centre of the sitting attendees, hollering loudly, ridiculously so.

Receiving a wink from Michaels, I simply grinned even wider, my cheeks heating at the attention.

Not seeing Michaels every day for the past month had sucked. But between my final month and Michaels being back at base, still hunting for the illusive Hornell, we made it work.

Weekend visits and late-night and early-morning video calls helped. But neither would I have to worry about again. In nine days' time—after my one week of leave—I'd be an official member of the ITU, as would Smythe, who'd since been brought into the fold.

Officially, I was joining the Global Response Shifter Force, a bullshit arm of the SICB. It was a department everyone thought existed. I certainly had. It made sense that would be my official unit, considering Michaels's official capacity in that division. It prevented any curious questions.

Watching the rest of the newly commissioned recruits, I applauded, happy they'd made it through. Smythe stepped onstage, and once his badge was in hand and the necessary handshakes made, I clapped a bit loudly, my mouth twitching when Kent stood, whistling.

The cyber whiz hadn't been bullshitting about taking Smythe under her wing. Her standing there with her wife, Jada, was just a fraction of how invested she was.

Smythe blushed beet red. Though there was no holding back his wide smile, which he directed at them.

I'd learned a lot about Smythe since the op, and he hadn't been joking about having arsehole parents. The fact that they weren't here today spoke volumes. But the man seemed content, happy with his lot, if not a little overwhelmed at first when Lucas discussed with him the true nature of the unit while asking him to join.

Fifteen minutes later, the official ceremony over, I shook the hands of those around me, hugged Richmond, Henderson, and Smythe, then made a beeline towards my parents and Michaels.

And wasn't that something. My folks and my official boyfriend here together.

Mum swooped me into a hug first. "I'm so proud of you, sweetheart." A kiss landed on my cheek before she edged away, eyes a little shimmery as she handed me over to Dad.

"Proud of you, son." He wrapped his arms around me, my size almost a mirror copy of his.

"Thanks, Dad."

He kissed my cheek before leaning back, his own gaze suspiciously watery.

My parents were amazing. They didn't quite know the extent of all that had happened, but they knew enough —just like they knew I was silenced by secrecy—and were proud of me. Funnily enough, learning I was joining Michaels in the Global Response Shifter Force, which on paper looked absolutely legit, eased my folks' concern.

Because of course he'd won them over.

It took less than five minutes for them to decide they adored him. Unsurprising, considering the man had won me over in about the same amount of time.

"My turn." His deep, throaty voice rippled over my skin.

I turned, all but launching at him.

Strong arms wrapped around me, and he breathed me in, his face tucked into the corner of my neck the way he loved to do. I expected I loved the gesture a little more than he did.

"Proud as hell, Jett." His lips pressed against my skin, waking fresh goose bumps along my arms.

These were the times I had to practice control, and with the way the arsehole chuckled against my neck, I wasn't doing a great job of it.

Sure, we were outside, the scent of gumtrees

circling in the air, but in a space filled with supes, there'd be no concealing my lust.

I pulled away, shooting Michaels the evil eye. Considering he smirked in response, he wasn't taking my threat too seriously. I quirked my brow in challenge. With just two hours to get through sharing a meal with my parents, boyfriend, Smythe, Kent, and Jada, I would so make him regret teasing me.

When the smile slipped from his face, his gaze heating, he seemed to get the message loud and clear.

"Right." I turned my back to him, smiling so big and with genuine happiness bubbling in my chest. "Are we ready to eat?"

"I think you should call in sick all next week. That way we can do this all night and day." I snuggled up to Michaels, content after he'd sucked me to completion.

"Not sure Lucas would buy me coughing down the line, pleading illness."

I chuckled, just imagining how that conversation would go.

"You've got a week of rest and moving to your new pad. Try and enjoy the downtime before the mayhem really starts." He punctuated his words with a kiss to my temple.

Michaels wasn't exaggerating.

Since the shutting down of the warehouse and the deaths of the two former trainers, there hadn't been a moment's grace.

This had become more than searching for Hornell.

While the SICB had managed to shut down the black-market transactions between Shadowfall and Beijing and Mauritia, and had copious records, samples, and evidence, that Hornell still had access to pertinent information and could strike again was a real concern.

Then there was the mysterious support ITU had received. There was no doubt in anyone's mind that the same person had sent the encrypted files to Thatch in the first place. The only thing we could deduce was that the software to break into the files hadn't been provided until they trusted us—or possibly brought Smythe into the loop.

We didn't know for certain, and poor Smythe was as flummoxed as he was a little flattered—something he'd confidentially admitted to me—at the possibility.

As for the unicorn code—a name that would live in infamy in the walls of the ITU—well, all traces of the code had disappeared. As in wiped. Completely and truly lost to the ether.

The unicorn hacker, the name of whom Smythe and I had joked around about and was kinda sticking—pissing Kent off a little—had removed everything.

The additional work Kent and Smythe had done on the coding? Gone.

The files saved on secure networks? Missing.

The additional notes on Kent's laptop that didn't even have network access? Lost.

The unicorn hacker had skills beyond my comprehension. And as angry as Kent was, her admiration that they'd managed such a thing wasn't lost on us.

But Smythe—if it was possible to form a crush on an unknown entity—he was sunk. He got this look of wonder in his eyes every time we talked about the unicorn hacker.

But hey, if the guy got a hard-on over coding skills, more power to him. I'd once gotten a boner when Michaels told me he was eating a custard tart, so I had no room to cast aspersions.

"How long did you say the contract on your new place was for?"

With a furrowed brow, I peered up at him from my position on his warm chest. Since he'd been with me to see the place with Smythe, he already knew this answer. It was a decent-sized, two-bedroom apartment about fifteen minutes from base. Smythe and I were going to be flatmates as of next week.

"Six months." I tried to capture his gaze, but with him staring at the ceiling instead of at me, Michaels wasn't taking it easy on me. "Why?"

The double thump of his heart had me pausing. Pushing up, I peered down at him, directly in his line of sight, concern zinging under my skin at the small tell that he was nervous.

"What's wrong?"

"Nothing's wrong," he quickly said, finally looking at me. "Just thinking of the future."

The galloping heart in my chest was a dead give-away that once again, he'd caught me off guard. He always did whenever he got this small glimmer in his gaze when he mentioned the future.

Rather than calling me out at my inability to control my reaction around him, he cupped my cheek. "Just thinking I like you in my space, in my bed. After six months, you moving in would be pretty cool."

Shock slammed into me even as I melted into him. "Pretty cool, huh?" I teased fondly, not even trying to hold back my emotion at how his words touched me.

"I think so."

"I think so too."

His eyes widened a fraction, as though not quite believing I'd accepted so easily. Two months of knowing the man felt like the best of lifetimes already. More of that and hopefully forever? Heck yes. I was here for all of it.

"Six months to settle into work. Six months to learn how to deal with all your annoying—"

"Hey." He grabbed my waist and flipped me. Hovering over me, he nudged my thighs apart. I spread willingly, loving nothing more than him being pushed up against me, naked cock nudging at my arse. "I don't have a single annoying quality."

A simple, slow arch of my brow was all I offered in response.

"But you love all my qualities."

As soon as the words filled the space between us, his gaze widened, brows shooting up high. Yeah, we totally hadn't been there yet. Kinda funny considering my heart beat for him these days.

And considering he'd just asked me to move in, his feelings were hardly a secret.

"I do." The loud thud of my heart sounded in my ears. "Love you that is. Everything about you."

He swallowed loudly, his breathing turning shallow.

"Even the annoying parts, like you being a weird snob about whiskey," I teased.

His laughter cut through the thread of tension, settling over me and warming me up. "I love you. Everything about you too."

I waited for the list of my annoying qualities, but none came. When he did nothing but stare down at me, his cock thickening, the air between us crackling, I lifted my head off the pillow and slanted my mouth over his.

He kissed me back, soft and sweet, with a gentle thoroughness that took my breath away.

"This," I murmured, pulling away a hairsbreadth, "seems like something we should celebrate with an orgasm."

His grin was wide, relaxed, his happiness reaching his gaze. And fuck if I didn't have everything I wanted in this exact moment.

And I'd keep it. Fight for him, for us. Work hard every single day to make this world we lived in a safer place while doing it.

In this, I trusted my instincts. Trusted his too. And as he pressed into me, still lubed and ready from his mouth working me over, I sighed into his touch, knowing that life was going to keep getting better and better and, I expected, even more interesting.

Enjoyed Michaels and Shaw's story? If so, I'd really appreciate a review. And don't forget you can read Callen and Thatch's story in **Thicker Than Water**.

What I'd also love to know is if you want more from my SICB world and the gorgeous agents. If you do, please reach out to me in my **Facebook group** (where I'm the most active), letting me know whose story you'd like next: Lucas's or Smythe's. Alternatively, subscribe to my **newsletter** for updates. It's also a handy way to hit Reply so you can reach out to me.

Looking for more Aussie MM romances from me? Why not check out **High Alert**—a delicious best friend's brother romance.

ALSO BY BECCA SEYMOUR

Zone Defense

No Take Backs | No More Secrets | No Wrong Moves

Fast Break

Rules, Schmules! | Facts, Smacts! | Regular Smegular

True-Blue

Let Me Show You | I've Got You | Becoming Us | Thinking It Over | Always For You | It's Not You | Our First & Last | Next For Us

Outback Boys

Stumble | Bounce | Wobble

Fangs & Felons

Thicker Than Water | Weaker Than Instinct

Stand-Alone Contemporary

Not Used To Cute | High Alert | Realigned | Amalgamated | Under the Blazing Stars

ACKNOWLEDGMENTS

This book is so very overdue. It was such a joy revisiting the world of SICB and I absolutely want to continue the team's stories.

You can all thank Lana Shanks and Cat Palmer for encouraging me to get this book off the ground. Their encouragement and love of book one was the boost I needed to finally work on Michaels's story. Thank you, both!

My team of Hot Tree Editing editors, my amazing admin, and talented cover designer are all wonderful. Each play an integral role in every book I publish. I'm so grateful to each and every one of you.

Readers, thank you for enjoying my stories and continuing to one-click. I appreciate you all so much.

ABOUT THE AUTHOR

Becca Seymour lives and breathes all things book related. Usually with at least three books being read and two WiPs being written at the same time, life is merrily hectic. She tends to do nothing by halves, so happily seeks the craziness and busyness life offers.

Living on her small property in Queensland with her human family as well as her animal family of cows, chooks, sheep, and dogs, Becca appreciates the beauty of the world around her and is a believer that love truly is love.

To check for updates head to Becca's website:
HTTPS://BECCASEYMOUR.COM
You can sign up for her newsletter here:
HTTPS://LANDING.MAILERLITE.COM/WEBFORMS/ LANDING/R9F0I4
Plus, join her Facebook group, which she shares with the awesome Louisa Masters here:
HTTPS://WWW.FACEBOOK.COM/GROUPS/ ROMMANCEWITHBECCALOUISA

facebook.com/beccaseymourauthor

twitter.com/beccaseymour_

instagram.com/authorbeccaseymour

bookbub.com/authors/becca-seymour

tiktok.com/@beccaseymourwrites